MERLIN'S GIFT

MERLIN'S GIFT

IAN McDOWELL

AVON BOOKS • NEW YORK

To Amy Goldschlager and Jennifer Brehl, for their patience and good humor in the face of both catastrophe and my own foolish lassitude, and to Robert "Dolemite" Adkins, the Ambiguous Mary (High Queen of Mars and six boroughs of Faerie), the peregrinating Mr. Cavin, and the luminous Kelli Bickman.

AVON BOOKS
A division of
The Hearst Corporation
1350 Avenue of the Americas
New York, New York 10019

Copyright © 1997 by Ian McDowell
Published by arrangement with the author
ISBN:1-56865-436-7

First AvoNova Printing: August 1997

AVONOVA TRADEMARK REG. U.S. PAT. OFF. AND IN OTHER COUNTRIES, MARCA REGISTRADA, HECHO EN U.S.A.

Printed in the U.S.A.

Reflections

Sharp winter is now loosed.

Horace, *Odes*

One

NONE OF this would have happened if Guinevere's little sister hadn't grown a penis. At least so I thought this morning, as I walked along the broken strand and watched the wave crests gleam like sword blades in the newly minted light, and when that daft insight struck me, all I could do was sit down on the cold sand, rest my forehead on my knees, and laugh till the tears came streaming down my face, salty droplets stinging in the lines my recent cares had worn there. I was tired and sore and bleary-minded, having enjoyed neither sleep nor any other comfort in the long hours before sunrise. Gwen and I had tried to fuck, knowing we wouldn't be getting many more chances, but I'd been unable to get it up, so we lay there in our separate silences until cockcrow, when I rose and came lurching forth like Lazarus, to walk the beach where so many men had recently died and pretend I was preparing myself for all the deaths to come.

Pardon me if I'm not at my best. I buried my brother Gawain yesterday, after killing him in battle two days before. Hadn't known who it was till I'd pinned him to the ground and suddenly recognized the stocky, grizzled shape writhing at the end of my spear. There was no point in pulling it out of him, so I let go of the shaft and held him in my arms and strove to make sense of the small wet sounds his mouth was making. Maybe he was trying to speak, maybe he just meant to spit on me, but what came out was a frothy red gush, and then he went limp, limp as my dick was last night, with rain

3

falling on his open eyes and tears pouring out of mine, and both of us all over mud and blood. It was a very wet day, and a cold one, and I've not been warm since. Captain Colwyn had to fetch poor Gwen to the battlefield, as nobody else could drag me away from the sodden corpse of one of the few people I've ever managed to love. I'm sorry she had to go through that, but then I'm sorry for a lot of things these days.

Ach, no, that's not the way I wish to begin this chronicle, with either self-pity or something that sounds like a vulgar joke. It's true that the chain of events that ended with me and my brother clutching the spear I'd just shoved through him can be said to have begun with poor Nimüe's transformation, but these dark matters run deeper than that, and go back further, to me and Gwen making love on a floor of human teeth, or half a decade before that, to Arthur recoiling in horror from me and the knowledge of who I was. But those are only reasons, not causes. For what has happened to everything Arthur built, and what will likely happen to Britain itself, I must accept no small blame. I made the decision to keep returning to Gwen's bed, and, more recently, the decision to go to war against the king who is her husband and my father. I've already told you, who probably will never exist, much less read my history, how the first business came about. Now it's time to write of the second and all that led up to it. There will be at least a few more sleepless nights before Arthur is in position to cross the Channel and engage what's left of our forces, and if the last evening is any indication, Gwen and I will prefer to remain apart, despite the love that still lives between us, she seeking some small comfort in lonely prayer and me left with the solace of this testament.

My cold morning walk done, I made myself eat something—I don't remember what—and gave orders to the remnants of our forces, an exercise in futility now that our strength is broken and Cuneda has decided to sit out further battles, doubtlessly so he can force terms upon the survivors, if there are any—damn me for a fool for allying myself with him in the first place, although my pain at being separated from Guinevere seemed to give me little alternative at the time. My prediction about Gwen was right—she's gone to chapel, to bolster her faith against what must surely come, and now I'm alone in the royal quarters of this old legion fort, sitting beside the tower window that lets me see the sun on the waves and struggling to regain some sort of authorial voice. I really should blot out these ramblings in favor of a more formal and elegiac preamble, but balls to that; I've already told the first half of my story without dressing it up in pompous finery, and besides, a messy style befits a messy life. But enough of this doodling; let us begin again.

It's been two years since I last put pen to vellum, and nearly ten since the events I've already chronicled. I've told of how I was born in storm-wracked Orkney, the realm of my mother, Queen Morgawse, and of sour King Lot, the man I thought my father. I've told of how I loved Arthur, King of all the Britons, long before I knew it was he who'd sired me upon his own sister, and of how he spurned my boyish devotion when he found out the truth of who he and I were to each other. I've told of how I hated my mother's husband, of how he slew her, and how she helped me avenge her slaying after she was dead. I've told how Orkney fell, Lot's palace hammered into weedy rubble by the storm I summoned up, and how Gawain and I journeyed to Camelot, me taking my mother's head with me in a box. I've told how that head counseled me when I met Guinevere, my true father's new queen, and found myself in love with her, and how I rescued Gwen from the Kingdom of Teeth. I've told how the price of her freedom from that aspect of the Otherworld was her virginity, and how once she gave it to me, my fate became more bound to Arthur's than ever. I've told how her safe return to Camelot restored Arthur's regard for me and how he accepted me as his son and gave me an honored place at court. And that is how I left my chronicle, with me possessed of some small simulacrum of joy and no knowledge of how everything must end.

I'm wiser now, if less happy.

I gave Gawain the Christian burial he'd have wished, for in recent years, the seed of faith that Arthur planted in him long ago had finally taken root, though without the thorns of doubt and guilt that so tormented the man who was his

uncle and my father. Bishop Gerontius was too astonished
to find himself summoned by me to waste his breath with
threats of damnation upon my traitorous heathen soul.
There'd been a temptation to treat my brother's head in the
manner my late mother had shown me, so that I could speak
to him one last time and perhaps even ask for forgiveness,
but no, I couldn't do that to him; he'd lived all his forty-one
years untouched by Mother's darkness, and the least I can
do for him now is spare him posthumous indignity. But by
Lugh and all the bloody Saints, I wish I could speak to him
one last time, if only to hear him curse my name.

For my part, I curse Merlin's. He's the architect of all our
calamities; that shriveled, smirking, aged-but-ageless boy has
undone us all. Merlin loved Uther, Arthur's father (and my
grandfather), and when Uther no longer desired him, helped
Uther conceive Arthur upon another man's wife. He later
had his revenge for being spurned by aiding my mother in
my conception, for I now realize he must have known that
I'd be Arthur's doom, or at least the doom of everything
he'd built. Either Arthur or I may just possibly survive the
coming battle, but Arthur's legacy won't. The Saxons are
waiting even now, to regain what my father wrested from
them.

Oh, Merlin, it was a wicked gift you gave us all. Who
would have thought, four summers ago, that it would come
to this. Taking up this chronicle again, I look back upon the
last few years and begin with the tale of Nimüe, the girl who
became a boy, and with how, in trying to undo that change,
Guinevere and I managed to unravel the very fabric of Britain. That sounds like the basis for a grand, sad story, doesn't
it? Well perhaps it is, if you're not one of the ones it happened to. Despite the weighty things I shall relate, I'll not
begin with portents or prophecies or battles, but with a
smaller thing, a gray-and-white cat with a missing tail and
the dirty little girl who wanted me and Gawain to catch it.

Ñimüe

The beginnings of all things are small.

Cicero, *De Finibus*

Two

I T Ⱳ⅍Ʃ a lovely summer day in Camelot, with a gentle wind sighing off the Usk and tumbling folded woolen clouds across a sky as polished blue as that expensive Egyptian pottery you can hardly get in Britain anymore. Gawain and I had spent the morning on the parade grounds, drilling our squadrons in mock battles with padded lance heads and dull wooden swords, but it was too fine an afternoon to waste on mud and bruises, and so we were off to the Capricorn, a favored tavern whose courtyard opened beneath a spreading apple tree, just the place to sit in the blossoming shade and fill ourselves with wine and sausages. However, we never made it there.

Coming from the storerooms, where we'd left our gear, we were crossing the colonnaded walkway of the palace's outer courtyard when something small and gray dashed between my legs, nearly tripping me on the paving stones. "What the hell!" barked my burly half brother, shaking peppery copper bangs out of his perpetually squinting eyes. "Was that a rabbit?"

"No," I said, watching the small furry shape streak out into the Via Principalia, "just a cat, I think."

"It didn't have a tail."

"Perhaps that's why it was moving so fast," I said, noticing fresh drops of blood on the slate pavement.

"Oh, stop her, please, stop her!"

Too big to pass between my legs the way her quarry had, the redheaded girl smacked into me, though fortunately with-

9

out sufficient mass to knock me down. Instead, she re-
bounded from my chest and went sprawling on the
cobblestones, to stare up at me with big green eyes that reminded me very much of someone else's. Despite her strong
tomboy jaw, there was more than a little of her half sister
Guinevere in her smudged face.

Chuckling, Gawain stepped forward and helped her to her
feet. "Mordred, you brute, you've knocked down poor little
Nimüe. I think you owe her ladyship an apology!"

"I never!" I said in mock outrage. "She ran into me!"

"A true gentleman always takes the blame," said Gawain,
gently brushing some of the dust she'd somehow acquired
off her worn but finely woven shift. "But then, we already
know my brother is no gentleman, don't we, Nim? Now why
were you chasing that cat, and what the devil is it you've
got in your hand?"

She dropped what she'd been holding with a look of horror, as if she'd not been aware of it before now. It was indeed
a cat's tail, or at least most of one. Her eyes watered, and
two big glistening droplets began to trace channels in the
dirt on her face. "Oh, no, I didn't mean to, really! Poor
Clymenestra! I'll never catch her now."

Gawain knelt beside her and dabbed ineffectually at her
face with the sleeve of his tunic. "There, there, child. You'll
never catch who?"

She stamped her scabby bare foot upon the paving stones,
and her wet eyes flashed with an emerald fire that would
have done credit to her half sister. "My cat, you big lummox!"

I tried very hard to look disapproving, but couldn't quite
manage it. "Really, Nimüe, big lummox he may be, but he's
also the King's nephew and Master of Horse, and a mere
Lady of the Palace shouldn't call him that, least of all one
that's only eleven years old."

"I'm almost twelve, and Guinevere says I should be free
to speak my mind, here in Camelot." Turning to Gawain,
her manner became less comically haughty. "But if I'm
sorry and call you nice things, will you help me find my
kitty? Please? She's hurt."

Gawain prodded gingerly at the tail, which didn't seem to

have been cleanly severed, but crushed and torn. "Yes, I suppose she is. Still, plenty of cats lose their tails and heal up none the worse for it. She'll be off to some hiding place to lick wounds, but eventually she'll come back to wherever her food dish is kept."

Nimüe took his broad brown hand in her small freckled one. "I wish she would, cousin, but she's not a very smart cat, and she's never been hurt like this before. She was sleeping on the warm flagstones in front of the stables, right beside the wheel of some stupid servant's oxcart, and he whipped the oxen forward without waiting for her to move. She screamed and ran, and I ran after her, and caught her when she was trying to climb the wall. I didn't mean to grab her tail, really I didn't, but it was all I could reach, and when I did, it came off in my hand just like a lizard's! She's going to hate me now; I'm sure she thinks it my fault! Oh, my poor kitty, what am I going to do?"

"I doubt she thinks it's your fault, sweets," said Gawain gently. "Cats generally don't think much at all, and less than that when they're panicking and in pain. Probably all she knew was that she was hurt and needed to get away."

Nimüe crouched beside him, her arms around his thigh and her face buried in the loose folds of his tunic, before looking up again. "Please," she said through the veil of her dirty hair, "help me find her. She's out in the city, and I don't think she's ever been outside the palace before. If she runs far enough, she may not know how to come back."

My brother looked at me with seriocomic resignation. "Now how can we resist such an entreaty as that? You once killed a giant cat, Mordred. Do you think you can help us bring a small one back alive?"

I sourly met his gaze, not quite believing he was willing to waste the remaining daylight on such a pointless errand. "You're only doing this because you lost at dice, and it's your turn to buy the wine, you silly git."

Nimüe turned her surprisingly steely gaze my way. "Cousin Mordred, please help me, too. You have fine horses and servants, but all I've got is one little cat. Won't you help me get her back? It would make the Queen happy."

I don't know whether it was her look or the mention of

Gwen, but I melted, too. Kneeling beside her, I brushed cobwebs from her unruly hair. "Ach, I expect it would at that, and we do all want Her Majesty to be happy. So, you'd have me bring her back to you?"

"Yes, please."

I looked at the ten inches of striped fur and muscle and bone that lay so pathetically on the pavement. It was the type of odd scrap that Mother would have found useful when she was alive. That gave me an idea for a better way of finding the beast than peering under the foundations of every barracks building, storehouse, and granary on the Via Principalia. I picked up the tail, holding it by the end that wasn't bloody.

"I think I can make her come back."

Nimüe peered suspiciously through her dusty scarlet bangs. "You can?"

"Yes, sweets. It will take me a while to prepare, but it's easier than peering down every culvert in the fortress. Why don't you run off and play, and meet me by the courtyard fountain just before vespers."

Gawain cleared his throat with a sound not unlike a mastiff growling. "Mordred, this isn't what I meant."

"No, of course it isn't," I said easily, "but she asked my help, and by Lugh and Jesus she shall have it."

"You're going to do magic, aren't you?" said Nimüe softly. "The King doesn't like magic."

The King didn't like a lot of things, but I didn't say that. "It's only a very small bit of magic, and Arthur needn't know." Fortunately, he was likely to be on the horse-training grounds until nightfall. The spot I had in mind would be as free from prying eyes as any part of the palace could be, as it was essentially Guinevere's private retreat, and she took some pains to see that she and I weren't disturbed by servants when we were alone there. For once, I hoped she was elsewhere, for though I normally more than welcomed her company, she might not like what I was going to do, and her disapproval carried more weight than Gawain's.

Nimüe thought it over for a moment, and her uncharacteristic pensive stillness gave me the chance to notice that she'd grown a bit since I'd last seen her, which I suddenly realized had been some time ago, and I found myself idly wondering where she'd been keeping herself lately. She was at least an inch taller than I remembered, with a hint of her sister's large bones in her frame, although at her present gawky stage she had nothing like Guinevere's fluid grace. Indeed, I couldn't yet tell if she was going to be as lovely as Gwen or as homely as Regan, the late lady-in-waiting whose duties she'd theoretically been given but in practice paid scant attention to.

"All right," she said at last, "if you can really get her back." And without waiting for my reply, she went dashing off, leaving me alone with Gawain's disapproving stare.

I leaned against a column and met his gaze. "That's almost as cold a look as your father used to give me," I said, referring to Lot, our dead mother's even deader husband, who had killed her and then been killed by me with her posthumous help. Lot had despised me long before he knew I wasn't his son.

Gawain's mouth twisted up at that jibe, and his big hands clenched for a moment, then his face softened and he looked like a bear disappointed to find no honey in the hive. "That's not fair, and you know it."

I looked down at the scuffed mosaic, feeling ashamed of myself for using our poisonous family history as something to prick him with. "I'm sorry for that. And for the magic. I know you don't like it. Go to the tavern, and it will all be over and done with when you get back."

He hooked a thumb in his belt and looked away. "Nah, I think I'll stick around. That way, if it doesn't work, I can help her find her stupid kitty."

I grinned. "Gawain, are you actually sweet on the child?" Other than the usual whores, whose custom his growing Christianity never seemed to interfere with, Gawain didn't take much interest in women, despite the fact that he was at an age where many men would have been married for a while. Even Arthur, who'd already lived like a monk in penance for years before he discovered his "sin" had been with his sister, had not remained unwed for such a length of time.

Was he blushing? "She's just a child, Mordred."

"Well, yes, but not for that much longer. Maybe by the

time she's a woman, you'll be tired of your bachelorhood.''

Surprisingly, perhaps, he didn't get offended. ''By Our Lady, Mordred, you are such a bloody, ach, what's the word, cynic? Yes, a bloody cynic, thinking everybody's got a selfish motive for everything. I like the child, is all, and don't like seeing her mixed up in such a dicey business as magic. So I'll stick around, if you don't mind, and make sure things turn out all right.''

Camelot, the jewel in the crown of Arthur's Britain, actually began to take shape over a generation before his birth, when my grandfather Uther Pendragon and his brother Ambrosius Aurelianus set to work restoring the deserted legion fort of Isca Silurum. Built upon the foundations of the old praetorium and questorium, the white limestone palace covers over one thousand square feet and consists of two flanking wings jutting out from a much taller central structure, a six-story rectangular edifice in which windows of yellow clerestory glass gleam like fragments of the sun, and above whose red-picked ramparts and gilded copper roof flies the writhing scarlet dragon of Arthur's united Britain.

The royal Hall of Orkney, the so-called palace where I grew up, would have fit inside this building's rear courtyard, which was large enough to contain a fountain, an ornamental garden, and a small stand of mulberries and dwarf oaks. This was where Gawain and I awaited Nimüe, in the blessedly cool shade beneath the sighing branches. Several marble benches sprouted like big square mushrooms among the tree trunks, but I sat on loam and root, with my back against mossy bark, listening to the wind-rustle and larksong that echoed back from the surrounding whitewashed walls and ignoring the rhythmic crunch of my brother's doeskin boots as he paced back and forth beneath the swaying boughs.

''This place is too peaceful for such restlessness,'' I said finally.

''You know what I think. No need for me to say it again.''

''No, Gawain, there isn't, and I wish you'd stop fretting. It's just a harmless bit of hedge magic. You're acting like you fear I'll conjure a demon here in the King's own arbor.''

Actually, I wasn't sure that I *could* conjure a demon if I

wanted to, but try explaining that to my brother.

"No, Mordred, that's not what I fear. Now why don't you just go ahead and do it?"

I held up the whistle I'd drilled from the biggest vertebra in the cat's tail, after having a perplexed cook boil the flesh from it. "The cat belongs to Nimüe, so she must be the one to blow on this and sound the note that will bring her pet back. Surely you learned a little about such things, back when you were small in Orkney, before I was ever born."

Gawain looked sourly at the small cylinder of bone. "Ach, I took pains to make sure it was very little indeed, and have often wished you'd done the same."

By the Dagda and a dozen buggered Saints, he'd be trying to bring me to Jesus next, just like Arthur had once wanted to. I loved my brother more than anyone but Gwen, but he could be a dolt sometimes. "Do you like Guinevere?" I asked idly.

That took him aback. "She's my Queen and my uncle's wife and a fine lady. What do you mean?"

"Do you like her? Are you glad that she's here, and that she and Arthur are happy?"

He scratched his nose, which was peeling from sunburn. "Of course I am."

I rose and stretched, wishing I had brought some bread and cheese with me from the kitchen. Some resinated wine would have been nice, too. "Then never forget that my magic, the magic I learned from our late mother, makes that possible. I got her back, when no one else could, from the Kingdom of Teeth. Do you think you could have done that?"

He sighed and put his hand on my shoulder. "Your point is taken. This isn't the same, though."

I looked him in the eye. "It's a small thing, but I'm helping in my way. Doing a good deed, even."

Before he could say anything else, Nimüe came padding up. She'd gotten no cleaner in the hours since we'd last seen her. Since she was here in Camelot ostensibly to serve Gwen, she might accompany her to the bath more often. Even I hadn't been such a dirty ragamuffin when I was small, and Camelot was much cleaner than Orkney.

"I'm ready," said Nimüe. "What are you going to do?"

I handed her the tube of bone. "I'm not going to do anything. You're going to blow through that."

"Ick," she said, apparently recognizing where it had come from. "I have to put that in my mouth?"

Children are like that, rolling in dirt one moment and poking merrily at dead things, oddly squeamish the next. "Yes, you do, if you really want your cat."

She crossed herself, no doubt more a reflex than anything else, and put the bone to her lips. The sound wasn't very loud.

"Good. Now do it again."

Again she blew, a soft sour note.

Overhead, the lark had stopped singing, and the branches were still. I could hear everyone's breathing. Nimüe gingerly twirled the bone between her fingers. "It's not working, is it?"

"Patience, child, even a cat can travel only so fast."

I couldn't read Gawain's face. Was he hoping I was wrong? Not that I was sure myself that it was really going to work, for all the confidence in my voice. Oh, well, if it didn't, it didn't. The whole thing had been much more trouble than it was worth, anyway.

My pessimism proved unfounded. There was a plaintive mew, and then a small gray-and-white cat with a fresh stump where its tail had been came scrambling over the courtyard gate. Nimüe ran to meet it and scooped it up in her arms. When she brought it back to us, I could see that the poor little thing was panting like a dog. Yes, she'd come a long way, and had been running all of it.

I picked up the bone whistle, which Nimüe had dropped. "You may want to keep this. If she ever runs away again, you can blow on it and have her back. But don't show it to anyone else, and say nothing about it. Will you promise me that?"

"Yes," she said softly. Still hugging her pet, who seemed too exhausted to resist, she reached awkwardly out for the whistle. "I just did magic," she whispered.

I gave her a conspiratorial wink. "Yes, that you did. Now

come along, Gawain. Let's leave Nimüe to look after her kitty.''

I still couldn't read his face, but his silence made his feelings plain.

And that's how it began, with something as pitiful but commonplace as a scrawny little cat whose tail had broken off like a lizard's. Or, to be more accurate, it began with the cat's owner, an equally scrawny little girl with unruly red hair and big hands and feet and eyes far more solemn and lovely than the rest of her. Truth to tell, I'd paid scant notice to Nimüe since she'd come to Camelot, for I generally found children to be the sort of annoyance that's best kicked or ignored, and since she was Guinevere's half sister (and more than half, in Gwen's heart, as Gawain was more than half brother in mine), the former was hardly a viable option. Guinevere had returned from a trip to her father's stronghold at Cornwall with the child in tow, saying that Nimüe was going to be trained as her lady-in-waiting. *You might as well train a monkey*, had been my thought at the time, and indeed I assumed the real reason that Gwen had brought her back to Camelot was as a sort of pet, a passing amusement. I'd been wrong in that, for the Queen was soon bestowing the kind of attention upon her supposed servant that royalty seldom shows to its own offspring, much less its cast-off lowborn siblings. Well, Gwen's always had a generous heart, and I couldn't really begrudge her finding room in it for the child.

As girls too young to be bedded by anyone not a degenerate go, Nimüe actually wasn't that much of a nuisance, being a quiet sort, seldom given to puerile prattle, despite Guinevere's generous indulgence. And as is true of so many of us, there was more to her than first seemed.

I got my first inkling of this a month and a half later, though at the time it appeared to be nothing more than childish obstinacy and the dislike of bathing that many of us have when small.

Three

THE PALACE'S front courtyard hadn't changed much since it was part of the original praetorium, with a roofed and colonnaded walkway lined with rooms containing the royal armory and arsenal, various workshops, and, facing the gatehouse, what had originally been the legion's Chapel of Standards. The armless marble statue of the emperor (*an* emperor; it was impossible to tell which one) had been long ago moved to another chamber, and on the raised dais now stood a life-size wooden image of the Virgin—well, "life-size" if you believe the Mother of God was a broad-shouldered Amazon taller than the average Jute, with tits bigger than my head and a nose like a boxer's. Of course, for all I know maybe the Virgin *did* look like a buxom gladiator—perhaps that's why only God wanted her. Aside from such eccentric artistic license, the figure showed a fair amount of skill, although the woodcarver's work was garishly painted, with the crude enamel outlines around her rather crossed eyes making her look inappropriately wanton.

Arthur wasn't praying, something which he seemed to spend less and less time doing these days, but instead stood critically regarding the icon's crumbling paint. As always, he was dressed in scuffed campaign leather and smelled of horse; a decade and a half of peace had done nothing to polish his rough edges. His short bowl-cut hair was almost all gray now, not unexpected in a man of forty-six, but there was no dimming of his blue-gray eyes, and his weathered

18

face remained handsome, despite the broken nose and jug handle ears.

"You were right," he said, "that time you tried to needle me by observing that the paintwork on this image of Our Lady makes Her look like some soldier's doxy. I expect that's afforded you no small amusement over the years."

I blinked. "If so, it was passing. I can't remember the last time I gave it any thought."

He peeled a strip of paint off the statue's cheek, exposing bare wood. "This would have felt like sacrilege, once. Images were important to me when I was younger. I even believed I won at Badon primarily because I wore Her likeness painted on my shield, rather than because they overextended their supply train."

This was a relatively new note. "Arthur, do you mean to tell me you're losing your faith?"

He crossed himself, though I'm not sure he was aware he'd made the gesture. "No, not exactly. I still believe. I'm just not sure I believe He cares. I hope He does, I really do, but a certain certainty is lacking. I've done so much, Mordred, over all these years, but it never seems quite enough."

This was not the sort of conversation I was used to having with my father. "Well, your faith was never exactly a comfort to you, was it?" Or to me, for that matter.

He looked away from the painted wooden eyes and into mine. "You know the answer to that. Too keen an awareness of my sins only led to my compounding them; I looked at you and saw what I had done, not who you were. I looked at the sky and saw God frowning at me. I looked at the world and saw nothing but the cracks and flaws and broken bits; I was like a man who walks a city street and can only think of the muck in the sewers underneath. Sometimes I think Guinevere has the right of it. Perhaps Bishop Julian's Pelagianism isn't such heresy after all."

Never good at just standing around listening to someone else talk, I shifted uneasily, wishing we were someplace where it wouldn't be gauche to sit down. "Arthur, I don't think you sent for me so we could discuss theology."

"I shall have to have Her repainted," he said, seeming not to have heard me. "I wish it were as easy to put a shiny new face on my convictions, to kneel before Her without feeling like I'm going through the motions. But yes, you're right, that's not why I asked you here. Come walk with me a while.''

Thank God and the gods for that, I thought. Not that this hadn't been an interestingly odd conversation so far. I followed him out of the room and down the colonnade. Soldiers in conical helms and polished ringmail saluted as we passed, but Arthur gave them no heed. ''Guinevere says you're the best educated man in Britain.''

I chuckled sourly. ''That says more about Britain than about me, and I'm not even sure it's true. Gildas and his ilk have me beat when it comes to Christian learning.'' Not that almost anyone who'd ever set foot in a church didn't. ''And of course there's Merlin, if he still lives in the Caledonian forest.''

Arthur made a rasping sound in the back of his throat. ''Since I'm the one who exiled him there, I can expect little aid from that quarter. Let's put it this way; you're the best educated man I have on hand.''

I nodded. ''True enough, I suppose. Not that it's ever done me much good.''

We were inside the great hall now, our boots echoing on the slabs of blue-and-white concrete, inlaid with gray shale, with which most of the ground level was floored. Servants were setting two places at the oaken table in front of the great hearth. ''I hope you're hungry,'' said Arthur. ''I've been so busy today I forgot to eat, and if I wait for Guinevere and the regular mealtime, my empty stomach's likely to make me ill company indeed, so I told the staff to lay out a light supper while the Queen is at the baths.''

''An odd hour for her to be there,'' I said mildly. It was customary for women to bathe in the morning, with the afternoon reserved for men.

''Ah, but as the Queen, Gwen can make her own hours, as those she's having turned out of the bathhouse are no doubt finding out. Like me, she dislikes arbitrarily using her power, but she's reached the end of her patience with Nimüe's disregard for cleanliness, not to mention the child's ability to break free from whatever poor servants are dispatched to wash her, and so has vowed to scrub the lass herself.'' He chuckled. ''I expect she's finding that as easy as it would be to bathe Nimüe's cat.''

Fortunately, despite his reverence for Roman institutions, Arthur had never adopted the custom of dining while stretched sidelong on low couches, something I'd found damned uncomfortable the time or two that Mother made the Orkney household attempt it. As usual for the King's table, the food was plain and homespun, for he spurned aristocratic delicacies like snails and fattened dormice. Indeed, Arthur himself was eating nothing fancier than a bowl of soldier's porridge, a bland if sustaining concoction of grain and lentils, but I was relieved to see goat cheese, crusty dark bread, and blood sausage on my trencher—a satisfying enough summer repast, though I'd hoped for a bit of mutton or maybe smoked oysters. Sipping the barley ale a servant poured into my fine Samian mug, I waited for my father to come to the point.

When he did, it was nothing I would have expected. ''I have need of your expertise in scholarly matters, for I've been doing a bit of reading lately.''

That surprised me, though I'd always been vaguely aware that he knew how. ''An admirable hobby,'' I said, reaching for another sausage. ''Has Guinevere finally gotten you to share her enthusiasm for Ovid?''

He snorted. ''She'll sooner teach my horse to fly. No, I've been plowing through *The Military Institutions of the Romans* by Flavius Vegetius Renatus. Ambrosius gave it to me when I was quite young, and I've been meaning to tackle it for the last twenty-five years. Slow going, particularly for as unpracticed a reader as myself, but useful enough that I regret not having dipped into it sooner. What else do you recommend?''

I looked at him, and it was a moment before I remembered to finish swallowing. ''What, you're asking me to recommend a course of study?'' Too bad Gawain and I had failed to dig Mother's library out from the ruins of Lot's palace, since she had ended up with most of Ambrosius's books. ''Arthur, I truly mean no disrespect, but I find it hard to imagine you sitting down with the Trivium and Quadrivium.''

He shook his head. "No, you misunderstand me. Philosophy, rhetoric, those are fine things, I'm sure, but not what I need at present. I wish to learn as much as I can of the history, campaigns, and tactics of the Roman army, particularly in the West. What I learned of such matters at Ambrosius's knee has served me well here in Britain, but now I want to know more. Any suggestions?''

I had to think for a moment, as Mother, for all her love of Roman matters, hadn't encouraged me in the study of war, afraid as she was that I'd follow Gawain's path into Arthur's service. Still, certain obvious choices presented themselves. "Caesar's *Commentaries*, for a start, though you're likely to find the combination of his bland style and cold-bloodedness repellent. After that, I don't know ... maybe Polybius or Flavius Josephus. Some Livy and Tacitus, certainly. That would be a sound foundation, were all of it readily available here in Britain." Much of it, of course, was not.

The soldier's habit of wolfing his food, as he never knows when dinner might be interrupted, dies hard, and Arthur had already finished his porridge. "Make me a list, please, so I'll know what to look for."

I had to smile at the image of me sending him out like a servant to market. "Look where? Guinevere dreams of a Bibliopola in every town square, but you and I both know that won't happen in our lifetimes. If Beortric and the Jutish mercenaries who now lay claim to Orkney might be persuaded to give it up, we could always dig in the ruins of Mother's tower, but I can't imagine that much of her library has survived the elements. Were you planning to go book buying on the Continent?"

He sipped his ale, the light from the rippled yellow window giving a greenish halo to his ashen hair, making him look like an incongruously homespun Lord of the Fay. "Essentially, yes, as I shall be crossing over to Less Britain in a few weeks, and have been in correspondence with the Bishop of Armorica. More learning has survived there than in the rest of Gaul, and with luck I can convince him to exchange some of his more secular volumes for holy works from Gildas's library at Glastonbury.''

I snorted. ''Gildas won't like that. He already accuses you of turning away from your youthful fervor.''

Arthur ran a callused finger along the rim of his cup. ''Gildas needs to remember who has kept most of the Christian throats in Britain uncut for the last two decades. More churches have been built during my reign than in nearly the whole century before me, yet still he scourges me from the pulpit. Were I a petty man, I would simply confiscate his library without payment. But no, he'll be rewarded for helping my cause.''

Sitting here in the yellow-green light, my belly full and the ale tingling in my head, I felt content. When had I started being so comfortable in Arthur's company? Some of the old walls had crumbled when I first brought Guinevere out of the Kingdom of Teeth, even though that act, and the feelings for her it revealed in me, added a new twist to the knot of our relationship. Despite the balm that the years had poured on old wounds, it does seem odd that I could be so at ease around a man whom I so regularly cuckolded. Well, perhaps it's just that one can only be unhappy for so long, though that's a thought I would have found inconceivable when I was younger. Arthur, too, had mellowed, of course—when I returned Guinevere to him and to this world, something thawed inside him, and at least part of the old guilt melted away like a patch of dirty winter snow.

''Just what is that cause?'' All his life, he'd carried the Roman torch that Ambrosius and Uther passed on to him, but this interest in past military glory was something new, for though he was a brilliant commander, there'd never been much of the scholar in his soldiering.

His eyes retained their distant sheen. ''I have an idea, Mordred. Perhaps it's folly, an aging warrior's silly dream. Yet lately I find myself thinking this. So much of my life has been weighed down by guilt and disappointment that it's been easy to forget what I've actually managed to do. I've brought the Saxons and Picts to heel, which is more than even Ambrosius ever did. Our borders are safe, at least a handful of our towns are thriving, and whether they wanted to or not, the petty chieftains have come together under the banner of Imperial Britain. Sometimes I am mad enough to think I might do for the Continent what I've done for this island. The Saxons seemed unbeatable once, but I beat them, and they were never at each other's throats the way the Franks seem to be. What if I could restore, not just this former outpost of Empire, but the Empire itself? Pick up all the broken pieces, clean off the muck, mend and polish them, and fit them back together again. Now *that* would be something, wouldn't it?''

I kept my face impassive. "So, this upcoming visit across the Channel is more than just a matter of routine diplomacy.''

He shrugged. "Perhaps, perhaps not. I need to see things firsthand before I plan further. It might prove to be mere fancy after all, a silly old man dreaming in the sun.''

I tried to measure out my words carefully. "You're seldom silly and a long way from old, but the things you speak of are not to be considered lightly. Gawain is doubtless a better one for advice than me.''

He shook his head. "Your brother is generally all too happy to follow me into any folly I might propose. You're a more practical sort, when you wish to be. Plus, you've never been afraid to tell me when you thought me a fool.'' He smiled grimly. "Or worse.''

As happened so often, it was his very reasonableness that I found irritating, though I didn't want to show it. "Maybe so, but despite your having generously made me a Commander of Horse, my knowledge of war and conquest is almost entirely theoretical. Asking me for advice in such matters is like asking Gildas how to satisfy a woman.''

He made a face at that, a hint of his prudish younger self. "Ach, lad, I'll be seriously needing your help. Don't spurn my offer for the sake of bawdy sarcasm.''

I met his level gaze. "I'm spurning nothing, just warning you not to put too much store in me.'' Not that anyone ever needed too much warning of that sort. "Have you talked to Guinevere about this?''

He rested his chin on clasped hands and looked pensive. "Oh, aye, I'd be a fool not to, for we both well know how sharp she is. Guinevere has her doubts, saying that much remains to be done here in Britain, and that I too readily forget that most of the country does not live as well as we do here in Camelot, or even next door in Caerwent. She's right enough, I suppose, but I rather think that such civil affairs are ones that she can manage well enough without me. And I trust you'll aid her in that regard."

Ah, he's getting restless in his middle age, now that the great wars were done, I thought; *the years of minor border skirmishes and harmless displays of force have dulled the memory of his youth's bloody work.* But perhaps I was being uncharitable, and anyway, his immediate plans were good news for me and Guinevere, and for that reason alone I really ought to encourage them. In old stories and certain Roman comedies, not to mention the histories of the Caesars, wives managed to cuckold powerful husbands with surprising ease and frequency, but our own opportunities had never come so often as that. Indeed, we were seldom able to chance a tryst more than once or twice each season.

"Of course, I'll be glad to help in any way I can," I said, being careful not to smirk.

His eyes narrowed, and for a lunatic moment I was afraid he knew what I was thinking. "That reminds me," he said as he stood up, idly wiping his hands on the front of his dirty tunic. "The last time Guinevere went to market in Caerwent, she came back quite irate about the state of the town streets, and Lord knows they've only gotten worse with the recent heavy rainfall. Marcellos the Artisan says that, while he can't build a sewer to match the one here in Camelot, he can do better than the crude gutters they have now. Do you think your squadron is up for a bit of engineering detail?"

I tried not to grimace at the thought. "I don't expect they'll be happy at the prospect, no."

He nodded, his lips pursed. "True enough. No matter how hard I try, I'll never make a Roman of myself, much less my men. They grumble enough about digging fortifications, let alone latrines. That's the problem with having an army of horsemen; they can range from coast to coast with a speed the old Augustan infantry could never manage, but they aren't half so willing to do the hard and dirty day-to-day work that was a legionnaire's expected lot. I've already sent notice to the Caerwent magister to have a work gang of prisoners ready on the morrow. So just take enough of your men with you to direct them.''

I saluted him, while inwardly groaning at the prospect of having to watch sweaty peasants labor in the sun. "It will be done.''

He clasped my hand. "You're a good man, Mordred. Thanks for your service.'' Despite our renewed familiarity of recent years, he seldom if ever addressed me as his son, and I just as seldom called him Father.

I bowed and made my exit, still bemused by the entire conversation. I've already made it plain that Arthur had changed quite a bit from when I first arrived in Camelot, becoming less guilt-ridden and more pragmatic. Most times, I gave little thought to those changes. Indeed, except when having to do so for the purposes of this testament, I spent much of my time not thinking of him at all, despite the fact that I saw him almost every day. My relationship with Guinevere had begun when I was still angry (no matter how much I denied it at the time) for the way he'd cast me aside upon learning I was his son, with me still smarting from the lashes of his guilt and sense of sin. When love turns to hate, or even just a sour bitterness, betrayal comes relatively easy, but what about when that bitterness fades? I still deeply loved Guinevere, and sharing her with her rightful husband had never become easy, and was harder now that I was no longer angry with him. For my own protection, I'd built a wall around my heart, for fear that in the absence of my old acrimony, something like affection might creep in again. I couldn't afford to let that happen, no matter how smoothly I went through the motions of easy familiarity with the man who'd sired me. I'd seen what guilt had done to his life; there was no way I was going to allow it to enter mine.

Thinking of these matters made me want to see Gwen, for no matter how confused or lost I felt, I could stare into her green eyes and find myself again, and her lovely lopsided smile was still, after all these years, a balm for all the turmoils of my spirit. On those all too rare occasions when we got to be alone together, I knew, absolutely *knew*, that what

I found in her arms was not petty vengeance on her husband, not some cheap self-serving consolation for the world's injustice, but something fine, and, as laughable as the word may sound in this context, relatively pure. I wasn't half so sure of that when we were apart.

It didn't take me long to find her. She was alone in the courtyard, sitting on the bench beside the fountain and sipping a cup of wine, her long red hair unbound and a sour expression on her pale, high-cheekboned face. At her sandaled feet paced Clymenestra, Nimüe's cat, with scabbed tail stump held high and mouth open in a repeated faint meow. "Poor little beast," I said as I bent to scratch her small flat head. "We spend much of our lives losing things we took for granted; you just started earlier than many of us, that's all." Clymenestra mewed again, then chewed gently on my thumb.

"Why the long face?" I asked Gwen as I sat beside her on the marble bench, which was still warm from the fading light. The sun had sunk below the palace's western wall, and shadows were spreading out from beneath the arbor like tendrils of spilled ink. In the darkness of the tiny grove, crickets had begun their nightsong, and swallows were diving low between the branches.

Guinevere rested her head on my shoulder, and I breathed in the scent of her freshly cleaned hair. "My sister is turning into a most difficult brat," she said. "Lord knows where she gets it. I certainly wasn't so obnoxious at her age."

Oh, bloody hell; I'd hoped to talk about something deeper than these petty squabbles with Nimüe. Still, Gwen seemed genuinely upset, and my sulking wouldn't help matters, so I forced myself to laugh. "Sure you were, love; probably more so. And really, what makes you believe you're not obnoxious *now*?"

She rapped my kneecap smartly with her knuckles. "Speaking of obnoxious, I should know better than to expect sympathy from you." She then stroked the knee she'd just bruised, and I bit my lip and fervently wished Arthur was already on the opposite side of the Channel rather than just at the other end of the palace.

If Gwen had similar thoughts, her tone of voice did not

betray them. "Why that child has such a terror of a simple bath, I don't know, but when she began to smell like a Jute, I resolved to get her to the bathhouse by sheer force, if necessary. Thinking she'd be less likely to bite or kick me than she would the servants, I took her hand and we set off, enlisting poor Gawain as our escort. The way I catch her looking at your brother sometimes, I thought she'd be more likely to behave if he was with us. Well, for a few blocks, she did, more or less, even though she trudged so sullenly between us that we might have been taken for guards escorting a condemned felon to the gallows. Still, we made it there, and outside the baths I foolishly relaxed my grip on her wrist, and suddenly she squirmed in my hand like an eel and was free, turning and dashing right through a band of Franks who were tossing a ball in the exercise courtyard. We set off after her and must have been quite a sight, your brother, myself and the clucking servants, all chasing a grimy little girl through half of Camelot. Plautus couldn't have written such a scene. Thank God one can't get one's crown revoked for possessing insufficient royal dignity—I wasn't particularly queenly, charging down the alleys with my gown hiked up around my knees."

I tried to sound sympathetic rather than amused. "How long did it take you to catch her?"

She picked up the meowing cat, who stared at me suspiciously from her lap. "Unfortunately, I didn't. She went scuttling under one of the big brick granaries. Luckily, a squad of Gawain's men had joined us, finding it funny as hell, no doubt, but helpful for all of that. They got the building more or less surrounded, while Gawain went under it after her. He suggested that I return here and wait, saying that I didn't need to be crawling on my hands and knees in the dirt with him, a sentiment with which I heartily agreed, as I already felt quite ridiculous. Besides, I was tired, and needed a bloody drink, and so I left him and his men to their hunting. I hope he's caught her, by God, I really do." She picked up the cat and held it at arm's length. "Clymenestra, I'm tempted to hang you from the palace wall in an iron cage, as a hostage to ensure your mistress's return." She put the cat down again, but it immediately jumped back into her lap, purring in blissful ignorance of her threat.

I took her hand in mine. "Pardon me for asking, Gwen, but just why do you bother? I mean, you treat her like she's your own child, rather than your half sister." Hell, she wasn't even royal, for Gwen's father, Lord Cador, had sired her on a serving girl.

Guinevere gave me a stare as enigmatic as that of the cat snuggled in her lap; no wonder she and the feline folk got along so well. "I don't know, Mordred; it seems I am not to be blessed with child, despite your efforts and Arthur's, and it may be that Nimüe is the closest thing I shall ever have. I wasn't sired on a servant, but my father never treated me much better than he treated her. Between him bundling me off to a convent and my late mother trying to sell me to a Lord of the Otherworld, I've never had anyone treat me like family. Maybe I want to give her what I never had." She smiled grimly. "And if there are times when I want to wring her neck, well, that's part of being family, too."

At that point I heard deliberate footsteps on paving stones and turned to see Gawain emerge from the colonnaded walkway, Nimüe squirming under his right arm. I'd not have thought it possible for her to be dirtier than before, but she was.

My brother smiled grimly. "Ach, Mordred, I could have used you just now, scrambling like a badger in the dark after this one. You were always better at wriggling your way into tight spaces than me."

Nimüe stopped struggling. "All right, Gawain, you can put me down, now," she said softly. "I promise not to run away."

Gawain chuckled sourly. "Aye, that's what the rabbit said to the poacher, right enough. Still, I don't see how you could have much wind left in you, and the fires are out in the bathhouse furnace, anyway, so it's not likely your sister will be taking you there again tonight."

"I just might," said Guinevere, gently pushing the cat from her lap and rising to her impressive full height. "A dunk in the frigidarium might be good for you. Instead, though, I think I'll just empty your chamber pot over your head and chain you outside for the night. If you like filth so much, you can sleep in your own.''

Gawain cleared his throat. ''For the love of Jesus, Gwen, that's harsh. She's just a child, after all.''

Nimüe stood there with downcast eyes, her bony shoulders slumped in defeat. ''Sister, I'm sorry, I really am. Have the servants fetch a bucket of water and some fuller's earth, and I'll clean myself. Just let me do it by myself, with nobody around me, please?'' Responding to her plaintive tone, the cat curled around her ankles, purring even more loudly than before.

Even in the gloom, I could see the pale triangle of Gwen's face soften. She knelt in front of Nimüe and tilted her chin up with one finger. ''So that's it, then, you'd rather wash in private? That's what all this silly fuss has been about?''

Nimüe nodded, her eyes still downcast.

Guinevere made a token attempt at brushing Nimüe's hair out of her face. ''Well then, you could have simply said so, and spared us all a lot of trouble.''

Nimüe turned away, nearly twisting her own head halfway around her neck like an owl's in an attempt to avoid meeting any of our eyes. ''Look, I'm sorry, really I am. I don't mind cleaning myself, I just don't want anyone around when I do it, that's all. They look at you in the baths. I don't like that. I don't want anyone looking at me.''

''She's modest,'' said Gawain. ''That's all it is, really; she's just modest.''

Guinevere straightened up. ''All right. I'm going to trust you to do it now, without me watching over you. Tell the servants that I said to bring you water and fuller's earth, and to leave you alone in chambers for a time. You'll have the devil of a job scrubbing all that filth away, with nobody to rub you down with hot oil and scrape you with a strigil, but I expect you to be thorough about it, no matter how raw you must rub yourself. I'll come looking for you after supper, and if I see or smell a trace of dirt on you, I swear, Nimüe, I'll have you stripped and scrubbed down with a horse brush in front of the palace guards. Do you understand me?''

Nimüe nodded. ''Yes, Your Highness,'' she said in a tiny voice. ''I really am sorry I ran away from you.''

Gwen motioned her onward. "Just go and do what you've said you'll do, and that will be apology enough."

Bowing awkwardly, Nimüe turned and went, the little cat trotting after her.

"So that's it," said Gwen, after she was gone. "I should have suspected as much."

"So that's what?" I asked.

"She's on the cusp of womanhood. If she's not started bleeding yet, she soon will. That's a difficult time for girls. You find yourself feeling very strange about your body when it begins changing on you."

Prophetic words, though little did she and I know the full extent of those changes.

Four

BEFORE RETIRING, I scratched a list of books that Arthur might wish to look for in Armorica onto a waxed bronze tablet, although despite the Bishop of Armorica's rumored literary treasures, I was dubious he'd find any of them there. From all reports, the real storehouses of learning, such as existed in our benighted age, were in Italy, North Africa, and Byzantium, with even poor Britain being better off in such regards than barbarian-ravaged Gaul. Ah, well, I told myself that it was not my problem.

As Arthur himself had intimated, Gwen was not entirely pleased with the direction in which her husband's thoughts had been turning lately. We talked about it the next morning, when I met her beside the tinkling fountain for an early game of chess.

"Can it be that he thinks the work that remains to be done here in Britain is too small for him?" she said as she took my bishop. "Really, I find myself half-hoping that the Saxons grow discontented with their present borders, or that their kinsmen across the sea raze one of the shore forts, just so that my husband will feel he's got himself a bloody challenge, one presumably more exciting than the mere labor of restoring broken roadways or reforming the government of the towns. Yes, he's built something glorious here at Camelot, but just go seven miles down the road to Caerwent and look at the crumbling facades, the poor squatters cooking their dinners in pits dug out of courtyard mosaics, and the pools of sewage in the streets."

I sighed, not happy to be reminded of what I had in store for me today. "Oh, he's not unmindful of that. Indeed, after your continued protestations about the sorry conditions at our neighbor city, Arthur has decided to do something about it. Unfortunately, that something turned out to involve delegating the whole bloody task to me. When I was a foolish boy dreaming of my heroic future here at Camelot, I didn't quite envision that my services would be put to such glorious use." Despite my sarcastic words, I spoke more lightly and with less bitterness than I would have once felt, for I knew Arthur intended no slight, something I would have been less sure of only a few years before.

"Now, now," said Gwen consolingly, "he hardly doubts your worth, but despite the heroic deeds you've performed, you've had little actual military experience, and that's why he prefers to use your squadron for civil engineering rather than on the Saxon border. Don't blame him for being practical."

She had a point, but I didn't feel like conceding it. "Bloody hell, Gwen, how am I to gain any real experience if all I ever do with my men is set them to digging sewers and latrines?" In reality, they would only be overseeing the poor wretches who did the actual digging, but I was in no mood for such distinctions.

She twirled a strand of her unbound hair between two fingers and made a mock pout. "Someone seems to have gotten up on the wrong side of the bed this morning. I would remind that someone that if he were actually given a duty of a more martial nature, such as manning one of the Saxon shore forts or riding the Wall, then he would be too far away to have me as a chess partner." The gleam in her oh-so-green eyes made me wish that we were alone. Well, there was a temporary remedy for that.

"Speaking of chess, I shall have to break off this game before much longer." I moved my rook, then looked at Brigid, Gwen's walleyed Irish maidservant. "But before I go, I think the Queen wants some wine and cheese from the kitchens. Am I right, my lady?"

Gwen nodded at Brigid. "What the Lord Mordred means is that he is hungry, and by mentioning his appetite wishes to distract me from his parting gambit, which I now foil by moving my queen." Damn, not much got past her. "But yes, go ahead and bring us some food, and some for yourself as well." Curtsying, Brigid put down her knitting and departed.

"I wish we could have sent her in search of something farther away," I said once she was out of earshot. "Though we can only dare so much while Arthur sleeps under the same roof."

She slipped her left foot out of its gilded sandal and stroked my ankle with her long, surprisingly prehensile toes. I felt myself get hard, a reaction that even after over half a decade of our furtive couplings, the briefest touch of her flesh upon my own could still engender. "Oh, I don't know. Sometimes I think Arthur simply chooses not to see what he chooses not to see, and it really doesn't matter how close or near he is, but then my sense of self-preservation tells me not to get complacent, for I'm hardly married to a doddering fool like ... what *was* his name, the Emperor whose wife cuckolded him at every turn?" She raised her leg higher, so that the ball of her foot was gently pressing against my crotch.

I tried to ignore the way the stiff head of my penis seemed to strain against the wool of my tunic, like a snake probing for an exit in the fabric of the sack in which a child has trapped it. "That could be several of them," I mumbled through teeth that I found difficult to unclench from around my lower lip. "Claudius, perhaps. And if you keep that up, you'll get me so horny I'll have no choice but to seek out a whore this afternoon."

She pressed her foot harder against my groin, bearing her heel down on the bulge of my testicles. "You better not."

I grasped her ankle, raised her foot so high in the air that she almost overbalanced, kissed it, then lightly bit down on her big toe, which made her choke back a sound that was half sigh of ecstasy, half squawk of protest. "Well then, you shouldn't play the cock tease, should you? How did a lady who grew up in a convent ever learn to be so wicked?"

She leaned back on the bench, her hands behind her buttocks, her long legs straight out in front of her, golden hairs glowing like fine copper wires on the exposed milky skin of her left calf. Time weighed lightly on my Guinevere, giving her slight hollows under her emerald eyes, sketching the faintest hint of laugh lines around her wide red mouth. Despite her big bones, she was still as lithesome as a cat, and there was no gray in the fiery cascades of her hair. "I came late to those skills, but I had a good teacher and proved a fast study." The slightly lopsided quality of her grin did nothing to diminish its charm, and I had to sit on my own hands to keep them from reaching out to her. *My life has been ruled by women*, I thought; *first Mother, now her. Ah, but this is a better servitude than my last.*

Two sets of footsteps sounded on the paved and colonnaded walkway, the heavier one measured and the lighter one skipping. Gwen quickly removed her foot from my crotch and slipped it back inside her shoe. I stuck my tongue out at her. Fortunately, while several windows in the upper stories of the palace looked out on this inner garden, the magnolia boughs that shaded our bench provided a convenient canopy against prying eyes, at least in summer.

Brigid appeared, carrying a small Castorware amphora and a wicker basket, Nimüe trotting beside her. "Has anyone seen Clymenestra?" asked the latter as she came skipping toward us."

"Still clean," I said to Gwen, *sotto voce.*

"So far, at least," she whispered back, sounding cautiously optimistic. Then, to Nimüe: "I've not seen her, dear, but I expect she's in the stable, breakfasting on mice."

Nimüe shook her head, and I noted that her hair showed a semblance of combing. "No, she doesn't go near the stable, not since she lost her tail, for she's too frightened of the oxcarts. I haven't seen her since yesterday, and am worried about her. Usually she's here, hunting lizards in the sunlight."

I spied a small rock in the garden soil at my feet, picked it up, and, turning where I sat, tossed it across the courtyard and into a cluster of ivy, pleased to see I'd not completely lost my childhood throwing arm. The impact of my missile sent an exodus of small blue-gray shapes scurrying across the whitewashed wall. "Well, there's plenty of game about, but I don't see your four-footed huntress. Sorry.'' Idly, I wondered if the loss of her own dorsal appendage had soured the cat on that typical feline pastime of snatching the tails off lizards, but did not voice this silly fancy.

Nimüe walked past us into the small stand of trees. "Here, Clymenestra,'' she shouted, adopting that irritatingly shrill tone that people unaccountably insist on using when calling their cats. "Here, kitty, kitty, kitty!''

Guinevere accepted the mug of wine that Brigid poured for her and nibbled on a wedge of cheese. "Really, Nimüe, that's hardly necessary—Lord Mordred and I have been here for the better part of an hour, and there's been no sign of your pet. It's really too nice and peaceful for you to be making such a racket.''

I gulped my wine and wolfed down my cheese less daintily than Gwen had. "True enough, Nim. I'm off to Caerwent to round up and supervise a damned work crew, and would very much appreciate a few more moments of stillness and quiet before I have to spend the rest of the day shouting at louts in the hot sun.''

Nimüe frowned and stuck out her lower lip. "I was just making sure she wasn't asleep.'' Saying that, she turned on her heel and started to stride away.

Gwen made a clucking sound. "Sister, you forget your manners.''

Nimüe pivoted and made a clumsy attempt at a bow. "Forgive me, Your Highness. I give you and Lord Mordred good day.''

Gwen sighed and waved her on. "I don't insist on formalities all the time, but we shouldn't forget them entirely,'' she said, to herself as much as to her departing sibling.

I stood up, wanting to kiss her lips good-bye, but in her maid's presence having to settle for her hand. "We'll finish the game soon, unless you want to go ahead and concede your inevitable defeat.''

She picked up several of the pieces she'd taken from me, rattling the quartz chessmen in her hand like a girl getting ready to toss the bones. "Inevitable, is it? I have your bishop, both your rooks, and your knight, as well as four of your pawns.''

Which was the only good thing about my having to leave at this point, as I despised losing, even to her. "Ah, but I prefer to be unencumbered by superfluous pieces. Unfortunately, time doesn't permit a further demonstration of my strategy." I bowed sardonically. "Give you good day, my lady."

"And you, my lord," she said dryly, brushing one of the chessmen against her red lips before setting it down again. "Happy digging."

Camelot was built from the ruins of Isca Silurum, former headquarters of the Second Augustan Legion. When I first arrived there, the amphitheater just outside the southeast wall was little more than an empty shell, a huge grassy bowl rimmed by broken brown-and-gray stones, used mainly by the lovers (or whores and their customers) who slipped out the gates on warm summer nights to lie together on the cool grass. This had puzzled me, for although Arthur had no love of blood sports, it seemed odd that he wasn't making use of such a suitable parade ground and drilling field. But no, back then he preferred to train his men in the muddy purlieus to the west, saying that, as they would fight in muck often enough, they might as well drill in it. He was, of course, making a symbolic gesture, just another attempt at turning the world into his own personal hair shirt.

It says something of how he'd changed that the amphitheater was now ringed by wooden bleachers and the once-verdant sward had been trampled into raw red earth, which was regularly raked and rolled to provide a level practice field. Today, it was my own cohort that drilled there, 480 men in rag-stuffed leather padding, their wooden practice weapons *whack-whack-whacking* against wicker shields while dyspeptic officers strolled about and shouted orders above the arrhythmic timpani.

I say "my" cohort, but real day-to-day authority lay in the capable, spade-shaped hands of Colwyn, my senior officer, a broad-chested thatch-haired Ordovici whose flat sun-baked face never seemed to harbor even the faintest trace of emotion. Although there were no few of my native *Scotti* in the company, over half the ranks were composed of Silures,

and not of the centuries-tame lowland variety. Although they
sweated through their morning sword drill with a rough approximation of Roman discipline, their intricately tattooed
arms and lime-stiffened mustaches marked them as close kin
to the wild-eyed hillmen who'd once raided the brown plow-
lands and green meadows of the Usk basin from their strongholds in the Black Mountains to the northeast. The nearest
of those ancient turf-walled uplands fortresses was now
manned by a cohort of Dumnoni from across the Severn Sea,
for Arthur practiced a miniature version of the geographical
prudence that once sent British legionnaires to North Africa
and set Scythians along Hadrian's Wall.

I sat on a folding camp chair on the raised dais that once
supported the officer's box and watched Colwyn pick the
two dozen men I'd need, nodding my approval each time he
pointed his hazelwood swagger stick at a likely candidate,
though truth to tell, for the work we were going to be doing,
I could just as well have taken the twenty-four men standing
nearest the dais. Still, since I was going to be in direct command of this lot, it was prudent to rely on Colwyn's judgment in choosing men who wouldn't try to cut my throat
and bolt once we were near the seedy fleshpots of Caerwent.
That wasn't a particularly likely prospect, of course, but for
all of Arthur's attempts at creating a professional and civilized army, these men were only a generation or two removed from the loose amalgamation of barbaric warbands
brought together by Ambrosius Aurelianus, and a certain
amount of care was necessary to see that they didn't revert
to their reckless ancestral ways.

"So you'll be leading these lads yourself, my lord," said
Colwyn, as he lined his choices up before me. "Are you
sure you don't want to take an experienced officer with
you?"

I laughed sourly. "Ach, no, I wouldn't want to risk any
of our most seasoned men in today's perilous duty. Indeed,
I hope these fellows have made arrangements as to which of
their barracks mates will get their most prized possessions,
should they not return. I expect we'll suffer a very high
casualty rate today, riding herd on a bunch of unwilling civilian laborers and making sure they dig their ditches deep

and straight.'' Clearing my throat, I punctuated this jibe by hawking a phlegm glob onto the cracked marble slab at my feet. Most of the men standing at loose attention below me grinned at this, and I knew I'd won them over. Ach, it was nice to know I was getting better at this sort of thing.

Grooms were waiting for us outside of the amphitheater with the necessary horses, and soon we were cantering along the Isca Road under an opalescent sky, the walls of Camelot dwindling behind us as we rode east beside the brown bird-tracked mudflats and slate gray waters of the sighing Usk. Looking out at the water meadows and low hills, and beyond these, the darkening uplands and haze-shrouded crags of Gwent, I was struck, for the hundredth or thousandth time, by how large my world had become. That may seem an odd thought, considering that since arriving in Britain I'd never seen more than the southwest tip of what had once been just the most far-flung of Rome's many provinces, but you must remember that I was born and raised in low-horizoned Orkney, where my known universe consisted of a narrow strip of seabound moor, and trees and mountains were little more than something I'd read about in books.

After a few miles, we came to a stone-and-timber bridge, which we had to wait for a farmer's mule cart to clear before we could cross. On the other side, the road ran between a double stand of willows for a quarter mile, then looped through meadows where furze and bluebell flared amid the dull green and brown sedges. The day had begun on the usual overcast note, but now the mud-colored, soggy-looking clouds were breaking up and bearing off toward the west without discharging their usual quota of rain, and when the road rose and dipped to reveal Caerwent ahead of us, it stood highlighted by shafts of rainbow light that rent the dissipating overcast, making that rather shabby city stand out from the sedgy meads with an atypical fairy glamour.

This magical first impression was belied when the wind changed, and I could smell the place. You'd not expect someone who grew up in rude rough-hewn Orkney to have such refined sensibilities, but remember, where I was born, there were fewer than five hundred people lodging within a mile of our stone-and-timber palace, and that included the royal warband. We weren't very sanitary but we weren't that numerous, and so nothing had prepared me, upon my first arrival in Britain, for the reek of a large urban settlement. At Camelot, where an approximation of Roman hygiene was enforced, things weren't so bad, but our sister city of Caerwent was a different story. Although Arthur rebuilt the civilian bathhouse here, which was actually larger than the military one in his fortress, the common townsfolk made scant use of it, even after the city magister was forbidden to charge them admission, and there was no equivalent to Camelot's ingenious legion latrines, which Arthur had also restored, and which his troops were compelled to use, with docked pay and a flogging for any man caught relieving himself in the street.

Caerwent covers about forty acres and is divided by a main street running east to west, with two parallel lanes, and four more north–south ones, arranging the town in a grid of twenty blocks. From a distance, it still looks quite impressive, with a high wall rising starkly from the smooth turf, buttressed by a dozen imposing polygonal bastions. As you approach closer, rents become visible in the outer stonework, and once you enter one of the three functioning gates (the south one having been blocked up over a century ago, when Irish raids spurred renewed fortification), the present-day decline becomes rather more evident. This had been one of Britain's proudest cities, with a grand basilica and elegant town houses with tessellated pavements and heated rooms. Now many of the latter were in ruins, some having collapsed down to the ground floor, with squatters lighting their cookfires on the broken walls, and crude forges and tempering troughs dug into the tiles of what had once been fine mansions.

Remember, though, that the history of Britain is older than that of Rome, for we were the Island of the Mighty when the Empire was a village of mud huts on a hill, and all this urban decline meant was that Caerwent had resumed its traditional role as the market town of the Silures, with fruit and corn and hides being sold amid the broken columns and crumbling storefronts of the basilica, rather than the silver ornaments, delicate figurines, lead vessels, and uniformly produced Castorware that had once been the merchant's stock-in-trade. And, of course, there was a lively business in soldierly recreation, with taverns and brothels taking more than a dozen of the city blocks.

And until I came here, there had been the amphitheater, but after our misadventure with the Palag Cat, Arthur shut it down, ending the games and beast baitings. Now it was used mainly as a temporary stockade for holding prisoners, with nearly a hundred gathered there today, squatting in their shackles on the garbage-strewn arena floor. They were the usual hapless lot—a dozen murderers, at least four times that many petty thieves, a few deserters from the army, some Saxon brigands caught sacking a Silure farmstead, and prisoners from a repulsed Irish raiding party. The senior Watch-Captain, a grinning, red-faced fellow named Drumlach, helped me pick men whose crimes warranted temporary labor, rather than the more dangerous ones destined for lifelong servitude in the uplands silver mines or the farm country to the south. The selection made, my men and I returned to the main street, where a cartload of shovels awaited us, courtesy of the town magister. In the time of the legions, each of my men would have brought his own shovel, as important a part of a soldier's kit as his sword, and would have used it to do his own digging, but as I have said, no matter what Arthur might want to make of us, we are not Romans anymore.

The main street of Caerwent was not paved like that of Camelot, just strewn with gravel, with a shallow gutter running down its center. This trough had become so choked with mud, garbage, and human refuse that it no longer carried away rainwater, and today we were going to take the first step in replacing this inadequate system of drainage with an actual sewer, albeit one lined with timbers rather than stone like Camelot's. We started just inside the eastern gatehouse, having staked out some four hundred feet of the main street, or about one-third of its entire length. The forty prisoners, still shackled, were spaced at ten-foot intervals in the center of the street and given shovels, each man responsible for creating a section of trench eight feet deep. Later, wooden handcarts would be brought up, and the excavated mud, filth, and gravel would be carried to a cesspit outside the city wall.

Four of my men rode up and down the line, lances ready, while the rest, their mounts hitched nearby, stood guard on foot, hands on hilts. It was in truth a tedious detail, standing there in the sun, shaded only by the canopy of flies that rose from the muck displaced by our charges' shovels. Townsfolk eyed us from shabby storefronts and the roofs of the newer, cruder stone-and-timber houses (many of the older houses not having roofs that it was safe to sit upon), but they got bored soon enough and went about their business.

You might think that Arthur was trying to punish me with such a lowly assignment, one that could have easily been carried out by Colwyn or any of my junior officers, but no, such was not his aim. Men from all the kingdoms of Britain, as well as no few foreigners, rode under the Dragon standard, and keeping them loyal to each other and to the officers they served, rather than their native principalities, was crucial. Whenever possible, Arthur made even his highest-born commanders rub elbows with the enlisted men, believing that too much stratification increased the danger of rebellion. Such matters had been less important in the old days, with the day-to-day threat of Saxons giving every Briton a common objective, but in this decade of peace there was far more opportunity for internal discord, and Arthur wished to keep his forces as cohesive and unified as possible. Commanders like Gawain and Geraint and Kay routinely accompanied their men on the meanest of details, though, it must be said, those details were seldom as rank as this one.

Riding up and down the line, I kept noticing one particularly large and surly-looking lout, with a squashed-looking nose and a scalp that was almost completely shaved, except for one small patch of carrot-colored hair. He, in his turn, kept glaring at me, as if I were responsible for his plight, which was hardly the case, for if my men had not come along today, the Caerwent watchman would have shipped him off to the silver mines or the farms, where his prospects would have been rather bleaker than they were here. If I remembered what the watch had told me when I was going down the list, he was technically a deserter from the fortress, although his "desertion" had consisted of getting drunk in a brothel and refusing to return to Camelot when his leave was up. His was the sort that, paradoxically, you are more likely to see in times of peace than war, someone who chafes and chafes under military regimen until he does something foolish and self-destructive.

Which is exactly what he did today, and in a quite spectacular fashion. Standing as he was in several feet of ditch, with a mound of excavated muck beside him, his body was invisible to me below the waist. When, with a sudden snarled oath, he raised his shovel above his head and brought it down toward his feet with a stabbing motion, I did not at first realize what he intended, nor recognize the resulting dull *chink* for the sound of links parting in his chain. Instead, stupidly, I actually reined my gelding closer just as the bastard came bounding out of the ditch, whooping like a Jute and whirling his shovel above his head.

Fortunately, the reflexes acquired in long hours of drill meant that I'd pulled my lance from its leather socket even before my brain realized that this idiot was actually charging me, and our mutual timing was such that, as I lowered my weapon in his direction, he obligingly ran right into it, the tip of its pyramidal iron head penetrating his left eye socket, pushing the eyeball aside and punching through the bone with a dull crunch. The old familiar shock ran up my arm, and I almost lost the lance, not having had time to couch it properly, but, squeezing it between my forearm and ribs, and gripping my mount's sides with my knees, I somehow managed both to retain my hold and stay in the saddle. My erstwhile attacker hung there limply, his knees buckled and mouth agape, and then he slid off my point and crumbled onto the recently shoveled muck. Looking at him lying in a pitiful heap, the displaced flies already settling upon him, I thought this was surely one of the more pointless and humiliating deaths I'd seen. *Grant my ending more grace than this sad bastard's*, I thought, as I wiped the point of my lance on his dirty tunic.

My men were whistling and clapping, as were, bizarrely, a few of the prisoners. "This poor sod's idiotic death hardly deserves applause," I said with mild reproach, though in truth some shameful part of me was pleased. I pointed my lance at the next man in line. "You there, did you know this man?"

Standing in a ditch beside a mound of shit and gravel, he didn't look particularly intimidated. "Just a little," he said in the accent of the Summer Country. "We were in your king's army together.

Ah, another deserter. "Why on earth did he do it?"

The man shrugged and brushed flies from his hair. "Bugger always had a hot temper. It got him flogged a few times, which is why he said he wasn't going back. Some folk just don't like following orders." He looked down at his feet, then grinned back at me. "And I guess there's just something about standing in chains, with shit piled up to your waist, that can rub a fellow the wrong way, if you'll pardon me for saying so."

I put my lance back in its socket. "You can say whatever you bloody please, but if one more man tries anything that foolish, you'll all go to the silver mines when you're through digging this bloody sewer, rather than get released as I intended. Do I make myself clear?"

The man in the ditch actually saluted. "Yes, sir." Looking back down the line, he raised his shovel. "Come on, boys, let's get this damn thing dug, and no more nonsense!"

The rest of the day passed without incident, as the prisoners fell to their disagreeable work with renewed energy, chattering and laughing among themselves and singing bawdy songs off-key. Apparently, the man I'd killed (or perhaps more properly, the man who'd managed to kill himself on my lance point) had been less than popular, and his fellows seemed gratified for the amusement afforded by his death. Also, apparently many of them hadn't realized they *wouldn't* be going to the farms or silver mines when this detail was over until I threatened to send them there if anyone else misbehaved, and thus were quite relieved to hear me say that, barring any more unpleasantries, they'd be set free when their work was finished. At any rate, they worked more speedily and cheerfully than I expected, and by day's end we'd gotten the entire trench dug and most of the muck carted off to the cesspit outside the east gate. Tomorrow we'd start laying the timbers for the sewer, and with luck would get that finished, and the whole structure tarred and covered up in gravel by the end of the week.

After the day's tedious, foul-smelling work, it was a relief to canter through clean, cool air that smelled of apple blossoms and fresh water, with whooshing swifts and the night's first bats diving low after the insects that flittered above the chuckling river, while the sun melted like red tallow behind the blue-black hills. My men sang as they galloped behind me, less bawdily and somewhat more melodically than the work gang had done while shoveling, that old song about the lad who went hunting fat rabbits on the green hillside, and the woman he met there, whose hair shone like the moon reflected in deep water. Although I enjoyed listening to them well enough, I did not add my voice to their chorus, for I couldn't carry a tune if it had handles, a mildly shameful fault in someone of our most musical of races.

Our hoofbeats echoed under the overhang of the gatehouse, and then we were back inside our home fortress, where the darkening air carried the smell of the charcoal fires burning in the cookhouses built against the west wall. Delegating my horse to the man who'd laughed the loudest when I lanced the hapless prisoner, I made for the bathhouse, my legs unsteady after a long day in the saddle, for I was eager to have the scent of Caerwent steamed and scraped from my body and to feel the relaxing balm of the masseur's oiled hands.

Alas, I never got the massage I craved, for I was still sweating in the calidarium when I heard, not the clack of wooden bath sandals, but the softer tread of boots, and looked up from my damp bench to see who was risking doeskin on the hot tiles. Coughing from the steam, which he parted before him by flapping his tartan cloak, Gawain loomed over me and threw my clothes into my lap. ''You're needed back at the palace.''

Not about to dress here in the steam, I clacked out to the changing room, Gawain padding impatiently behind me, and hopped from leg to leg while pulling on my breeches. ''What is so important that it couldn't wait until I finished my bath?''

"You'll see," he growled like the bear he resembled. "It has to do with Nimüe."

"Lugh's balls," I grumbled, "what's she done now?"

"It's what you've done, brother, not her," said Gawain, as I pulled my woolen tunic over my head. When I could see again, his face had softened slightly. "Look, Mordred, I'm sorry to be a bloody pain, but it's easier to show you when we get there than explain. Now get your boots on, and let's be off." With that, he turned and shambled toward the door.

Uncomfortably sweaty in my woolen tunic, I cursed softly at being denied the benefit of oil and strigil and plunge bath—oh, aye, I'd become quite the pampered fop during my few years here at Camelot. Striding along uncomfortably behind my brother, I suppressed the urge to kick him and stalk back to the bathhouse, for aside from the obvious fool-hardiness of such a gesture, I knew that Gawain wouldn't be acting this way without good cause. *Nimüe*, he'd said; what on earth did some fresh difficulty involving Gwen's unruly sibling have to do with me?

I found out when we arrived back at the palace. Servants scurried out of the way, all whispers and saucer-eyed stares, as my brother led the way to the inner courtyard. It was more crowded than it had been this morning, for a dozen guards stood at somewhat uneasy attention, the light of their torches glimmering off their greased ringmail. In their midst was Arthur himself, pacing restlessly in his usual scuffed leather, his long sword bare in his hand with dark stains gleaming near its tip. For a moment, I was transported back to that horrible night when I'd been summoned here to find that Guinevere had been carried off by Melwas, Otherwordly lord of the Kingdom of Teeth. But no, the cause of this evening's uproar wasn't quite so momentous.

"What's the matter?" I asked when he turned toward me. "Gawain said there was something about Nimüe . . ."

He cut me off with a gesture, pointing silently behind him. My eyes followed the direction of his finger to where something small and dark moved faintly on the flagstones about ten yards away, halfway between the fountain and the grove of trees. Uncomprehending, I walked closer to it, and it resolved itself into several smaller pieces, all of them stirring feebly. I motioned for a guard to bring up a torch, which he was loath to do until Arthur nodded for him to comply.

By the guttering light, I made out what remained of Clymenestra, Nimüe's cat. If I'd thought the poor beast unlucky when it lost its tail, its present state was so unfortunate as to be almost grotesquely comic, for the animal had been hacked into at least three pieces, the nearest of which was its flat little head. When I nudged this with my toe, its glassy eyes blinked and its jaws opened in a soundless yowl.

Behind me, I heard a light footfall on the flagstones, then Guinevere's voice. "I put Nimüe to bed. Did Gawain bring Mordred?"

"That he did," I said without turning around. "What the hell happened?"

Arthur made a coughing sound before he spoke. "I tried to put the poor creature out of its misery, something which does not appear to be possible."

I turned back to him. "You tried to kill it?"

Guinevere answered before he could. "It was dead before he took his sword to it, Mordred, if that word has any meaning for something that won't lie down and be still. Take a look at it again."

I walked back to the remains and knelt beside them, fascinated. Picking up the cat's head, which continued to gape in my hand, I turned it over and over in the torchlight. Close inspection revealed saliva-matted fur and bloody holes, very much as if the skull had been gripped between canine teeth. Putting it down again, I gingerly examined the body, to which one of the hind legs was still attached, kicking feebly. A loop of pale gut glistened where the torso had been opened by something less precise than a sword. Wiping my hand on my tunic, I stood up, once again wishing I was back at the bathhouse or the tavern.

"I came when I heard Nimüe screaming," said Guinevere grimly. "She'd been looking for her cat all day, and I'd told her not to blow her damned whistle inside, so she'd come out here again. When I came running to her, I saw the cat. It was mostly in one piece then, but clearly in no shape to be walking like it was, not with one leg gone, and its head hanging limply on a broken neck, with its guts dragging behind it.''

"It must have gotten out of the palace again," I said, understanding at last. "And run afoul of the barracks dogs." Many of the men kept dogs as pets, or for hunting, or even as a form of livestock, for when they weren't able to catch rabbits and had gambled away the silver they'd use to buy grain. "They caught and killed it, somewhere out there on the streets."

Guinevere stepped forward and handed something to me: the crude whistle I'd fashioned from a joint of Clymenestra's tail. "You gave Nimüe this?"

I looked at Gawain, where he was hanging back under the colonnade. He met my stare impassively, with no accusation. My brother had never been one to rub it in when he was right, not that this ever made me more inclined to forgive him for being so. Perhaps he sensed this, for with a parting nod, he turned and strode back into the palace. *That's right, Gawain, slink off somewhere else, just like you used to do in Orkney*, I thought unfairly. *If you're going to the bathhouse, I hope you slip and hurt yourself.*

I was wasting time with such uncharitable thoughts because I didn't want to answer Gwen's question, but of course there was no help for it. "Yes," I finally said. "I gave it to her, and told her to blow it if her cat ever ran away again."

Gwen's eyes glittered icily, and I realized, maybe for the first time, just how protective she was of her half sister. "And when she blew it enough times, the cat came back, even though it was dead. Is that what happened, Mordred?" No, I did not like this new inflection she gave my name.

"It shouldn't have." I held up the whistle. It tingled warmly in my hand, and smelled like the air where lightning has struck. Yes, there was true power here. "She shouldn't have been able to do that," I said in dull astonishment. "Not her, not with this. She shouldn't have been able to bring her cat back after it was dead."

Arthur cleared his throat. "That's the point, Mordred. If you hadn't given her that sorcerous token, she'd not have been able to do such an unnatural deed. You know how I feel about these things. This does not please me."

More importantly, it displeases your wife, I thought, searching for some hint of reprieve in the torchlight-dappled triangle of her face. A distant part of me wondered how long it would be before I lay in her arms again, and I wanted to kick myself for creating this barrier between us, right before Arthur was due to go away for a while. He'd be across the Channel in Less Britain, and I'd still sleep alone, all because I'd been too fucking lazy to go searching for a cat. Ach, but as you must know by now, I've never needed much excuse for self-pity.

"No, you don't understand," I said, frustrated even as I spoke by the realization of how this was going to sound. "She still shouldn't have been able to do such a thing. What I gave her was magic, yes, but not so strong as this. I don't think I could have brought the cat back to life no matter how hard I tried, not without . . ." I broke off before I could say *not without Mother to help me.* My late mother was not a subject easily broached around Arthur, and this was no time to be reminding him of what he considered the dark and pagan side of my heritage.

"Then why didn't Clymenestra stay dead?" asked Gwen impatiently. "How is it that the poor creature still moves after my husband cut her into pieces?"

I looked back at the remains. Well, she wasn't moving *much,* but it was no help saying that. "I don't know," I mumbled. "It wasn't just my magic."

"If not yours, whose?" said Arthur, with more mildness than I would have expected from him.

The answer was obvious, though hardly credible. "Nimüe's, I think. Some people are gifted that way, without ever being trained in the art, or even being aware of their own abilities. Gwen, your own mother was a sorceress; you must know something of these things."

She came closer, and I was relieved to see the cold fire in her eyes had dimmed slightly. "My mother, not hers. My mother died before Nim was born. I don't see how she could have passed her gift on."

Arthur was hanging back, aloof from all this, and though I was grateful enough, I wished he wasn't there at all, for I dearly wanted to take Gwen's hand. "That's my point; it doesn't really have to be 'passed on'—it just crops up, the way some children are born with a hot temper or a lisp or a gift for music. Gods, if she were formally tutored, she could be quite powerful.''

Arthur made a rumbling mastiff sound, but then spoke in a voice he kept low and even. ''That will not happen. I may have drifted somewhat in my faith, but I'll not have magic studied here.''

He was being foolish, I thought, doubly so for a man who'd needed (and more importantly, accepted) magical aid on at least one crucial occasion. But no, Arthur associated such matters with my mother, who'd seduced him with her arts, and with Merlin, the prophetic and preternaturally aged-but-ageless boy who'd been his father's catamite, and whom he'd exiled to Caledonia upon becoming King. Apparently, the pragmatism he'd acquired in middle age only went so far, which is not surprising; who among us is ever truly rid of his younger self, a nemesis that he spends his adult life growing away from, but which forever hounds his track?

Arthur continued to speak in low, measured tones. ''Mordred, when I told you that I'd lost something of my old convictions, I was not asking to be shocked back into them, nor did I mean my confession of weakness as leave for you to be taking up your mother's black arts. Now get rid of this unholy mess.''

There was no arguing with that. I unpinned my tartan cloak, silently cursing the fact that it was my best one, and spread it on the ground, then picked up the twitching pieces of resurrected cat and tossed them on it. Grinding the bone whistle under my heel, I scooped up the resulting fragments and dropped them on top of the remains. Tying the cloak up in a sack, I handed it to a guard. ''Please burn that in one of the furnaces.'' Whatever latent magic Nimüe possessed, it could hardly be strong enough to reanimate ashes.

Arthur nodded, and the man stalked off, holding the bundle at arm's length like a bag that contains a snake. I went down on one knee. ''I apologize, Your Highness, and to you, My Queen, and must beg your forgiveness.''

The tone of Guinevere's voice suggested her eyes were flashing again, which made me thankful my own were downcast. "It's not me, or even Arthur, to whom you should apologize, but poor Nimüe. She's suffered the most in this. The child is likely to have nightmares for weeks."

Aid came from an unexpected source. "Now, now, Gwen," said Arthur, the calmness in his voice sounding less forced. "All of us have known worse, and at a younger age. Mordred made a mistake, one I daresay he won't repeat. Nothing is gained by further reproach." Something in his voice made me wonder if he was jealous of the attention she lavished upon her sibling.

I looked up to see him wave the guards away. "Back to your posts, everyone; let us put this nasty bit of business behind us. And you stand up, Mordred; you were never one sincerely to go down on your knee to me or anyone else. Let's all be about our evening's business, and with luck, there shall be no cause to speak of this again."

Everyone swept out of the dark courtyard with him except Guinevere, who in the absence of torchlight was a tall, long-haired shadow. She strode to me, but until her hand touched my face I had no idea of her mood. "I should still be angry with you," she said quietly. "Indeed, I am still angry."

Safe there in the shadows, I pressed her hand against my cheek. "I only meant to do the child a kindness, Gwen. Don't use that as a stick to beat me with. I'm no hero in a story, to languish mournfully because I've lost my lady's favor."

She actually chuckled. "Ach, no, you're all barbs and thorny nettles, same as ever. You once told me I must accept you for yourself, with no hope of changing you. Now as then, I seem to have little choice."

I brushed my lips against the side of her hand. "There's always choices, Gwen."

"Perhaps," she said with a low sigh, "but some cannot be unmade, and you and I are one of those."

Though I knew this was true, I didn't like hearing it, for there always remained that part of me that did not want to be bound to anyone. "We could stop this, now or tomorrow or next week, and never touch like this again. Our lives might be simpler and more safe."

She chuckled again, more ruefully this time. "Oh, aye, we could do that. But you know we won't."

And then, kissing me quickly, she turned and hurried after Arthur, leaving me alone in the dark courtyard. The crickets and tree frogs that dwelt in the small grove resumed their nightsong, and I listened to their chorus and thought that things could have turned out much worse, and that there was really no cause to be unhappy. Ach, but I seemed to be telling myself that quite often, these days. Well, there was no help for it but to get drunk, for all the misery that a hangover would add to the morrow's renewed labors.

Five

P ROBABLY BECAUSE Arthur's own room was small and spartan as a monk's cell, Guinevere maintained separate and rather more luxurious chambers at the other end of the fourth-floor hall. When they fucked, which I gathered wasn't all that often, they presumably did it in her comfortably large bed, as I couldn't imagine them coupling sweatily on his narrow pallet (actually, I preferred not to imagine them coupling anywhere, but that's another subject). The Queen's quarters consisted of a furnished antechamber that opened on the hallway, a curtained-off inner bedroom, and beyond that, a railed balcony that afforded a good view of the red tile roofs and gridiron streets of Camelot, the less orderly cluster of timbered shops and row houses beyond the southeast wall, and encircling all, the gray-green ribbon of the Usk as it wound its way from the stone-and-bracken uplands to the glistening mudflats of the Severn estuary.

Nimüe normally slept on a low, narrow but well-cushioned cot in the tiled antechamber, but this morning she lay huddled in a gold-and-green-patterned wool blanket on Gwen's fine oak-frame bed, her fever sweat staining the expensive linen sheets. More like an attendant than a queen, Guinevere sat beside her on a padded stool, softly humming the tune that the folk of the Summer Country call "The Courtship of Bronwyn" (though it must have at least a dozen names and as many different lyrics), occasionally dipping a square of woolen cloth in the bucket at her bare feet and using it to wipe her sibling's brow.

53

"Ach, you should let me do that, my lady," said plump little Brigid as she ushered me into the chamber, the beaded curtain rattling behind us. "I've had plenty of practice caring for sick brothers and sisters, and all nine of them lived, even though fever was bad in the bog country where I was born. Here, I've brought Lord Mordred for you."

Guinevere did not look up. "Thank you, Brigid, but I'll do this for a while longer. And it was for Nimüe that I asked you to bring Mordred."

The child opened her dark-circled eyes, bigger than ever in her drawn face. "Hello, cousin," she said, her voice somewhat raspy.

"Hello, yourself," I said as I went down on one knee upon the huge bearskin that covered most of the room's floor. "I've come to ask your forgiveness and to bring you something that will make you feel better."

In the week since the unfortunate return of her dead cat, Nimüe had fallen ill, a result, no doubt, of sleeplessness and a lack of appetite and the general shock to her sensibilities. And maybe more than that; I've already said that the little whistle I carved for her should never have contained the power to bring even a small animal back from the dead, for all its potency in summoning a live one. Whatever deeper magic Nimüe had unknowingly wrought, she might have used up a tiny bit of her essence in doing so.

"You don't have to apologize," she said with that gravity that sometimes came over her and belied her years. "You were only trying to help me. If not for you, I wouldn't know I could do magic."

Guinevere frowned. "Love, we've agreed there'll be no more talk of that. I thought I had your promise."

Nimüe coughed into the blanket. "Maybe, but promises are different when you're sick. You have to be nice to me and let me talk about whatever I want."

Guinevere's scowl exaggerated itself into a teasing frown, though I could tell from her eyes she was still peeved. "Ach, I have to be nice to you, do I? If that's the way of it, then you better not plan on getting well again, for I shall have quite a storehouse of meanness ready when you do."

Nimüe smiled and reached out and took her hand. "I

know it's naughty of me to tease you when you're taking care of me like this, but I can't help thinking about it, for it just keeps going round and round in my head. If I can do magic, I can change things. Maybe even change myself.''

Figuring I might as well be comfortable, I sat cross-legged on the floor. ''And what would you change, then?''

Nimüe looked up at the plaster ceiling, which was painted with colorful but crude nymphs and dryads. ''I'd become a beautiful lady, like in stories. The kind a handsome warrior looks at once and loves forever. Gawain would be visiting me now, if I could change myself into that.''

Gwen and I exchanged looks, mine somewhat more amused than hers. I'd teased Gawain about having a soft spot for this child, but hadn't realized that the attraction I'd jokingly attributed to him was reciprocated. ''I'm sure he'd be here, if he'd not gone to London with Arthur, to see him off to Gaul and then to make sure the South Saxons are behaving. And anyway, what's this 'handsome' talk? I'm here, and I'm much better-looking than my brother.''

Nimüe laughed, though it looked like it hurt to do so. ''Gawain is like a noble bear, a sweet one, but bold and brave. You're more like . . .'' She broke off, her drawn pallor giving her grin a rather forbidding aspect.

Guinevere mopped her brow again. ''Like what?'' she said with the easiest amusement she'd shown so far. ''Just what sort of animal is it that Mordred reminds you of?''

The raspy sound Nimüe made was probably a giggle. ''I don't know, a sleek, quick weasel, or maybe a fox. Something wicked and cunning.''

Sick or no, if she'd been alone, I would have thumped her. ''You do me little justice, good lady.''

''I don't know about that,'' said Guinevere slyly. ''Children can be so wise sometimes. Nimüe, if you like, you may call Mordred 'Lord Weasel' from now on.''

I looked into those damnable green eyes of hers and did my best to maintain my frown. ''If she calls me that, someone shall be spanked.'' Turning her face so that only I could see it, Gwen responded by sticking out her tongue. For neither the first time nor the last, I wished we were alone together. Ach, but with Arthur away, opportunities would certainly come, and then so would we.

"At any rate," said Gwen, turning back to her charge, "you are already a beautiful lady, so there's no need for any magical transformations."

"No, I'm *not!*" said Nimüe with unexpected shrillness. Closing her eyes, she rolled over on her side. "I'm not, and I never will be, never never never!" Her face was hidden in a handful of bedsheet, but from the way her thin body shook, it was clear she was silently sobbing.

Gwen looked at me with renewed concern. "Poor child; she's delirious. I was afraid of this."

Brigid was still hovering solicitously. I stood up and handed her the small Castorware jar I'd brought with me, its mouth stoppered with a plug of wet clay. "Here, take this to the kitchen and mix a pinch of it with a small amount of boiling water, then put it in a cup with some wine and honey. Make sure she drinks it all, and give her another cupful in a couple of hours. She won't like the taste, but it will ease her fever." Brigid looked from me to her mistress. "It's medicine, not magic," I explained, though that was not entirely true. Guinevere nodded to her servant, who went hurrying from the chamber.

Gwen gently stroked Nimüe's shoulder. "I don't care what it is, actually, as long as it makes her well."

"It should help," I said, trying to sound confident. For all her often formidable skills, my mother had never been very adept at the healing arts, with more aptitude for poisoning people than curing their ailments (indeed, in at least one memorable instance, her attempt at the latter had led to the former). Still, this particular philter had proved reasonably effective in the past and had damned well *better* work this time, considering the trouble I'd gone to in compounding it. The proper roots and bark hadn't been too hard to find, but catching a fat male toad and boiling it alive in order to skim off a small portion of the resulting liquor had proved both tedious and unpleasant. However, Guinevere had requested my help, and, as usual, she could have practically anything she asked of me.

Nimüe's body relaxed as her shut-eyed sulk gave way to

drowsiness, and in a moment she was softly snoring. Guinevere stroked the child's brow, then reached out and took my hand. "I expect I don't want to know what's in your medicine."

I brought her fingers to my lips. "No, I expect you don't," I said, punctuating my sentence by brushing lips across her knuckles. "Just know that it will ease her aches and get her over the worst of it. It always worked on me when I was a child. She'll be up and about by the time I get back from the North."

Guinevere rested a bare foot on my right buskin. "I wish you didn't have to go."

I ran one finger along her slim pale ankle. "Ach, me too, love." *Careful you fool*, I thought to myself, *you can't be sure that Nimüe is really asleep.* "But somebody has got to collect the royal tax." Indeed, it was just such a mission as periodically brought Gawain back to Orkney when I was small, though I doubted anyone in Gododdin would be as glad of my visit as I used to be for his, in those dreary island days of my boyhood. "I just wish the wealth of the Votadini was measured in coin instead of cows. Last week, my men and I were digging ditches. Now, we are to be herdsmen. When I was a child dreaming of my future service here in Camelot, the prospect seemed rather more glamorous."

Hands clasped behind her head, Guinevere arched her back like a cat and stretched the kinks out of her long frame. The brocaded sleeves of her green-and-orange-checkered gown were rolled up, and the morning light limned the fine golden hairs on her bare forearms, turning her pale skin translucent and revealing a tracery of delicate blue veins. Watching a sunbeam kiss the milky hollow of her throat, I wished that I were kissing it, too, and silently cursed Arthur for this duty, and then myself for not having thought of a good excuse for refusing it, as I could hardly have said, "Please, sire, I want to stay in Camelot and fuck your wife while you're away." Still, I'd be back from Gododdin long before he returned from Gaul, and by the time I was, Nimüe would with luck be well or dead, and either way not taking up time that Gwen could be spending with me.

Shaking crimson hair from green eyes, Guinevere looked

from the drowsing girl to me, and I was pleased to imagine that a trace of regret at Nimüe's presence crossed that lovely, lopsided face. "And for my part, I'm well glad that the days of glory are behind us. If you must be away from me and here, I'd much rather it was on some routine administrative duty, not leading your squadron into a forest of enemy spearpoints. I wouldn't like to lose my favorite chess partner."

I stood, for Brigid would surely be back soon, so there'd be no opportunity for a truly satisfying leave-taking. "Arthur's wars were over before I ever came here, but Gawain remembers them, and he says that I should count myself fortunate for having been born too late to see those bloody days. The deeds that bards sing of were done out of desperate necessity, and are glorious only at a safe distance. Don't fear, Gwen. I don't envy men like my brother the excitement of their youth, and am glad to be living in this Britain rather than that one."

This was true enough much of the time, but not always. Unlike Gawain and Geraint and Kay, I had not helped Arthur finish what Ambrosius and Uther had begun, and could never quite be as at home here as those who built this place with blood and sword. I was like the guest at the feast who sits quietly in the corner, enjoying the wine and the music and the gaiety well enough, but still somehow aloof and all too conscious of the gulf between him and his fellow revelers.

Guinevere also rose and clasped my hand in hers. "Sometimes I think my husband wishes those old days were not over, and that he had Badon and Celidon to fight again."

I did not wish to spend these last few moments in her company talking about Arthur, but tried to keep the displeasure from my voice. "Perhaps. Britain was Arthur's first love, and like many a man, his eye may wander now that the wooing is long done and the bloom is off his conquest." The expression on Gwen's face kept me from pursuing that line of thought, and instead I backpedaled. "Ach, my prickles are showing again, and I'm being unfair. Whatever his faults, Arthur is too complicated for such a simplistic pronouncement. Don't fret yourself over his intentions in Gaul. He's human, and so wants something of his youth back, but he's not going to risk what he's built here, or leave the job half-done.''

The oak and leather-strap framework of the Queen's bed creaked, and we turned to see Nimüe sitting bolt upright, her brow glistening and her eyes burning in their hollows. "Take more than one squadron with you today," she said in a low voice that I would not have recognized as hers if I hadn't seen the words form on her cracked gray lips. "In Pictdom, you will need spear and sword and horse and your own smooth tongue." Her body quivered and her eyes rolled back to their bloodshot whites, and for a moment I feared I would need to shove something between her chattering teeth, but no, the seizure passed and she collapsed limply back onto the sheets. At first her breathing was a rattling gurgle, but then it resumed its previous soft rhythm, and, except for the sheen of fresh sweat on her flushed brow and sallow, skinny arms, she looked just as she had before whatever it was came over her.

Guinevere crossed herself, and I was startled to realize that I'd done the same, which is what comes of living too long among Christians. "Shit!" I said, with questionable gentility.

Gwen walked slowly back to the bed and sat beside her half sister. "Nim, please tell me that you were playing a game with us just now. I promise I shan't be angry, if you only tell me that."

There was no response until she gently shook the child's bony shoulder, at which point Nimüe rolled over without opening her eyes. "I'm so tired," she said in a soft and mumbly but quite normal voice. "Must I take my medicine now?"

"Not just yet," said Gwen, her face still strained. "Brigid hasn't come back with it."

"That's good . . . I'll just sleep a little more."

"It's no use," I said in Gwen's ear as I rested my hands on her strong, tense shoulders. "She won't remember anything of what she said. Not when she's awake, or even when she's better." Assuming she did get better; prophecies were a bad sign.

For a moment, the visage that Guinevere turned toward

me was as nearly as pale and drawn as her sibling's, but then she mastered herself and looked at me with a cat's unreadable eyes. "Whatever this means, we can't afford to ignore it. I'll send Geraint to Gododdin in your stead."

I stood there, in mote-filled sunlight that had suddenly gone all bleached and cold, as if the season were high winter rather than early harvest, and pondered that tempting alternative, but only for an instant, for I had a small store of pride mixed in with my practicality. Nimüe's prophecy, if that's really what it was, did not say that ill would befall me, but only that I should be prepared for trouble. *In Pictdom, you will need sword and spear and horse and your own smooth tongue.* More of the former shouldn't be too difficult to authorize, and I'd have brought the last with me, regardless. While this mission wasn't supposed to take me to "Pictdom," those realms of the painted tribesmen beyond the Antonine Wall who'd never bowed to Rome, the kingdom of Goddodin did indeed butt up against their southern border, and a hundred different imaginable calamities might require me and my men to cross the turf wall that separated Brit from Pict. That prospect wasn't as dangerous as it would have been fifty years ago, or even fifteen, for the forty-mile rampart running from the Firth of Forth to the Clyde now demarcated an agreed-upon border rather than a war zone, but if trouble was brewing there, crossing it with only one squadron at my back might not be entirely wise.

Gwen, it appeared, had similar thoughts. "Take the whole bloody cohort," she said grimly. "I rule in Arthur's absence, and can authorize that."

Maybe, but it would take some damned fancy explaining once he came back. I'd come up in the world since arriving here, with Arthur first acknowledging my parentage and then giving me my own cohort after I brought Guinevere back from the Realm of Melwas. This meant I nominally commanded six squadrons, each consisting of between eighty and a hundred horse, although without the provocation of an enemy raid it would require more than my say-so to up and move all of them from one end of Britain to the other. Even with Gwen giving me the crown's blessing, the thought of depriving Camelot of one-fifth its strength for what was supposed to be a routine tax collection was not a happy one.

"I'll take two squadrons," I said, "and maybe part of a third. That should be enough to get me out of trouble if the Picts start anything."

Guinevere might have argued the point, but Brigid had come back with the medicine, and Gwen's attention returned to Nimüe, whom she managed to awaken long enough to down the acrid-smelling brew. I well remembered its vile taste from the fevers of my youth and was surprised to see the child drink it with more grace than I'd ever managed, though that might have been because her illness made her too weak to be disagreeable. As I'd suspected, she had no memory of making any oracular pronouncements.

Six

KING CUNEDA of Gododdin was a grandson of Patern Pesrut, or Paternus of the Red Tunic, one of the last tribunes of the North, and his heritage was evident in the sort of long Roman nose one sees on old statues. He'd lost the tip of it, either to a sword or someone's teeth, but this only made his face look even more like it belonged on some imperial monument, now defaced by time and vandalism. His patrician features contrasted with his characteristically Gaelic shock of red hair, graying only at the temples despite his age, and the sort of lime-stiffened British mustache no proper Roman would ever have worn, which he fingered in nervous agitation as he paced before me, his hobnailed boots clacking on broken tiles, then thudding softly on the rugs and skins spread over the worst of the damaged floor. His palace here at Din Eidyn in the ancient stronghold of the Votadini had once been his grandfather's villa, though it looked more British than Roman these days, the frescoes long since crumbled from walls where the paint had been replaced by intricately patterned fabrics, tapestries, and brocades, their richness in stark contrast to a few bare spots where the timbers showed through the ravaged plaster like exposed ribs.

"It's Gwid of Fortriu," he said, naming the chieftain of the nearest of the Pictish tribes that lived north of the Antonine Wall, the hollow end of his nose adding a whistling echo to his words. "He has Teged, my only son."

I'd only arrived at Din Eidyn that morning, and here we

were already talking of Picts. So much for dismissing Ni-müe's prophecy as a child's delirious babbling. "He was taken on a raid?" I asked from where I sat cross-legged on a particularly impressive bearskin, drinking wine from a bronze goblet and trying to ignore the way my thighs and bum ached from so many days of riding, the punishment for not having taken part in more cavalry exercises with the troops. This news did not help my sour mood; any serious Pictish incursion into Gododdin would require sending word to Arthur, and I didn't relish the prospect of his premature return. Of course, if I dealt with the matter here and now, that wouldn't be a problem.

Cuneda stopped and scratched his nose, actually inserting his thumb into the scarred hole that was its tip. "Aye, it was a raid, though Teged was the one doing the raiding, the lovely fool. Gwid has many fat cattle, and my son and a few of his comrades thought to snatch some, to pay your Arthur's fucking tax. Through bad luck or folly, they ran into a hunting party composed of Gwid himself and all his war captains. My boy and his companions were outnumbered, but being young and hot-blooded, chose battle over sensible surrender. Teged killed no few of the Painted Men before they brought him down. His silver neck torque marked him as a prince, so the Picts spared him for ransom. They also set his surviving comrade free, to bring me the news of my son's capture and their terms." He paused for a moment, then spoke more slowly. "The man they spared had been stabbed in the thigh with a Pictish boar spear, then bludgeoned senseless with its haft, and was delirious from his injuries. Because of this, he told me something that he might not otherwise have spoken of."

Ach, this explained why Cuneda so often paid his taxes in cattle, even though Gododdin minted its own silver, a rare thing in Britain, and rarer still so far from the South. Livestock raids were the ancient sport of warrior princes, and acquiring booty in that way no doubt took the sting out of having to send it to Camelot. How long had Gododdin been paying its taxes by robbing its neighbors? Now probably wasn't the time to ask.

"And what did he tell you?" I asked, intrigued to see hesitancy in such a forthright man.

Cuneda stopped pacing and squatted before me, eyes burning. "They buggered my son, right there on the sward, laughing while they did it."

This wasn't too surprising, from what I knew of the Picts. Actually, the practice occurred among some British tribes as well. Despite our long Romanization, we Brits can't match the Latin appetite for sodomy, but we don't have the Saxon taboo against it, and beyond the obvious recreational appeal, a good buggering is considered by some folk to be the ultimate way of humiliating a captured enemy. Still, a king's son was usually afforded better treatment.

"Even savages are usually more gentle with royal captives," I said, rudely wondering just how many Picts had actually taken part in the buggering, and whether Teged's arse was as raw as the eleven-day journey from Camelot had made mine. "They must have been particularly upset." Either that, or Teged simply had a particularly attractive bum, but this last was too impolitic for even me to say aloud.

Cuneda cleared his throat, or maybe actually growled, it was hard to tell. "Yes, they were angry because he fought so well and killed so many of their comrades," he muttered, continuing the pacing that was rapidly getting on my nerves. "The boy had put his spear through the brother of the Pict who led the buggering. No doubt they thought the shame of it would keep him silent, as indeed it probably would have. As I've said, even Teged's surviving comrade would likely not have spoken of it if his wits weren't rattled by his injuries." The fire dimmed in Cuneda's bloodshot eyes as the aggrieved father gave way to the calculating ruler. "My anger aside, this presents a problem."

"How so?" I asked, probably sounding less solicitous than courtesy required. "You pay the Picts what they want, they give you your son back, and that's that." I thought of Cuneda's rumored plans to marry his son off to the daughter of Malcolm of Strathclyde, an alliance which would make Gododdin the most powerful of the Northern kingdoms. "It's not like he's a girl, and loses market value with his virginity." Christ and the Dagda, I was being particularly obnoxious today, and to someone it wasn't terribly wise to offend. Well, I've already said I was tired and sore, and this made me even less receptive than usual to the sort of problem that Cuneda's foolhardy whelp had dumped into my lap.

At least my crude levity stopped his pacing, for he hunkered down in front of me, one grimy thumb idly tracing the intricate workmanship of his golden neck torque, the other tapping the enameled pommel of his ceremonial but quite practical dagger, which had been worn smooth from years of idle fingering. "When I was a boy," he said in his deceptively soft Northern burr, "we were always fighting Dalriada. Those days gave me little love for Scots, and even if I were not already angry, I would not care to be insulted by one, Arthur's envoy or no. Have care, Lord Mordred."

Not caring to piss him off further, I nodded in apology. "Indeed, I am being ungracious, and must beg your indulgence. However, tactless or not, the gist of my question remains. What is the problem of which you speak? Beyond the immediate one of paying the ransom, I mean. Do they demand too high a price?"

His right hand moved from his dagger to his mustache, which he again began to tug and twirl. A particularly large flea appeared momentarily on the horny yellow surface of his thumbnail, before hopping back into his graying whiskers. "No, they want the usual forty cows and ten bulls, standard value for a captured prince. Cattle raiding is sport, and being taken for ransom is as much a natural hazard of that sport as a sprained ankle is for a boy playing kick ball. However, being buggered is not. I'm old and practical, and can live with the shame, but I doubt Teged will be able to. He'll want vengeance, and that's the start of a blood feud. I can play that game, too, but if I do, it will surely bring Arthur down here with his damned horsemen, like a schoolmaster breaking up a fight. I don't like paying his taxes, but accept them as the necessary price for keeping the Saxons in their borders. I'm less willing to accept the South sticking its goddamned high-and-mighty nose into my affairs." He grinned at me with more yellow teeth than humor. "And there's my frankness to counter yours, making us equal in discourtesy. I want my boy back, and will have him, by God, but my problems are just beginning when it happens.''

I found myself warming to the man, who was clearly not a fool. *Christ's balls*, this was a bloody fine mess to have stumbled into. If Cuneda's judgment of the situation was sound, the quicker it was dealt with, the better, if only so that I could tell Arthur it was over and done with in the same report in which he first learned of it. Well, I'd slain monsters, and journeyed to the Otherworld and back again; surely this was a mere diversion. At least, that's what I tried to tell myself.

''Well, let's give Teged his blood feud, then,'' I said, finishing my wine, which had proved finer than I'd expected. ''Or rather, let's preempt it, by giving him nobody to feud with. If the fight is finished the same day it's begun, Gwid's Pictish neighbors are much less likely to get involved. How large is the Fortriu warband?''

Cuneda stopped his impatient fidgeting and became suddenly attentive. ''If you only count the warriors in Gwid's stronghold, and not those he can muster from other forts, he has slightly more than five hundred. From my warband here, I can immediately send seven hundred against them. Almost double that, if I take the time to call upon the shore garrisons.''

I shook my head. ''The more time you take, the more time Gwid has to call upon his own outlying forces, not to mention his tribal allies. You want to fight him, not all of Pictdom.''

Cuneda grunted impatiently. ''I know that, but it doesn't matter. Whether I fight him now or next week, he'll kill Teged at my first attack.''

I nodded. ''Almost certainly. However, I think I can get your son back and destroy the Fortriu warband, without you having to fight him at all.'' That would keep Gododdin clear of any blame, and perhaps prevent reprisals against the North Britons by Gwid's allies.

Cuneda didn't move, but his eyes glittered. ''That's a finer gift than I ever expected of a *Scotti*. What's your price?''

He hadn't asked me how I intended to do it, which I hoped meant that I sounded more confident and formidable than I felt. ''Not much of one. Just your memory of this, should I ever need the North on my side." Oh, yes, I was learning to play the political game well.

His expression told me that he'd expected as much. "Can you ride on the morrow?"

I stood and stretched, trying not to frown at the prospect of another day in the saddle. "That's the plan. However, I'll need fresh mounts for all my men, the cattle that Gwid demanded of you, and two cartloads of this fine wine—no, make that your most potent mead, as there's no need to waste good wine. Can you have all that ready for me by dawn?"

Standing, he clasped my hand in his callused paw. "Aye, if I must, though the mead will be the hardest to part with. You'd best be as good as your word, Lord Mordred. Bring Teged back to me and I'll be forever in your debt. On the other hand, if your plan kills my boy, that's the end of my allegiance to Camelot, and you can take that news back to Arthur by way of your kinsmen in Dalriada, for you won't be safe returning through my lands. Are we understood?"

It became real, then, the opportunity for failure and sheer disaster which my scheme afforded. Well, balls to that, I tried to tell myself, for if my often turbulent life had taught me anything, it was not to fear Fortuna's vicissitudes, fickle bitch though she might be.

The tribal stronghold of the Fortriu Picti was a timber-laced ring fort covering about five square acres atop a flattened rise in the midst of rolling moor country, the eastern face of its twelve-foot rampart looming over a sprawling cluster of low beehive-shaped, thatch-roofed roundhouses, the smoke of their cooking fires marking the settlement for miles. Around us, the bracken-carpeted hills stretched away, the closer ones lifting gently like great smooth shoulders, the more distant rising in sharp peaks and rocky ridges, and in the northwest, tumbling upward into mountain. Here and there stands of birch and ash broke the monotony of stone and heather, and to the east of the fortress were great tilled patches of Pictish farmland, where cornstalks danced golden in the winds that blew between the North and Irish Seas. Nearly a day's ride past the ditch-and-sod rampart erected by Antoninus, I was uncomfortably aware that we were well outside that part of Britain that had ever officially submitted to Rome or anyone else.

Pictish herdsmen had spotted us soon after we mounted that grassy boundary, so time-eroded and gently sloping it could scarcely be called a wall anymore, and had gone scampering to distant stone-and-turf homesteads, the main houses of which appeared unnaturally low owing to being partially underground. Before we were a mile beyond the wall, we'd acquired an escort of painted spearmen, naked except for cowhide breeches and the plaid blankets they wrapped around their stocky bodies, who rode bareback on their shaggy ponies, the growing body of them keeping pace with us while a few galloped on ahead. At first those who remained with us hooted and clacked their hafts against their oxhide shields, but when this began to spook the cattle we drove before us, they promptly stopped, which was a good sign. If the livestock hadn't marked us as something other than a war party, there might have been resistance long before we reached Gwid's fortress, and I couldn't risk that.

Our progress had been good, considering that we were slowed down by fifty cattle and two heavily laden wagons. There was no Roman road here, but the ancient cart and chariot track served well enough, at least in this dry weather. So far, Fortuna was with me, for although we'd come through plenty of rain on our way to Gododdin, the local countryside had seen nary a drop of it for over a week, which Cuneda told me came close to constituting a drought in these parts. Bad for crops, but good for us; I hadn't relished the thought of getting bogged down and having night fall before we reached Gwid's stronghold.

We stopped a half mile from the settlement, on the banks of a narrow winding stream where a pack of naked Pictish children had splashed until our approach sent them scurrying toward the fortress. Allowing the cattle to graze freely, we watered our horses and calmly pitched our tents, as if there was no throng of barbarian warriors gesticulating from the distant wall while their peasants poured from the thatched huts below and drove their pigs and chickens through the timbered gate. Colwyn, my second-in-command, rode back and forth supervising the work, telling the men to ignore the prancing spear bearers on the stone-faced earth rampart. ''Wish we'd brought stakes with us, sir,'' he said as he went past, a slight frown his only indication of concern at our grossly undefended position. Stakes would have allowed us to erect a palisade around our camp, but we'd been too pressed for time, and I wanted it make it clear our intentions were not hostile.

We didn't have to wait long. A tall gatehouse of crudely dressed limestone had been built into the fortress wall, and now the timber portals swung open, issuing forth first a cluster of spearmen, then some sort of rattling cart drawn by four white horses, taller and finer than the ponies of the Pictish outriders. As it left the spearmen behind and rumbled toward us, I saw it was a war chariot, a thing almost obsolete in the rest of Britain. I'd read Caesar's account of such vehicles and was fascinated to see that it consisted of little more than a plank balanced between two large iron-rimmed wheels, though the horses were richly bedecked, with silver and enamel in their harness and horned bronze caps strapped to their heads, the latter making them look like a team of fabulous monsters.

As it drew nearer, leaving the other warriors behind, I saw that its two riders were even more outlandishly decorated than the horses. The charioteer was very small and dark, which was typical of the Pictish peasant class, and nude except for his broad leather belt and a necklace of cow's teeth. His penis and balls were painted bright red, while his arms and legs were decorated with yellow stripes, and a white crescent had been daubed across his barrel chest. His head was shaved except for a beribboned topknot, and he lacked the usual mustache.

The warrior who stood behind him was a head taller, with an equally broad torso and much longer arms and legs. An orange, black, and green plaid blanket was fastened at his hips with a golden brooch, but his upper body was bare, except for the silver neck torque that marked his nobility. A mixture of lime and woad had been worked into his bushy hair, turning it into a nest of spiky blue quills, and his stiffened mustache stood out from his face like a cat's whiskers. Although he was not painted like his charioteer, an intricate scrollwork of indigo tattoos crawled across his arms and hairless chest. At his right hand bounced a wicker tube containing what looked to be at least a dozen spears, their barbed iron heads glittering in the wintry sunlight.

"Best get some of the boys between you and him," said Colwyn as he reined in on my left. "Be just like a Pict to put a spear in you when you come forward to parley."

I shook my head. "Ach, I think they're more honorable than that." Indeed, I was counting on it, as I was the one planning on treachery. "It will be me he wants to talk to, so there's no point in sitting here gawking." Saying that, I spurred my roan gelding forward before Colwyn could intervene. Behind him, I heard over two hundred men catch their collective breath, for they'd evidently not expected their commander to ride to meet the chariot alone. Well, assuming it didn't get me killed, today's activity would gain me fresh respect in their eyes, and perhaps make them consider me as something more than a necessary evil.

I was wearing helmet and mail, of course, but my shield was slung across my back where it would do little good, and my lance remained in its socket. I had, however, laid my wicked little composite bow across the front of my rectangular four-horned saddle, and my quiver was positioned for easy reach. Given to me in my boyhood by Gawain, the bow was fashioned of layered horn and wood bound together with sinew, its Eastern workmanship making it an anomaly in Britain, at least since the legions withdrew and took their Scythian archers with them. Fifteen years ago, when I still practiced regularly, I could have likely snatched it up and fired a shot while the Pict was still reaching for a spear, but now . . . well, with luck, we'd not put each other to the test.

The charioteer had stopped, and he and his master now watched me come, the peasant's expression wary as a watchdog's, his lord's a haughty mask. I held up an open hand to show I meant peace, and prayed they didn't think I was answering some sort of archaic challenge to meet in a combat of champions. And, of course, there was the possibility that Colwyn was right, and they were planning treachery, for I wasn't such a fool as to think so-called barbarians were honorable simpletons. My troops were a hundred paces behind me now, and that seemed miles away. Midges, our constant torment these past few days, swarmed about my head and neck, and I resisted the urge to swat them away, not knowing how sudden movements might be interpreted. And then, rather too soon, I was only a couple of yards from the chariot, and so had to rein in, feeling stupid because I still had no idea what I was going to say.

Fortunately, the silver-torqued Pict spoke first, and to my relief I could understand him. "I am Tarain of Fortriu," he said with an accent that reminded me of Gaul. I'd known that the Pictish aristocracy, who are more akin to their Southern neighbors than their own smaller and darker peasants, spoke a form of British, but had been worried about the dialect. "My father King Gwid wishes to know who you are, and why you are here."

"I am Mordred Mac Arthur," I said, sitting tall in the saddle as I could. "I come as an envoy from *my* father, the High King of Britain. He is angry with Teged, son of his vassal Cuneda, whom you now hold captive, and wishes to punish him for trespassing in your lands and for breaking his peace. He also brings greetings to your father, as well as gifts. This, however, I must tell King Gwid in person."

"My father is brave," said Tarain, "but he did not reach his age by being a fool. He wonders if you wish to lure him out so you can kill him."

I gave him my best smile. "Look at the men behind me. Surely your people remember the legions, and know these for the same sort." Which wasn't strictly true, as Roman troops would have been largely infantry, whereas Arthur, like Ambrosius before him, depended almost entirely upon horsemen, but the point was that my men looked like drilled soldiers and not some ragtag warband. At least, I hoped they did. "Was there ever a fortress that could stand against a legion?" Not in Pictdom, but that was irrelevant, as I lacked the sappers and engineers so vital to the Roman military, and there had been no time to knock together ballistae or other siegecraft. "But forgive my fierce words, for I come as a guest, not a warrior. And as a guest, it is seemly that I should go in to meet Gwid, rather than he come out to meet me. Will you lead the way?" That was foolishly bold, right enough, but the less time this took, the better our chances.

Apparently having expected more caution and dickering on my part, Tarain seemed quite taken aback by my apparent eagerness, but, to his credit, he quickly recovered his composure. "Follow me then, Southman, if you dare to come alone."

"Why should I not dare?" I said easily. "Is your father not a man of honor?" I certainly hoped he was, for I intended such honor to be his downfall. Turning in my four-cornered saddle, I waved back at Colwyn with more bravado than I felt and, despite my unease, took satisfaction in noting that his impassive mask had finally cracked, for I could see his scowl from where I sat. Well, I'd be scowling, too, in his place. If the Picts did indeed kill me, my frowning senior officer faced the unhappy choice of either mounting an ill-prepared retaliatory siege or beating a humiliating retreat back to Gododdin. Though it wasn't the most prudent alternative, I rather hoped he'd attack, should worse come to worst. At least that way my whole company might get wiped out, and there'd be no one left to tell Gwen and Gawain that I died in such a foolish manner. Ach, but it's good the men watching me in surprised admiration could not read my selfish thoughts.

The charioteer got his team turned around, moving them in a much tighter radius than I would have expected, and I followed close behind, the shadow of the wall stretching to meet me in the afternoon's fading light. That barricade consisted of a double palisade of upright timbers, packed dirt filling the space between them, and the outer shorings faced with blocks of sod, against which had been pressed crudely fitted stones. Though its rough slope formed rather less than a ninety-degree incline, it was still a formidable barrier, made more so by the sharpened, tarred, and fire-hardened stake points that projected from its surface at two-and three-foot intervals. Any force trying to scramble up that steep bank must be widely dispersed, for if too close together, they'd press each other against the stakes.

And of course Gwid's warband would be waiting atop the wall, as indeed so many of them were now, their large, oval, chalk-washed oxhide shields decorated with the now familiar vertical-barred crescent, its color (either rowanberry red or woad blue) presumably denoting the shield owner's station. Each man had an eight-foot spear driven haft first into the earth beside him, so that their points formed a visual picket line, although in actual practice these would, of course, be reversed and hurled down into the foe. The bulk of them also had long, old-fashioned swords, their squared points indicating they were more for cutting than thrusting, and a few carried axes or even spiked clubs. Unlike Tarain or the riders who'd escorted us, many wore some kind of hauberk, though scale mail was more common than rings, with bronze or even sections of cow horn as likely to be sewn onto their leather coats as iron. Only a few wore helmets, usually topped with bronze spikes, which, along with the blue quills decorating such scalps as went uncovered, meant that the Picti could have as easily been called the Pointy People as the Painted Men.

As we passed through the gates, I took careful note of their construction. Each was fashioned of eight thick timbers—really, barely dressed logs—that had been lashed together with cowgut, then nailed to three thick crossbeams, with more gut providing reinforcement. The hinges were of black iron, larger than my forearm, and of good workmanship, their skilled forging in contrast to the image most Southerners have of Picts, which is of crude savages in animal skins, like something out of Pliny. We tend to forget that Picti are very similar to ourselves, at least as we were before the Romans "civilized" us, although it's said that their peasants have the blood of an older race, one that lived in these isles before the Britons came over from Gaul.

Glancing down at the dung-strewn earth beneath the stone-and-timber gate frame, I saw that years of tramping feet and trundling cart wheels had packed it down into a shallow depression, leaving over a foot of space between it and the portal's bottom edge, which was a useful bit of information. A man could squeeze through there when the gate was shut, if he didn't mind crawling on his belly. Well, neither Caesar nor his successors had been much impressed by native British fortifications.

Inside the wall was a disorderly cluster of thatch-roofed

stables, barns, and roundhouses, all surrounding a much larger building shaped like a double oval, or two mashed-together tits. Its size and central position made it likely this was the royal palace, despite being at no point more than six feet high, with pigs rooting in its sod roof. Knowing that the Picts constructed many of their buildings partially underground, I suspected that the interior was rather more impressive than the exterior, but was not particularly eager to find out.

Yapping, dust-colored dogs followed us through a cluster of black and yellow chickens, drawing back with bared teeth when we stopped in a clear area bordered by four upright slabs of sandstone. These were about ten feet high and covered with carved figures, stylized but quite recognizable. Most depicted groups of spearmen, some battling each other, others hunting stags, but there was also the recurring motif of an odd animal that looked like nothing so much as a duck-billed horse. And then, of course, there were the preserved human heads, which hung by their hair in clusters from iron hooks driven into the stone, balls of brightly enameled clay shining in their empty eye sockets. Many British tribes also kept heads, both of enemies and revered ancestors, so this ornamentation did not shock me, although both the Brits and we Scots usually took better care of such trophies, and did not so expose them to the elements, preferring to hang them over our hearths, or from the roof beams of our halls. These had been dipped in tar or pinesap for preservation, making their race somewhat difficult to determine, but their woad-dyed scalps suggested all were Pictish and not the fruit of border raids, a testament to the peace that Arthur had enforced south of the wall.

Someone awaited us amid the head-draped stones. He was tall for a Pict, with bowed legs and a great slab of belly, his sagging chest and long, gnarled arms decorated with the most intricate tattooing I'd yet seen. I recognized the barred crescent, the double oval, and even what looked to be a simplified version of the duck-billed beast from the standing stones, with a mirrored pair of the creatures facing each other across his drooping man-tits. His eyes were set deep in nested wrinkles, and there was much gray in his mustache, but I couldn't guess his age, and his rolling swagger and straight back bespoke strength and vigor. His dyed hair was not blue, but a color very close to the Imperial purple, presumably obtained by mixing woad and the juice of rowanberries, and I wondered if the shade indicated his royalty, for this clearly was King Gwid.

He wore a tartan blanket, pinned at his hips with an ornamental brooch and tossed over his left shoulder, and a trailing cape of otter skins. His finely wrought neck torque was of gold, as were the circlets on his arms, and he also wore two necklaces, one of silver Roman coins, the other of enameled cow's teeth. In his right hand, he held a six-foot rowan staff, atop which had been fixed the skull of a centurion, recognizable by still being encased in its crested helmet. Molten gold had been poured or brushed over this trophy, but there were large spots where the original bone and bronze shone through. I wondered how long this heirloom had been in Cuneda's family, and whether the hapless Roman had been one of Agricola's officers. *Be careful, boyo*, I said to myself, *else your own noggin ends up on a stick*. Out of the corner of my eye, I saw Tarain grinning from his chariot. The bastard was no doubt remembering the glib comparison I'd just made between my squadrons and the legions.

Ignoring that feral smile, I slipped from the saddle. Gwid was flanked by a half dozen painted spearmen and several smaller, darker servants. Handing my reins to the nearest of these, I bowed, then turned up my open palms. "I have gifts for you, Your Highness, but they are not of the sort I can carry with me, so I hope you will forgive my empty hands."

"You have also brought many armored horsemen with you," he said mildly, his soft and rather high voice at odds with his fierce appearance. "I am not used to gifts from someone who comes with such a warband behind him."

With luck, my smile was bolder than I felt. "Cattle raiding seems quite the sport in these parts," I replied, "and I didn't want any of your neighbors getting greedy. After all, it was a bit of such greed on the part of Teged of Gododdin that brought him here, and me after him, to clean up his mess."

Tarain jumped from the chariot, stalked to his father, and

whispered in his ear. I waited, swatting idly at the damned midges, while the shadows of the standing stones lengthened around us. Come on, you lot, I wanted to shout at them, let's get this nonsense over with.

Gwid played with his mustache, which left a sticky residue on his fingers. "What have you brought me?"

I crooked a thumb toward the open moorland on the other side of the wall. "Those forty cows and ten bulls out there, as well as twelve barrels of mead. I must take Teged back with me, though."

Gwid's eyes narrowed. "My son says you speak of punishment."

Finally, we were getting somewhere. "Oh yes, for breaking the High King's peace. In fact, I can begin it here. Will someone give me a horsewhip?"

Again, Gwid muttered with his son. We now had quite a crowd surrounding us, though at a respectful difference. They, too, were whispering amongst themselves, and all seemed very interested.

Finally, Tarain gestured at his charioteer, who threw me his whip. I gave it a trial crack in the air, then pretended to look satisfied. "Good. Now bring Teged to me."

More frowns and muttering, and then two warriors went trotting toward Gwid's palace. I continued to swish the whip through the air. Bloody hell, but it was getting late; the sun was little more than a red glow beyond the broken hills.

Finally, the warriors came back, dragging a fair-haired young man between them, his bands bound behind his back with leather strips. When they brought him closer, I decided that the Picts had more than anger as a motive when they buggered him, for he'd been stripped to his wool breeches, exposing a lithe torso on which the skin looked smooth and hairless as a girl's. Despite his dirt and bruises, he was quite handsome—pretty, even, with green eyes that weren't quite the equal of Gwen's, but came close, and long hair that looked like it would flow in honey-colored waves once someone washed the dust and dried blood out of it. The boy had spirit, too, for there was defiance in his emerald eyes and a sneer on his cracked lips.

Turning to Tarain, I muttered in Latin, too soft for anyone

else to hear, "I hope he had a firm, tight bunghole." That was stupid, really, for it was best that the Picts not suspect I knew what had really befallen their captive. However, my gamble that they did not speak Latin paid off, for Tarain stared at me without sign of comprehension.

Not bothering to explain what I'd just said, I walked forward and spoke more Latin, my voice still low but with an apparently harsh inflection. "Listen to me, my Noble Prince, and I'll get you out of here. Do you want revenge?"

Nothing on the faces of those watching hinted they'd understood, and besides, I'd practically whispered in Teged's ear. "Yes," he said, his own Latin having a lot of North British burr in it. "I'd give anything for that."

"A few more minutes of humiliation is all I ask," I said, flipping the whip back across my shoulder. "That and some pain. Bear with it."

Taking a half-step back, I pointed at the ground and spoke loudly in British. "Prince Teged, you have offended Arthur Pendragon, my lord and yours. Before taking you to his realm for punishment, I shall give you a small taste of what waits for you. Now kneel, lest I decide to leave you at the mercy of King Gwid and his warriors."

Teged was no fool, and did indeed kneel, his eyes locked on mine and his face impassive. I walked around behind him and laid the whip across his bare back, rather enjoying myself, for one seldom gets to treat royalty in such a fashion. On the second stroke, I drew blood, and all the watching Picts but Gwid and Tarain yipped like dogs to see it. I thought that might bring some protest from Teged, but no, he simply grunted, so I laid on with vigor and gave him eight more, each slap of the whip accompanied by hoots and barks from our audience, who grinned and jostled each other in their excitement, like British townsfolk watching a horserace or beast baiting. To his credit, Teged never cried out or even swayed. Lugh knows, I'd have been limp and howling before it was over.

Tossing the whip back to Tarain's charioteer, who sniffed it with interest, I turned back to Gwid and his son. "I bring you further word from my lord and father, Arthur, King of all the Britons. In a year's time, he will come here to parley

with you. He is concerned that the Saxons may settle upon
the coast of Pictdom, and wants your permission to move
through your lands and fight them, should they do so. To
this end, he might even build a road like the one on the other
side of the old turf wall that separates Pictish soil from British, should you allow it." Gwid, of course, had no way of
knowing that this was beyond the engineering capabilities of
Arthur's warband.

Many of the tribal nobility hissed, but Gwid was silent for
a moment, leaving me to stand there swatting midges and
eyeing the lengthening shadows. "I do not think I will permit such a road," he said at last.

I bowed again. "That is truly your prerogative, but I do
not come here to discuss it now. If that is your answer in a
year's time, Arthur will accept it. For now, he wishes you
to know that he plans to visit you after the winter and his
business across the sea are done, and that he will come in
peace. For my part, I must be returning to my camp, as we
go back to the South in the morning. Prince Tarain, I must
ask you to take this man to my camp, while I wait here." I
gently kicked the still kneeling Teged, who rose somewhat
unsteadily, his face still impassive, though there was fresh
blood on his mouth, from where he must have bitten his lip.
"When you do so, my captain will send the cartloads of
mead back here. In the meantime, your herdsmen can be
rounding up the cattle I've brought you."

Come on, you fucker, give the order, I thought silently.
This was the crucial moment, when he had to decide whether
or not to release his captive. The whole nonsense about Arthur wanting to come here and negotiate with him was intended to throw him off his guard and make him think that
there were larger matters to be considered than relations between his tribe and Gododdin and what would happen once
Teged was returned to his people. If I'd merely come with
gifts, he might have been suspicious, thinking me too readily
generous. Instead he was busy contemplating the prospect of
having Arthur to deal with in a year's time. It's easier to
trick a man in the present when you've got him worrying
about the future.

The good portion of his warband that had been gradually

assembling around us shuffled in growing excitement, muttering amongst themselves, their interest obviously piqued by my mention of the mead. That was something I'd been counting upon. These were not disciplined troops, which are hard enough to control when carousing becomes a real possibility, but warrior aristocrats out of Homer, and, as their chieftain, Gwid was expected to provide them with such opportunities. It was going to be difficult for him to refuse my offer.

He seemed to realize this. "All right," he said with the slowness of a man not eager to stop weighing his options. "Tarain, take Cuneda's whelp back to the Southmen's camp, and lead the mead carts back here." At this, most of the assembled Picts beat their spears against their shields, whooping and yelping. Gwid remained impassive, ignoring the din, but Tarain continued to give me a suspicious glare.

I caught Teged's eye and winked, then took him by the elbow and helped him into Tarain's chariot, which would be quite crowded with three men in it. Tarain looked like he would have preferred to drag Teged behind the vehicle, but voiced no actual protest as he squeezed in between the driver and his soon-to-be-former captive. Once again, I admired the skill with which the small dark charioteer got the horses turned around. Soon they were trundling toward the gate, Teged's bound wrists making him look more like a felon on the way to the gallows than a man moments away from deliverance.

My close proximity to the Picts had already given me fleas, and I dearly wished I could scratch beneath my mail coat, but at least the midges seemed less numerous. I badly needed to piss, but didn't relish the thought of doing it in my wool breeches, for all that it wouldn't be the first time. Leaning against a standing stone, I ignored the heads dangling above my own and grinned at the assembled warriors. Christ, but there were now a lot of the evil-looking bastards gathered round the open square. A few moments' wait seems much longer when you've got several hundred painted, half-naked, heavily armed and quite ferocious men staring at you, their expressions ranging from openly hostile to contemptuously amused. Gwid himself stood silent and statue-still, tattooed arms crossed on his tattooed chest, his face as unreadable as those on his preserved heads, and for the life of me, I could think of no suitable small talk. It was one of those awkward moments.

Blessedly, it eventually ended, for I heard hoofbeats and creaking wheels, and then the assembled Picts parted to let the mead carts through. "Easy, lads, we're almost done here," I said to the two drivers, who looked in sore need of such reassurance, their eyes skittering in clenched faces and hands white-knuckled on the reins. Walking to the nearest cart, I slapped one of the barrels. "Perhaps there are some strong men watching who will help a poor British weakling unload these."

A score of Gwid's warriors came jostling forward, not waiting for their King's consent, and a few sweaty, grunting moments later we had all dozen barrels sitting on the ground. "Open them," I yelled, and the Picts eagerly complied, prying the lids off with their spears. Tarain had also returned, and now he jumped down from his chariot and strode to join his father, into whose ear he intently whispered. I distinctly caught the word "poison," but little else. "Stop!" yelled Gwid at his warriors, some of whom were starting to quaff the sticky liquid from cupped hands. "Let the British lord drink first!"

Ach, I'd hoped to avoid this, since any trustworthy demonstration would require me to sample all dozen barrels, and I would be needing my wits about me later. Still, I had to prove Tarain's concerns groundless, reasonable though they might be. Untying my chin strap, I removed my iron helmet and walked among the barrels, dipping my improvised bowl into each one, raising it to my mouth, and taking a swallow of the sweet, thick, amber-colored liquid. "To your health and good fortune, King Gwid," I said before the first one, "and that of your warband, the boldest in the North" before the second, and so on, toasting his horses, his noble ancestors, his gallant Prince, the unbroken spirit of the Pictish kingdoms and Lugh knows what other nonsense. Taking only one drink each time, I emptied the rest of the helmet into each successive barrel, but I was still feeling a bit tipsy when I was done, most likely because I'd not eaten all day.

Bowing again, I put the dripping helmet back on my head, not having any other place for it, and looked for my horse. The Pict who'd taken my reins had tied them to one of the iron hooks in the nearest standing stone, and I had to reach in amongst a cluster of grinning, enamel-eyed heads to free my gelding. Climbing into the saddle, I wiped a trickle of sticky mead from my brow and nodded to Gwid. "Now my men and I shall return to our camp. In the morning we go south to Camelot, taking Cuneda's son with us for his punishment there." Looking at the nearest cart driver, I said softly in Latin, "Prince Teged *is* safely in our camp, I hope." The man nodded, looking very eager to turn his horses around and be out of there, for which I couldn't blame him.

That was perhaps the hardest thing, or at least the most arse-clenching, trying to canter nonchalantly toward the gate, which to my huge relief proved still open, with the stares of the assembled fortress boring into my back and me not knowing if spears would follow. However, even before we were past the wall, I heard an excited rumble as the Picts swarmed over the mead barrels, their fellows scrambling from the wall to join them, and I knew their attention was no longer upon us. No one molested us except a cluster of naked brown children, who laughed as they threw clods of dirt and cow shit at us with annoying accuracy, and the dogs that yapped at our horses' heels. Then we were past those nuisances and through the gate. The sun was gone behind the stony hilltops, and shadows lay heavy across the bracken as I and the two drivers urged our horses toward the camp, where fires were already burning.

Colwyn waited for me beside his grazing horse, his creased face much calmer than before. "It worked, by God," he said as a groom took my reins and helped me from the saddle. "I wasn't truly sure it would."

"Thanks for your confidence," I grunted as I squirmed out of my mail coat and fumbled with my woolen breeches, for my bladder demanded immediate attention. "However, the hard part hasn't started yet."

Colwyn politely ignored the stream of my piss pattering on the dry sod. "Maybe not so hard. I don't see a single

sentry standing on their wall, despite us still being camped
so near. Except for the horsemen they sent out chasing the
cows we gave 'em, I expect every man of Gwid's warband
is jostling for space around those mead barrels. Like enough,
they'll all be drunk as Irishmen tonight.'' He looked at me
with new respect. ''You're a crafty one, sir, and that's the
truth of it.''

I shook the last drops of urine from my cock, then pulled
up my breeches. ''It's not very honorable of me, I suppose.
We could attack now, while they're still mostly sober. Make
it more of a fair fight.''

Colwyn spat, then gave me one of his rare grins, his gray
teeth nearly invisible in the fading light. ''Fair's for fools.
There's twice as many of them as us, and they have a fortress
to fight from. I'd say kill 'em in their sleep if we could.''

Clearly a man after my own heart. ''That's not going to
be practical, but with luck, we'll be able to lure them outside
their walls. Not for a while yet, though. I suppose I should
pay my respects to Cuneda's idiot son, since he's going to
be the main power in the North once his da passes on.''
Though truth to tell, Cuneda struck me as too tough to be
dying anytime soon. ''Meanwhile, have somebody make me
some food, and bring me a cup of wine.'' Ach, but no, my
head was still reeling from the mead. ''Actually, make that
water from the stream, though I suppose we should offer
wine to the Prince.''

I found Teged crouching in front of the largest campfire,
wrapped in a wool cloak someone had given him. I could
tell from the way the fingers on his outstretched right hand
curled and uncurled over the flames that they hungered for
a weapon.

''How fare you, my noble lord?'' I said as I sat beside
him, drawing my own cloak around me as the evening dampness crept out of the earth.

He didn't look at me. ''I'm fine,'' he said in a toneless
voice. ''And I thank you for obtaining my freedom. All the
time they had me, they were arguing about killing me, saying
that they couldn't let me go after what Tarain and his comrades did, that there'd be war with Gododdin for sure, so
why not start it now? It was clever of you to whip me, for

then they believed what you told them about taking me back to Arthur for punishment. Now, how are we going to kill them?''

I sighed, foreseeing trouble if he wanted to play a part in the upcoming attack. "*We* aren't going to do anything, my lord. I've not gone to such trouble getting you back just to risk having you killed."

His outstretched hand clenched and made a downward thrusting motion, and from the play of muscles in his golden-haired forearm, I guessed he was imagining shoving a spear through some tattooed torso. "Better I should die than be denied vengeance."

Fuck that, I thought; for I'd rather have a dozen dicks stuck in me than a single spear. Still, there's no talking sense to some people. "Look here," I said, trying to keep my irritation out of my voice. "You're back, and you're safe. They captured you and treated you roughly, but such is the risk any warrior takes. Now be a man and put it behind you." Ach, perhaps that wasn't the best choice of words, but I went on, pretending that I didn't know what had befallen him upon being captured. "Surely the most humiliating thing that happened was today, when I flogged you in front of them. Unless you're trying to tell me you suffered worse?''

He looked at me, searching my face for clues as to what I knew, then stared back into the flames. "No, that's it. I was captured and beaten, that's all.''

As Cuneda had suspected, pride and shame would seal his lips. Good, for that made him easier to argue with. "So now it's over. Eat some food and drink some wine, and when you return to Gododdin, you'll bear Gwid's and Tarain's heads at your knee. Isn't that enough?''

"It is," he said at last, though not as if he believed it. Well, as long as he stayed out of harm's way, I didn't really care what he thought, but I'd have the fool hog-tied if it looked like he was going to rush off into battle. A subaltern brought us an upturned helmet full of steaming soldier's porridge, that perennial gruel made from flour, lentils, leeks, and mutton fat, along with two wooden spoons, a tarred water-skin, and a wine flask. Teged proved more interested in the wine than the food, which was fine with me, as the more he drank on an empty stomach, the less trouble he would be able to make for me later. Sure enough, after a silent while he was dozing by the embers.

The night wore on, the sounds from the distant fortress getting fainter, while bats chased the great pale moths drawn by our fading firelight, and owls hooted in the farther dark. Eventually, I, too, dozed for a time, confident that Colwyn would wake me at any sign of trouble, and knowing, as all soldiers quickly learn, that sleep should be embraced whenever she presents herself, for there's no telling when that soft lady will smile your way again.

A few hours later, I was crawling through the cold dewy heather in my scuffed leather surcoat, having doffed my heavy mail for speed, hands and face blackened with soot from the dying campfire and twenty handpicked men slithering behind me. Colwyn had protested my intention of leading this party, but nobody else in the entire company was as good a shot as I hoped I still was with my little Eastern bow, a skill which might be crucial once we were all inside Gwid's fortress and one of us had to cover the others while they strained to pull back the heavy bar. It had been a slow, gut-knotting crawl through the gorse and bracken that grew thick beside the rutted cart track, but now we were almost there, for the wall was an inky mass ahead of me, blotting out the clustered stars. I smelled pig and horse and cow shit, wood fires and midden heaps, all the mingled odors of the looming settlement. There were distant muttered voices, but none seemed close, with the nearest human sound being the snores that came from somewhere on the wall above me. Ach, but that was a good sign.

You might think the Pictish warriors fools for not keeping a better watch, with over two hundred armed strangers camped little more than a stone's throw away, but you must remember that when we crossed the Antonine Wall we left any vestige of once-Roman Britain behind us, and entered a time-frozen realm much more like that described by Tacitus. In Pictdom, life went on as it had before ever the legions came, and no Saxons had yet set foot this far north, as either raiders or settlers, to disrupt the ancient status quo. The Picts were quite bloodthirsty when it came to harrying the South, but here in their ancestral lands, intertribal war was highly ritualized, a game played by clearly understood rules, and even on those rare occasions when one clan seriously tried to wipe another from the face of the earth, they did so with posturing formality, announcing their merciless intentions well in advance. Gwid's tattooed nobility saw nothing wrong in stealing cattle, burning outlying steadings, and butchering foreign peasants, but the idea of treacherously sneaking into the ancestral stronghold of some neighboring band of painted aristocrats was quite alien to them. As bloody-minded as they were, living lives built around armed raids, single combats, and grisly trophies, they lacked the ruthless practicality of more civilized men.

Now where was the bloody gate? Ah, there, to my right. A brief scramble across a few feet of open, rutted ground, then I was rolling under the rough timbers, holding my breath like a diver against the piled dust. That was the worst of it there, wriggling into the fortress like a spider scuttling under a closed door, neither my clutched bow nor my sheathed sword any use in that moment of cramped vulnerability, and me with no idea of what waited for me on the other side.

Trying my damnedest not to sneeze, I squinted in the faint light that made me feel terrifyingly exposed and vulnerable. The first thing I saw was the flickering source of that illumination, the dregs of a distant bonfire framed between two closer huts, a cluster of dark figures slumped around the embers. Very much nearer to me, silhouetted by the far glow, something pale rose and fell to the accompaniment of rhythmic grunts. The sight was so incongruous that it took me a moment to realize I was looking at some poor Pict's bare arse, thrusting away a mere ten feet or so ahead of me. Not knowing what I'd face, I'd come up from under the gate with an arrow gripped parallel to the bow in my left hand. Now, rising from my crouch so I could see directly past those pumping buttocks, I made out a shrouded torso and spiky-haired head, and the gleam of a silver neck torque. Creeping so near that I practically stood on his heels, I fitted arrow to bow, aimed just above that pale glimmer and let fly. The close range compensated for the faint illumination, and my broadhead crunched into the base of his skull. He made a sort of strangled cough and pitched limply forward on top of whomever or whatever he'd been fucking. Though no death is a good one, his was arguably better than many.

I bounded forward, sword out, wanting to silence the recipient of his favors before she, he, or it could raise an alarm. It proved to be a woman, her age and comeliness difficult to determine in the gloom, who had apparently drunk so much mead that she'd passed out while her lover was still thrusting away on top of her. I prodded her slack-mouthed face with the point of my sword, ready to drive it into the hollow of her throat if she showed any sign of reviving, but no, she barely stirred, not even when I smacked the flat of my blade across her cheek. Well, her inebriation saved her life, though she'd doubtless have a bad awakening later, when she found a dead man on top of her, and I tastelessly wondered if he was still hard inside her, or if he'd come before he died. If there'd been time, I'd have done her the kindness of rolling the corpse off of her, but there were more important matters at hand.

Behind me, my men grunted and groaned as they scrambled through the gap beneath the gate, and I cursed silently, wishing for a bit of catlike stealth on their part. Besides their swords and spears, the first six carried quivers of arrows, each man passing his to me as he came through. Grabbing the arrows by the handful, I stuck the shafts point down into the ground at my feet, creating a kind of miniature picket in front of me, though the real purpose was easy access to ammunition. Then I slung the last two quivers across my back, put two arrows in my mouth, and notched a final one in my bow. I heard my soldiers, who were surely as frightened as I was, fumble with the heavy bolt, and one fool actually cursed aloud as he strained against it, but I resisted the urge to turn and direct their labors. My guts were churning more loudly and painfully than ever, sweat poured down the back of my neck like blood from a wound, and I very much needed to pee.

It was, of course, inevitable that the Pictish dogs should

become aware of us, and we were actually fortunate that they'd not sounded an alarm while we were still on the other side of the wall. Yapping furiously, a score of smallish four-footed shapes bounded out of the darkness to my left, their barking chorus taken up at several points farther inside the fortress. I'd seen their like during the day, mangy dun-colored herders and hunters, nothing so fearsome as the huge wolfhounds of the Irish or the man-killing mastiffs that guarded Southern villas, so I didn't waste any arrows on them, judging them more likely to stand there stilt-leggedly baying than attack. Of course they awakened the sentries who'd been sleeping atop the wall on either side of the gate, and even as the first Pict yelled, I took four steps forward and spun around, aiming high. I wasted an arrow firing at the sound of his voice, but my second one caught him some-where in the throat or head, and he went spinning away, either to fall atop the wall or go rolling down its sloping outer face. His comrade on the other side of the gate im-mediately threw himself flat, taking him out of my line of sight, so I turned back toward the distant bonfire, where shadowy figures were rising groggily to their feet, swords and spearheads glinting in the light of dying embers.

I counted seven men as they came at us in a clumsy sleep-and-drink-addled rush, and the snap of my bowstring was an almost musical accompaniment to their stumbling charge. My aim was helped by the fact that they ran straight on, rather than having the wit to move in a zigzag fashion, and I blessedly managed to put every arrow into flesh. I wounded more than I killed, but all went down, most at the first shot, for I aimed at groins and stomachs, knowing it's the rare man who keeps coming when he's stuck there. One actually did get up again, although I don't know whether he was just exceptionally tough or if the blanket wrapped around his waist blunted the impact of my shaft, but since he was hold-ing his spear out in front of him rather than raising it to throw, I let him get so close that even in the dim light I was able to shoot him in his open mouth, cutting off his banshee yell.

Behind me, there was the unmistakable thunk of a spear into flesh, followed by a gurgling scream from one of my men. The remaining sentry atop the wall had obviously found the weapon he'd dropped when throwing himself flat, but he really should have hurled it at me, for when I looked up he was quite nicely framed against the stars, and this time my arrow slapped into his upper torso and he once more dropped from sight, with luck not to be getting up again.

More Picts were lurching forward from the remains of their bonfire, many of them with torches in their hands, which made them easier targets. I dropped at least eight, maybe more, before they broke. A small figure leapt like a rabbit from the inky darkness to my right and went scurrying through the dead and writhing wounded. It was a child, age and sex impossible to determine, but before I realized that, or that it was running away from me and thus no threat, I'd wasted an arrow on it, and he or she dropped amongst his or her adult fellows, squalling like a cat. The entire fortress was a cacophony of barks and yells, and some sort of horns were sounding. "Get that fucking gate open!" I yelled at the men behind me, concerned that they'd give up and make a break for it by scrambling back the way they'd come.

Four Picts were approaching behind interlocked oxhide shields, moving in a tighter and more disciplined formation than I would have ever expected. Dropping to one knee, I aimed for their legs, but these proved a difficult target, and I wasted five arrows and let them get halfway to me before I finally caught one in the knee. Roaring, he naturally lowered his shield, and I was able to put another arrow in his face, which had the gratifying effect of making the man on his right run screaming at me, shield thrown back to counterbalance his raised sword arm as rage overcame discipline, and of course I shot him in the face as well. Then the other two were almost on me, and I yelled at the men behind me for help as I dropped my bow and drew my own blade.

"Step nimble as a dancer," Gawain had once said, "and use the bloody point, don't just chop with the edge," advice that's always served me well. I dodged to the right, taking me around the shield arm of the right-hand Pict, and my point grated on his hipbone as I drove it into his side. Before he could stumble I followed the thrust with my foot, kicking him into his fellow, hoping to send them both down in a heap, but the other Pict was damned quick and rolled away, though he left his shield behind him, his wounded comrade having reflexively grabbed hold of it as he went down. Seeing him so vulnerable, two of my men pressed forward with spears, one feinting to draw his sword while the other ran him through the body. The Pict I'd wounded was finding his feet again, but slowly and unsteadily, and I had no particular difficulty putting my point into his throat, though it was lucky no other Picts were close at hand, as the arterial spray blinded me for a moment.

Wiping my eyes, I cursed to see the largest cluster of Picts yet, too many to count, most without shields, but with their spears raised for throwing, and I was certain we were dead. Even as I considered scrambling under the feet of those behind me and squirming under the door, leaving my men to their fate, Fortuna proved herself still moist for me, as a chariot came bursting through the Picts' main body, the driver and warrior so eager to get at us that they nearly ran down their own comrades, who only saved themselves by leaping to either side, so that their charge was effectively broken from behind. The two horses made a much better target than the driver, and upon taking my arrow in its chest, the left one screamed and reared, causing the chariot to veer sharply to the side, then flip over, spilling its occupants amongst the men they'd almost run down.

Behind me I heard the sweet, wonderful music of wood sliding on wood, followed by the lovely groan of hinges, and the air stirred at my back like a longed-for caress as my men threw themselves at the gate and it swung grudgingly open. And that was the cue my horsemen on the other side had been awaiting, for as we dashed out into the blessed night, throwing ourselves into the heather on either side of the cart track, a score of riders came charging in, lancers at their head and torchbearers behind them. They'd been as busy outside as we'd been within, for many of the huts that clustered on the southeast side of the fortress wall were burning. Inside, they'd find more tinder, for although Gwid's palace was all turf-roofed stone, many of the other buildings were timber and thatch, and I thanked every god I knew by name for the dry weather.

I rose and ran through the heather beside the cart track, away from the fort and the light of the burning outbuildings, the men around me laughing and whooping in triumph and me surprising myself by shouting with them. By God and all the gods, that had been bloody stupid of me, risking my life like that, but there's nothing like the feeling when such an action is over with and you're safe, that pumping exhilaration that surges through you with the headiness of strong ale, the joy of having your head still unbroken and attached, of guts still coiled inside your belly. Behind us sounded shouts, screams, whinnies, trumpeted alarms, the ragged timpani of weapons smacking into shields, and a crackling whoosh as smoldering thatch went roaring into flame.

The mounted figures waiting farther down the track proved to be Colwyn at the head of another formation, extra horses ready. A quarter mile beyond him, a bonfire burned in the very center of our camp, the men having gathered fuel for it all night, and even thrown their tents upon it, keeping it blazing strong in the hope its beacon would draw a Pictish counterattack. "Glad to see you safely back, sir," said Colwyn, grabbing my reins while I climbed into the saddle and thus halting a bite from my nervous gelding, the cavalryman's most common wound. "Your men had us worried, taking so long to get the gate open." Actually, we couldn't have spent more than a couple of minutes inside, but it had felt like hours to me, too. Damn, but it was good to have a horse between my legs—I'd had enough crawling on my belly for a lifetime.

The raiding party was returning from the fortress, for the last thing I wanted to risk was having them penned up inside, unable to make use of the crucial maneuverability their mounts afforded. Within the ramparts, everything seemed a sea of flames, smoke curling into a faint white blossom against the oily black sky, but that was an illusion, for Gwid's stone-and-turf den and the vaulted chambers beneath would surely remain untouched, and there were plenty of open spaces between the burning huts. No, their eyes and lungs might suffer from the smoke, but the Picts could safely remain within their wall, or better still, atop it, if they wanted to. If they came out to meet us, it would be by choice.

And that was a choice I was counting on them to make. It was unthinkable that such a grievous assault would go unanswered, not with the fire burning in the middle of our camp such a taunting reminder of our presence. The sky was brightening to the east, but that was all right, as most of the work for which we'd need the cover of darkness was done. I did hope we could finish this before the morning was over, though, for all those flames would be visible for miles, and there was no way of knowing if riders were already speeding to other tribal strongholds. It was crucial that we destroy Gwid's warband before any of his neighbors got here.

A man on foot approached, and I recognized Teged's voice. "You got your men inside," he said reproachfully. "Why bring them out again?"

Because I want to keep them alive, you git, I thought but didn't say. "Because the Picts will spare us the trouble now by coming out to meet us," I instead explained in the tone of voice usually reserved for children and simpletons, though he didn't seem to notice my condescension. "There's over twice as many of them as us; to get full value for my cavalry, I must leave them room to maneuver."

"If Gwid had any craft, he'd refuse to send his warriors after you," said Teged, proving himself not a complete fool after all. "Instead, he should set them atop his staked wall and dare you to make another sally."

"That's what your father would do, but not Gwid," I replied, trying to sound more certain than I felt. "And it's less a question of his craft than his control over his men." Gwid did not command disciplined troops, but the sort of Homeric band that thrives on boasts and oaths and heroic hyperbole, with battle for them representing a series of single combats, not cooperative action. That's a simplistic reduction, of course; the four Picts who'd come at me behind interlocked shields had proved themselves capable of intelligent strategy. However, with the fortress roused from drunken slumber by what they must surely consider the most craven of assaults, there would likely be few such cool heads in evidence.

We'd lost a few men, but not many, and as the raiding party returned to our main body, Colwyn rode up and down our line, getting them into position, no easy task in the gloom. All about me were shouts and whistles and hoofbeats on sod, and I despaired of making sense of it all, but fortunately my captain and his junior officers had sufficient experience to wrest order from this chaos. By the light of the burning huts, I could see Picts massing before the fortress gates, and guessed maybe five hundred men were gathered, perhaps more, shouting and shaking their weapons as they leapt about in ritualistic fury. *That's right, you lovelies*, I thought. *Get yourself all worked up, then come for us after you're all nice and winded.* Between the drink and these hysterical exertions, they'd be in fine shape for slaughter, or at least so I fervently hoped. At my order, trumpets were sounded so they'd be doubly certain of where we were.

Well, where some of us were. By prearranged signal, two groups of eighty horsemen each had split off from our main body, and were positioning themselves in the darkness forward of our left and right. Meanwhile, torchbearers rode up and down our front line, giving yet another indication that we were gathered here and ready for battle.

Fortunately, I was right, and the Picts accepted our invitation, their entire body moving toward us at a shambling jog, shrieking and waving swords and spears, a few charioteers and horsemen among them, but most on foot. The sky was paler now, and I feared that at any moment the predawn light would reveal the positions of our wings. That proved a needless worry, for the Picts were so groggily battle mad that I doubt they even bothered to look to either side, but bore straight toward our flaring torches, their fury so apparent even at this distance that I imagined I could hear them panting in their eagerness to close with us. Oh, this was better than I'd hoped; they actually seemed to be running, even though they were still over a furlong away. *That's it, my lads*, I thought, *please tire yourselves out and make our job easier.* I wondered whether Gwid was with them in one of the chariots, stupidly urging them on, or if he was lagging behind, impotently shouting for them to slow down and conserve their strength, or if he'd even given them the signal to charge. I never did find out.

On and on they came, the sound of their progress a low

rumble not unlike a distant rockslide, until they were squarely in the jaws of our trap. Two sharp trumpet blasts signaled the lancers Colwyn had sent ahead. First the right wing charged, then the left, in a neat scissoring maneuver that I would have loved to have been better able to see, though visibility was increasing every minute. Riding into a shadowed body of men is quite risky, and even in full daylight you can't gallop straight into a tightly packed formation, as your horses simply won't stand for it, and will throw their riders or veer off. However, as I'd anticipated, the Pictish advance came in a scattered, stumbling surge, with plenty of gaps between the loping men, and our scissoring wings swept right through them from both sides, leaving death and confusion in their wake, turning the enemy column from a rushing dragon into a snake that had been cut into three writhing sections.

That one pass from each wing was enough to break the Picts' momentum, as those in front belatedly turned after the horsemen who'd just gone charging through the ranks behind them, the men at the rear slowed at seeing their fellows in front of them cut down, and the hapless middle reeled from the impact of having one group of attackers sweep their front while others charged from the opposite direction through their rear. The double pass could not have killed or wounded more than a hundred Picts, at most a fifth their total strength, but although it might seem we'd only pricked them, that pricking had magically bled away their fierce purpose, leaving them a confused and dispirited mass.

Daylight was spreading over the moor, melting the pooled shadows, but that was to our advantage as well, for cavalry achieves its best effects when the foe can see it coming. Another trumpet, and the troops lined in front of me, half my total force, started forward at a trot, then a slow but still earth-shaking gallop, iron lance heads gleaming in the budding sun's first rays. Already distracted by the carnage behind them, the forward Picts lost their spirit then and turned to run, crashing back into their still reeling middle, suddenly sober panic rippling through their disorganized ranks. And that was the end of them, as it always is. The heaviest casualties come when men break and try to run away, for if you ever walk through a corpse-strewn battlefield, you'll see that the majority of the fallen received their death wounds in their backs. Most of Gwid's forces were still alive and unhurt, but they were now strung out in fleeing groups, some heading for the fortress, others scattering across the heather. None, however, could outrun a horse, and for my troops it rapidly became a kind of game, not unlike those cavalry exercises where you test your skill by skewering fleeing dogs, piglets, or other expendable livestock. As if it had been waiting for the dawn, rain came hissing over the bracken, dousing the smoldering torches that had been thrown aside once no longer needed, and putting out the fires in the distant fortress, its patter softening the death cries of Picts and the exultations of my men. I turned my face upward to receive the sky's cool blessing, grateful beyond measure that the worst was over, the animal thrill of victory coursing through me. Was this the pride in their butcher's work that Arthur and Gawain had felt after all their battles? If so, it was indeed a potent draught.

A dappled mare cantered past, eyes rolling and blood on her empty saddle, evidence that even the easiest victories have a price. Teged caught her reins and swung himself up before I could ask what the devil he was about. All my men were busy chasing fleeing Picts or fighting those small groups who'd chosen to make a last stand, so there was no one in earshot to send after him. Spurring my mount, I yelled for him to stop, and a hundred paces on, he seemed to hear me and obey, for he reined to a sudden halt and leapt from the saddle. However, when I caught up to him, it became apparent that he was only looking for a weapon. "Leave me alone!" he shouted as he picked up a dead Pict's spear. "I must find Tarain!" I still had my bow, along with a fresh quiver at my saddle horn, and I was tempted to stop him by putting an arrow in his thigh, but however satisfying that might be, it was too damn risky—even if my aim proved true, there were many ways a minor wound could turn fatal, and I well remembered Cuneda's warning about what would happen if my actions caused his son's death.

My hesitation gave Teged the chance to scramble back on top of the mare, and we were off again, me dreading that at any second some wounded Pict might roll out of a clump of heather and put a spear into the belly of his horse (or worse, mine). Then we mounted a hilltop and I saw that the God of Fools must have heard Teged's cries, for a hundred yards away careened a war chariot drawn by two familiar white stallions. Tarain crouched behind his painted little driver, both of them somehow managing to stay aboard despite the way their vehicle bounced over the uneven terrain.

Tarain saw Teged almost as soon as Teged saw him, and when he whispered in his driver's ear, that naked little Pict turned his stallions around with a skill that was truly beautiful to watch. Then the mounted warrior and the chariot-borne one were on a seeming collision course, the outcome of which would be all too predictable, as Teged's spear was couched underarm, whereas Tarain's lighter one was poised for throwing, with five more in the wicker sheath at his side. There was only thing to do, and I had to do it now. When I was still a boy, Gawain had given me my little recurved bow and a shaggy barbarian pony, and told me I could impress Arthur by learning to shoot from horseback, like the Huns to whom weapon and steed had once belonged. There'd been a time when I could actually guide my mount with my knees and fire without seeming to take aim, but lack of practice had dulled that skill, and so I wasted precious moments by reining in, sighting along my horse's neck, and letting fly. It was still a damned difficult shot, and it's no surprise I completely missed the Pictish prince, but Fortuna still favored me, for she sent my arrow deep into the driver's torso, causing him to convulse back into his master, who dropped his spear and teetered for one arms-flailing instant before pitching out of the chariot and rolling across the broken sward. Ignoring the vehicle as it careened past, Teged bore down on its former occupant, who was trying unsuccessfully to stand. Apparently realizing that his unarmed opponent was injured, Teged jumped from his horse and stood there, spear balanced on his shoulder, his back to me but his posture suggesting a cat that's just clamped its paw onto the back of a juicy mouse.

Tarain made one last attempt to rise, but one of his legs must have been broken, for he collapsed back in a sitting position, growling in agonized frustration. I'd caught up to them by this time, and, as I dismounted, Teged raised his spear and drove it into Tarain's stomach. The Pict doubled over with a sound like a loud wet burp, his face pressed against the shaft as if he was trying to kiss or bite it, while his killer leaned on the weapon, driving it so far into him that the point was surely emerging from his buttocks and pinning him to the blood-and bowel-stained earth. Letting go of the spear, Teged took two steps back and looked at his handiwork, pale lips set in a thin smile. Tarain's face was downcast, obscured by the spikes of his woad-dyed hair, his broad, short-fingered hands flopping at his sides like crabs in a boiling pot. The sound he was making might have been an attempt to form words.

"I wonder how long it will take him to die," said Teged with grim satisfaction. "Shall we wager on it?"

"No, my noble lord, we shall not," I replied as I drew my sword. Having no desire to look into Tarain's eyes, I walked gingerly behind him, careful of the foulness pooling there. Even though I used both hands and put my back into it, I didn't quite cut his head off, something which despite boastful stories I've never known anyone to manage in one blow, but when my blade chopped into his neck the poor bastard immediately went limp. Apparently wanting a trophy, Teged crouched beside the still-upright corpse and fumbled at the Pict's blood-splattered harness until he found a knife. The edge must not have been very sharp, for he was still sawing when I got back into the saddle and rode away.

It took another hour to gather up our wounded and get them into the former mead carts. Only twenty-three men were too injured to ride their horses, more than half of them looking like they might survive being carted back to Gododdin. Another thirteen were dead, with nine close enough to it that there was no point in moving them. Since Arthur didn't allow his men to take trophies, we were denied a conveniently literal head count, but we appeared to have killed well over two hundred of Gwid's warriors. We could thank the mead for that, for if the Pictish warband hadn't gotten so drunk, our casualties would have been much higher, and even if we'd won, more of our foes would surely have escaped across the moor. Still, between three and four hundred had presumably gone to ground somewhere out there in the rain-washed heather, and there was no telling if or when more might arrive from other tribal strongholds, so there was no time to dawdle.

Not that we could leave just yet, for you don't set off on a day's ride with mounts that have just been through even a brief battle, not without resting, feeding, and watering them first. I wanted to make sure that Gwid was dead, so I and a fifty-man escort gingerly approached the quiet-seeming fortress on foot, leading balky horses behind us in case we had to beat a quick retreat. Pictish corpses littered the cart track and the heather on both sides, most bearing diamond-shaped puncture wounds between their shoulder blades, fatal evidence of the folly of trying to run away from lancers. Every so often, one of the bodies would still be wearing a silver neck torque, and I diplomatically allowed those of my men who hadn't already claimed such booty to draw straws for it. No one had appeared atop the fortress rampart, although as we grew closer I could hear faint noises, both human and animal, from within. About four yards from the gate, we found Gwid.

He lay sprawled facedown on the stained gravel, several large black flies already exploring the familiar hole in his back, the butterfly spray of blood suggesting that the shaft had gone right through him. One of my bolder lancers must have spiked him right off the back of his chariot when he was just yards away from a safe retreat. At first I wondered who'd done it, but when I saw that he'd been stripped of his gold and silver, I decided that not only would I know soon enough, by the killer's boasts as well as his new ornamentation, but that he had made such a good haul that I was spared the tedious and expensive gesture of having to offer him any further reward. The Pictish love of precious metals was certainly proving lucrative for my men, which I supposed was a good thing, as their loot, coupled with the seemingly careless bravery I'd shown, must surely elevate me in their eyes. *Ach, Gawain*, I thought, *my cohort may soon love me as much as yours loves you.*

Sometime during the battle, the fortress gate had been

closed again. Wary of what might still be lurking inside, I'd sent two groups of fifteen men scrambling between the stakes and up the sloping wall on either side of the gatehouse before even pausing to inspect Gwid, and had not approached until they'd give me the all-clear. Now, I shouted up at their captain, a tall Iceni whose size and fair hair hinted at Saxon blood. "Ho, Brennios, what's going on in there?"

"There's plenty of their peasants milling about," yelled Brennios, tugging at his blond mustache in a way that suggested he didn't like being such a prominent target. "No warriors in sight, though, and none of the peasants have picked up so much as a pitchfork. A lot of them are climbing up the far wall and scampering down the other side—I think they're afraid we're coming in. Wait a minute, what the hell is this? You down there, keep back!"

"What is it?" I asked anxiously, wondering if I should give the order to remount and be ready for a quick retreat.

"There's two little Picts approaching the other side of the gate," said Brennios. "No, wait, one doesn't look like a Pict, and I think both of 'em are just boys. Want us to put arrows into them anyway?" Several of his men had straight yew bows, bigger and clumsier than my little recurved one, but deadly enough.

"Are they armed?" I asked, relieved that they didn't sound like a serious threat whether they were or not.

"Nah," said Brennios, "not that I can see. The one that doesn't look like a Pict has a rope around the other's neck, and is leading him. That's all either has in his hands."

This sounded intriguing, even if I didn't need the distraction. "Let them come, then."

There was a scrambling under the gate, which I'd expected, as there was no way the pair that Brennios had just described could get the portal unbarred and open by themselves. At first I thought that the head peering up at me like that of a badger from its den was so fair-haired that its owner must be part Saxon, but no, despite the fluid grace with which he slithered to his feet, his short curls were not blond but the dead and faded white of clean dry bone, and although he had the stature and slim-limbed, large-headed proportions of a ten-year-old child, the ruddy skin around his wet rheumy eyes bore a delicate tracery of wrinkles. He wore a short simple woolen tunic that scarcely covered his crotch, although this left him better covered than the dark blank-eyed boy he hauled after him, who was naked except for a heavy coat of dirt.

I was too surprised to be truly frightened, even though I instantly recognized him. Although I'd only met him once and briefly, when I was scarcely older than the young Pict he'd leashed like a dog, there was no mistaking that high-domed brow, those slender limbs, the moon white hair that so contrasted with the bright pink skin. "Merlin," I said, my voice calmer than I felt. "I did not expect to find you here."

"You're older, Mordred," he said lightly in a high voice and very pure Latin, standing on one foot while propping the other against his knee like a stork, and flashing fine white teeth. "Bigger, too."

"You're not," I said unnecessarily. "Why are you living with these Picts?"

The boy tried to crawl back under the gate, but Merlin halted him with one effortless flick of the rope, despite being just as small and rather less muscular. "You confuse a brief visit with residence. I still live in the forest of Strathclyde, where I've lodged ever since your father exiled me because he didn't like being reminded that I was once his father's catamite. Which allows me to ask you something I really couldn't when we first met. Does it bother you that I used to fuck your grandfather?"

This was not a question I'd expected to be asked today, or ever. Still, I knew better than to get angry with this smirking ancient boy. "I wouldn't care if Uther had used his dick to let the gas out of bloated sheep. But I do want to know why you're here in Pictdom."

Merlin idly bit his thumb and looked coy. "Oh, come now, you're the smartest man in Camelot, now that I'm gone." He again flicked his wrist, and the Pictish boy stumbled forward and collapsed at his feet, "Isn't it obvious? I knew that you'd be coming here, as I know so many things, and thought I'd stop by and say hello. And of course I knew you'd win, and that in the aftermath of your victory, there'd be easy pickings, like this sweet brown lad. He'll keep me warm this winter, and when I tire of him, I can write verses on his skin. I've written many poems while in exile. Would you care to hear one?"

"Not really," I said, wishing one of my archers on top of the wall would put an arrow into this creature, but unwilling to give the order or offer any other violence. Christ's balls, how had Arthur ever faced him down, when he exiled him right after ascending to the throne?

"Humor me," he said, idly tracing in the dirt with one prehensile-looking toe. "Then you can go, for I know you must be anxious to get Prince Teged and his sore rectum back to Gododdin. This was very clever of you, by the way. When the time comes, you'll have the North on your side. I didn't foresee that much, when we first met. Of course, you were small and quiet, and I was too busy thinking about your soft skin and imagining the tightness of your bunghole. A pity your mother interrupted."

"I didn't think so," I said through clenched teeth.

Merlin's laugh reminded me of a yipping fox. "Nor do you now, I'm quite sure. I rather wish we had more time to reminisce, but I know you and your men must be on your way. Shall I recite my poem now?"

I shrugged. "If you wish." Anything to get him far away, and quickly.

Grabbing the Pictish boy by the hair, he pulled his head forward, holding it under his arm and petting it like a dog's, the child grimacing in obvious terror but not resisting. Throwing his own head back, Merlin shut his eyes and began to declaim, and I briefly hated my men for not having the initiative to spring forward and attempt to cut him down, though I knew quite well that anyone who tried that would most likely fail, and die horribly in the failing.

> *"A budding secret sprouts between*
> *the seeming girl-child's thighs;*
> *Remember what I tell you now,*
> *when you see it with your eyes.*
> *Only Merlin has the craft to make*
> *true women out of men.*

*So seek me in the mossy wood
if you'd have him be her again.''*

Having no idea what to say to such gibberish, I could only stare. Merlin shrugged and grinned, dimples spreading under watery bright eyes. "Yes, I know, it's pure doggerel; despite the prophetic spirit inside me, I fear I lack the bardic gift. But you'll remember it and come seeking my aid. Oh yes, for all you scoff now, and recoil from my presence, the woman for whom you would do anything will learn she needs me, and upon this knowledge will send you to fetch me back from my long exile, with not even prim and pious Arthur able to gainsay her, for he loves her, too. Love, love, love; is there any magic greater? I loved your grandfather, you know. He was neither handsome nor witty, and his clumsy Roman affectations made him smell of garlic, but I loved him, and would have eaten my own filth if he'd asked me to. Love does that, even to me. It's the knife that wounds the world.''

I couldn't believe that I was standing between a corpse and a burned fortress, talking to this creature about love. "You said you'd be on your way once you recited your verse.'' Christ and Dagda, but I almost wished for a Pictish attack, any diversion from this most unwanted encounter.

Merlin took a step closer to me. "Ah, but perhaps I've changed my mind. You really are going to come seeking me, you know, so it might be convenient if I simply joined your party now, and went South with you.''

I think it was the prospect of such unwelcome company that spurred one of my men into action. Lowering his spear, he pointed it at Merlin's face. "Please, sir,'' he said to me, the quaver in his voice suggesting that he had a good idea of the futility of his threat, "give me the word and I'll kill him, or at least die trying.''

Merlin laughed his yipping laugh and extended a hand wrapped in cold blue flame. Taking the tang of the spear in his burning but unburned grip, he pulled the iron head to his face and stuck it all the way into his mouth, shoving it back farther than should have been possible without piercing the back of his throat, sucking on it for a long obscene moment, clearly mimicking a sexual act. The cold fire flickered out, and his hand was just a hand again, but when he drew the spearhead back from his wet lips, it was no longer a thing of stiff straight iron, but flexing scales, for the shaft now ended in a living adder's head, along with a few inches of its neck and body, the twisting snake form sprouting from the wood.

The impulsive soldier threw down his weapon as if it was red-hot, and he and his comrades all drew back several steps, leaving me feeling very much alone with Merlin. Up on the wall, Brennios began to pray, which would have surprised me if I'd had room for such an emotion, so few of my men being Christian.

Merlin tapped the writhing end of the fallen spear with one long pink toe, not flinching when it tried to bite him. "Examine it after I'm gone. You'll find it's still part snake, and that the transformation was no conjurer's trick. It will continue to twist and hiss until it dies from being unable to eat and drink, and then it will rot, and when the putrescent meat sloughs away, there will still be fragile snake bones sticking out of the reeking wood. I can change things for real and forever. That's why you'll need me. The seeming transformation you'll want me to undo is the result of no spell, but a perfectly natural process. All along, the apparent girl was truly a boy within, the secret growing inside the child like a seed. It's very rare, but it happens with some that seem to be born female, the tender shoot of manhood emerging at about the time they would start bleeding, were they genuinely women. As much as I dislike Arthur's beloved priests and saints, I know that many wield real power, but they will be of no help, as they might be if the child was simply bewitched. Many a learned man or woman can lift even the strongest spell, given the right mental effort and some luck. However, it takes a rare gift indeed to change something's true essence. Of course, we both know how stubborn Arthur is, and he will have that constipated-looking bishop of his send for a particularly smelly hermit before he concedes defeat. Remember that I told you this."

With that he pulled the Pictish boy to his feet and gave

me a low bow. "Uther was also stubborn. Indeed, the quality must run in your family, for I see by the expression on your face that you, too, prefer to do things the difficult way and don't want my cheery company, even though it would save you much time and trouble if I simply went South with you today. Still, if having the gift of prophecy teaches one anything, it's that there's no point in getting mired down in ifs and onlys. Besides, it would be awkward for me to come to Camelot before I'm asked. So go on and get your men back across the Wall of Antoninus before any of the late Gwid's neighbors decide to try to avenge him, and I'll traipse merrily back to my forest, to resume the sweet Arcadian life until you come looking for me. When you do, you'll remember that you could have spared yourself the trip."

Whistling, he struck out across the moor, his leashed captive stumbling after him. I'm not a sentimentalist about children, feeling no particular horror at having probably killed the one I accidentally shot last night, and once, when young and drunk in Orkney, I'd fucked an even younger and less than willing stableboy. But despite such transgressions, I very much despised myself for not trying to stop Merlin from taking that poor child with him. I thought about yelling for one of the men on the wall to put an arrow into the brat and thus prevent his imminent misery. But no, Merlin would be able to prevent the shaft from reaching its target, or worse, would not be able to prevent it, and would be peeved that he'd been denied his pleasure.

I knelt beside the spear haft. Its end still writhed, just as Merlin had said it would. From behind me came the sound of someone scrambling down from the wall, and when I looked, I saw it was Brennios, his tanned face pale under a sheen of sweat.

"I didn't tell you to come down yet," I said mildly, more from want of anything else to say than because I cared.

He stared after the small departing figures and spat, still too shaken to be mindful of my implied rebuke. "I'm sorry, sir. I wish I could have helped, that any of us could have. But we've all heard of Merlin, and . . ."

I stood up and looked back toward our camp. "Never mind him, soldier, he's gone. I think we should be, too."

It was a somber band that led our horses back to our main body, which was still preparing for departure. "Bad news, sir?" asked Colwyn when he saw my face.

I didn't feel like explaining, but simply hooked a thumb at the lowering sky. "This drizzle is going to get worse. I think our luck with the weather has run out."

He didn't say anything, just got the troops in order, and my prediction proved accurate, for by the time the whole company was finally moving, much too slowly for my liking, the rain was coming down in great hissing sheets, sweeping mercilessly across the writhing heather, turning the broken track to mud and dropping a cold gray veil over even the nearest hills, hiding anything more than a hundred yards away from view. We all had hooded, coarsely woven cloaks of oily, water-resistant wool, of the kind that Britain had once routinely exported throughout the Empire, and I pulled mine tight around me, the weight and weave soon causing me to itch and sweat despite the sopping chill, and quietly cursed the sucking ooze that fought our every step, the downpour that masked the sight and sounds of possible pursuit. Yet in a way, I was grateful for the discomfort and the danger, for it kept me from thinking too much about what Merlin had said.

Seven

GUINEVERE LOOKED up from her knitting when her maid issued me into her inner chamber. "Thank you, Brigid. Now please leave me and Nimüe alone with Lord Mordred." Brigid nodded and shut the door behind me.

Our Southern nights had begun to acquire a slight autumnal chill, although thankfully not so much of one as to foretell a particularly harsh winter. A three-legged brazier engraved with a coiling dragon smoked in the corner, for Gwen hated to make slaves toil in the basement furnaces until absolutely necessary, ignoring my sybaritic observation that there was little point in having such a painstakingly restored Roman-style heating system if we didn't make good use of it. But then, I was particularly sensitive, as two weeks of riding through rain and mud had given me a nasty cold.

Nimüe seemed to have recovered from hers. She squatted cross-legged on the floor, wearing a particularly fine green woolen gown that Gwen must have made for her in my absence, playing with the tiny tortoiseshell kitten half-hidden in its folds, also a new possession. Surprisingly, there was a large mug of mulled wine beside her, and her strong-jawed and atypically clean face was quite flushed, her freckles burning as brightly as the coals in the brazier.

I sneezed a wet, honking sneeze, then wiped thick green snot on my brocaded sleeve. "Damn this nose," I muttered hoarsely.

A smile flickered across Gwen's solemn visage. "As refined as ever. I'm glad the rustic North didn't blunt your manners.''

''Or anything else,'' I said as I settled in a chair, my bones too cold and fever sore for me to care that the wicker was dangerously close to the brazier.

Gwen's amusement faded. ''I'm glad to see you, too, but I fear this is no time for crude teasing. I need to—*we* need to talk to you about something very serious.''

Nimüe was staring at the top of her kitten's flat little head, pointedly avoiding my eyes. ''Yes, Mordred,'' she said in a tiny voice that sounded far younger than herself. ''I really, really need your help.''

Ach, so Gwen had discovered Nimüe's secret, something she surely hadn't known about when I departed on my eventful trip north. Merlin's prophecy had not been terribly oblique, and of course I'd put some of the pieces together by now, for all my attempts at not thinking about it during the journey back from Gododdin. Still, it wasn't as if I could just up and ask if the child had unexpectedly acquired a penis, and I could only wonder just how they'd broach the subject. Had I been less concerned about Gwen and the distress this must be causing her, I'd have found it all grotesquely amusing. Indeed, only Arthur's presence could have made the scene more farcically awkward, and I almost regretted that he was still in Gaul. My old bitterness toward my father was gone, and there were times when I even allowed myself some affection for him, but there was still a part of me that derived amusement from seeing him made uncomfortable.

Keeping my voice as bland as possible, I said, ''Yes, dear ladies, tell me what's the matter.''

Guinevere arose, giving her long arms a nervous shake, the brazier's glow reflected on her pale skin, her unbound shining hair. I would say that the light suited her, but then, almost any light did, the same way she'd be glorious in fine linen or dirty rags (and even more glorious naked and in darkness, but this was not the time for those particular thoughts). ''I think that Nim and I both need to drink a bit more wine first. Will you have some, too?''

''Of course, ladies.'' The occasion was as good a one for

drinking as any, though I'd never needed to lubricate my tongue before broaching unpleasant subjects.

Nimüe drank clumsily from her mug, spilling a bit on her gown and on the kitten, which rolled over and started cleaning itself, a comically sour expression on its tiny face. Gwen found me a goblet and filled it from the large red amphora beside the brazier, then refreshed her own. For a couple of minutes there was no sound other than the hiss and pop of the coals, the faint rasp of a feline tongue on fur, and our own sips and swallows.

"I'm glad the Lady Nimüe is better," I said at last, wishing that my phlegmy palate allowed me a better appreciation of the vintage. "I fear I shall need to partake of the remedy I prescribed for her when I was last here."

Nimüe hiccuped. "Good. It tasted awful. I'm glad you'll have to drink it, too. I hope it makes you throw up."

I laughed, though it turned into a sneeze. "And very grateful you are, I see. It did, after all, make you better."

She rested her shining face against her bony knees, ignoring the kitten batting at her lank red hair. "But I'm not *better*. My fever is gone, but I'd rather be sick again, sick near to death, than like this."

"Like what, my lady?" It felt cruel to make her say it, but really, there was no way I could express what I'd deduced from Merlin's unsubtle hints, not without likely making her feel worse.

Nimüe retrieved her hair from the cat and used it to wipe her eyes. "I'm sorry, Mordred, I don't mean to be such a baby, not when you're the only one who can help. I'm drunk, or at least I think I am. I've never been drunk before. Why do people like it so much?"

I blew my nose on my sleeve again. "A good question, that. We grown-ups are often a silly lot."

Guinevere knelt beside her sibling. "Sweet Nim, I think maybe this is a mistake. If you like, Mordred and I can talk about this alone, and then you can talk to him, or I can just tell you what he says."

Nimüe shook her head, and in her tight-lipped resolve I saw some of her sister's tough spirit. "No, Gwen, I must tell him. Please help me stand. My legs feel like I've left them somewhere else.''

With a smile that mingled sadness and pride, Guinevere extended a hand and pulled the girl to her feet, the ease with which she did so hinting at the considerable strength of her deceptively slender frame. Nimüe stood there, swaying slightly, her eyes half-shut, while Gwen brushed a few strands of the wet hair that the child had let trail into her wine off her flushed face. Then, with a clumsy half turn, Nimüe faced me, bent to grab the folds of her gown, and hiked it up about her waist, almost but not quite tipping over.

She was even paler down there, with fewer freckles, which accentuated the scabs on her prominent knees and the rash of pimples on her skinny thighs. It took me a moment to focus on her crotch, for what dangled there, although undeniably present, was hardly prominent. Her penis was no bigger than the first joint of my little finger, which aside from its coloration it vaguely resembled. Beneath it nestled a tiny scrotum, like twin white mushrooms sprouting amidst the fine moss of her pubic hair. The flesh around it was pinkish, and somewhat puckered, as if the vaginal canal had somehow turned itself inside out when disgorging her true sex. (And yes, I will continue to use the feminine when speaking of her, despite the obvious incongruity of a construction like "her penis.")

I looked at Gwen, whose expression made me wish I could hold her and tell that everything would be fine, that I could fix this and make Nimüe her sister again. I'm not sure whether or not being forewarned by Merlin made it any easier; the confusion and helplessness I would have felt might have been preferable to the unpleasant certainty of from whom I would have to seek aid. "I see it, Nimüe," I said gently. "You can lower your gown now."

Nimüe slumped to the floor, legs drawn up protectively in front of her, looking at me through disheveled hair and half-closed eyelids. "I've become a boy. I mean, I have . . . I have a . . . you know, you saw it." The tears came then, and she buried her face in her gown.

I got out of the chair and sat beside her, my arm around

her in an uncharacteristic and awkward-feeling attempt at comfort. "Yes, child, I saw it."

She slumped over into my lap, bony arms hugging my knees. "Don't tell Gawain. Please, whatever you do, don't tell him. I'd die if he knew, I'd kill myself, really I would."

Guinevere sat beside us, stroking her sister's hair. "Hush, Nim. Don't fret yourself that way. Gawain won't know, we promise." She looked at me, her eyes warning that the promise had better be kept.

Merlin, I said to myself, *I hope you were merely using your gift of prophecy when you told me I would need you, and that you were honest when you said this is no magical transformation. If I discover that this is somehow your work, I will have to find a way to kill you.*

"She's been that way for a while, but I only just found out," said Gwen. "When poor Nim was ill, so weak in her bed she couldn't move, I went to bathe her, and saw the change. I'm not sure she would have told me, otherwise."

Nimüe's gawky body shook with a new round of sobs. "I'm sorry, I thought maybe I could keep it a secret, that I could even pretend the thing between my legs wasn't there. It's only happened since my last birthday, I swear. I used to be a girl, I promise I did . . ."

Gwen smiled. "I well know that, sweets. In Cornwall, when you were little, you liked to wear nothing at all. I can't count the times I pulled you naked from some mud puddle, your shift wet and crumpled beside you. This is some evil magic, but we'll set it right, I promise."

Gently as I could, I extricated myself from Nimüe's grip and eased her off my lap and onto Gwen's. "You need some more wine, sweets," I said, sliding across the floor to refill her mug. It would be easier for Gwen and me to talk about the apparent realities of the situation after Nimüe was asleep, and wine would speed that process. With Gwen's help, she sat up, taking the mug in hands so shaky I had to steady them with my own. After a few more swallows, she put it down again, her eyes fluttering shut, and I picked her up and put her in Gwen's bed, although I would have preferred to carry her to her cot in the outer chamber. Mewing inquisitively, the little kitten jumped up beside her, kneaded her shoulder with its claws, walked a tight circle, and then curled on top of her chest, purring more loudly than should have been possible for such a tiny thing.

Gwen rose and stretched, running fingers through the flaming cascade of her hair, spreading it out like crimson wings. "I saw your face when she pulled up her gown. Were you somehow expecting this, or is it just that nothing magical surprises you anymore?"

Behind me, Nimüe had begun to snore. I wished I could get that drunk on three cups of wine. "It's not magic," I said softly, pulling off my buskins and flexing my cramped toes. "Things might be easier if it were, but it's not. She's truly a boy, and has been one inside, all along."

Gwen sat in front of me, hands crossed on knees and chin balanced on knuckles. "What do you mean by that, my love? She didn't used to have a penis. Now she does. If that isn't magic, I don't know what is."

I stretched forward and took her hands, which were bigger than my own, if softer and more graceful. "Someone—a very learned man—once told me about such transformations. He said they were very rare, but entirely natural, with nothing of magic in them. He said that sometimes children are born who appear to be girls, but are really boys inside. When they are on the first cusp of adulthood, their true sex emerges, like a plant putting forth a tender shoot. I neither like nor trust the one who told me this, but I've no reason to doubt him, for he's far wiser than me." I hoped she would not ask me who had told me this, or when, for then I would have to tell her what else Merlin had said, about being the only one who could help. That was a boon I'd rather not seek, someone in whose debt I would not have my loved one be, not now or ever, though of course I was foolish, thinking any of us had such a choice. I suppose it's inherent in our nature that we resist prophecies, that we struggle against their inexorable tide, like a salmon trying to swim upstream in a flood. The wine had gone to my already cold-addled head, and some part of me imagined that perhaps Nimüe could learn to like being a boy, and Merlin could rot in his forest.

Gwen cocked her head and looked at me with her green

cat eyes. "You're the wisest man I know. I can't imagine anyone wiser."

I somehow managed a grin. "I'm clever, my love, not wise. Sometimes, not even clever."

She slid forward, squeezing my knees between her own, though the gesture spoke more of tenderness than libido. "You went to hell for me, or a place very much like it, and brought me back. Who else could have done that? Or do you mean to say that a wise man would have left me there?"

I reached out and stroked her slim white calf, wondering if I could suggest that we move the child so as to have the bed for ourselves, but deciding against it. "No, that's not what I meant, and you know it. Perhaps a genuinely wise man never lets himself fall in love, but that's another matter." *Truly*, I thought, *if I weren't more than half a fool, I would never have wrapped myself in these chains.*

The lamp on the intarsia table flickered out, leaving the faint glow from the brazier as our only source of light. Gwen's face was a moon white triangle in the gloom, shadows accentuating the crooked line of her wide mouth, the pooled darkness of her large eyes, yet even this stark and irregular mask was somehow lovely. "Help her, please, if you can, and even if you think you can't, please try. Even if it's no magic, but an accident of birth that makes her what she's become, find a spell that will change her back into what she once seemed to be—into what she *should* be. I know I've no right to ask you for anything in this life, not after what you've done for me already, but I ask this anyway."

I ran a finger through the valleys between her soft toes, over the ridged ball of her foot, and along her ankle, where I traced the pulsing vein. "I know this is a strange idea," I said, speaking slowly and carefully, not sure how to best shape the words, "but think on it just the same. When I brought you back from the Kingdom of Teeth, you talked of why you were going to wed Arthur, even though it was me you loved. 'There's not much for a woman in this life,' you said. You married a man you didn't love because you wanted a modicum of comfort and control, the power to be something more than a bartered prize. Were I able to give little Nimüe her cunt back, would she be even that? She'd be marrying no kings, I think. You said you envied me the freedom given me by what hung between my legs, that I owned more of myself than you ever had. I think you love that child as if she were your own, rather than your half sister. Would you deny her this chance at the liberty of my sex?''

Gwen rested her face in pale spread hands, which she then ran through the shadowy torrent of her hair. ''That's a clever net you've woven from my words, I'll grant you, but she's been a girl for almost twelve years, with childhood nearly behind her. I don't she think could learn to be a boy, not after having come so close to womanhood. No, she'd be a woman with a cock, like some monster displayed at a village fair. At least, that's what she'd feel herself to be, deep in her heart, which is the only place it really matters. She loves your brother, you know. Some men can love other men in such a way, but I don't think Gawain is one of them.''

The backs of her thighs were warm against the tops of my feet, her breath smelled slightly but not unpleasantly of wine, and her voice was a lulling murmur in the gloom. I wondered if I would still feel this way if we were man and wife; would such secret intimacy seem half so precious were it less rare and fleeting? How much time had we really had, since I brought her back from the Kingdom of Teeth and surrendered her to Arthur? Would the individual moments we'd stolen down the years total a day, a week, a month? Surely no more than that, and likely less. An idle but subtly terrible thought struck me then, that only sharing her with Arthur had kept my love so fresh, that I would have tired of her long before were she entirely mine. But no, I told myself, rocking against her closeness in the dark, I could never tire of this, for I would rather feel one of her fingers on the back of my hand than fuck any other woman in the world, an insight I somehow found both terrifying and a comfort.

''Who was it that told you these things, about boys who are born as seeming girls?'' Gwen asked, breaking my reverie.

''Merlin,'' I said glumly, my inability to dissemble a measure of her power over me. ''I met him on the Pictish moor.

He told me what Nimüe is. That's why I wasn't surprised when she showed herself to me.''

Gwen was silent for a few heartbeats, and when she spoke, there was new iron in her voice. ''The aged boy magician whom Arthur exiled when he claimed the throne? I didn't know he was still alive. Why would he tell you this?''

I was glad that it was too dark to read her expression. ''He said that only he could change her back into what she'd once seemed to be, and that I should seek him in the Caledonian wood, when I decided—when we decided—that we needed him. He said he wanted to come South again.''

The hiss of her breath was like a knife leaving its sheath. ''Did he now? Are you sure this change is not his doing, despite slippery words about boys sometimes being born as apparent girls? By God, Mordred, if I thought he did this to Nimüe, I would not wait for Arthur to return from Less Britain, but would send the entire warband to the Caledonian wood, if that proved necessary, to chop it down, and Merlin with it.''

That's what it would probably take, I thought but didn't say. ''No, I don't think it was his doing. Were he able to work his power at such a distance, I believe he would cast it directly upon Arthur, not a child he's never known. I know enough of magic to be sure that, to have wrought such a change, he would need to be close to her, and I don't think he has been. Also, lying is likely the only sin he's never committed.'' Ach, did I just use the word *sin*? Well, it was late, and I was tired.

''Then we must bring him here and have him work his magic.''

I laughed sourly. ''Oh, yes, as easily as that! Gwen, aside from the fact that I would almost rather enter the Kingdom of Teeth again than to seek Merlin in his lair, or spend a minute in his company, there is the trifling matter of your husband. To summon Merlin here without his leave would be to invite—well, I'm not sure what, but I am sure it would not be good.''

''Then we will get his leave,'' said Gwen with a finality that would have brooked no argument were she speaking of anyone else.

Well, Merlin had said I would come seeking him, but while I did not doubt the efficacy of his foreknowledge, it would surely not be as easy as all that. "Arthur's changed, right enough, since either of us first met him, but he's not changed *that* much, surely. It would be bad enough that Merlin is a wizard, in Arthur's eyes a tool of that entity called Satan, whose power seems to concern Christians more than that of their vaunted carpenter . . ."

"Some Christians," said Gwen.

"Most Christians," I continued, "even if not so much you Pelagians. Anyway, completely aside from his connection to the Otherworld, there's the matter of what Merlin used to do in this one, when he was Uther Pendragon's little pet. You know Arthur feels that all his life has been a struggle out of shame and degradation. Maybe not so much now, but such feelings can never be entirely shaken off, not by a man like my father and your husband. It took a longish time for Arthur to accept me and be comfortable around me, even though I could logically share no blame in the supposed stain of my conception, and whatever my faults, I am certainly more pleasing company than Merlin. Be sure you understand the task you set yourself."

Gwen sighed and leaned forward to rest her head upon her knees, her hair spilling into my lap, where I gently took a handful of it and breathed in its soft fragrance. "I will not fail Nimüe," she said softly. "She needs this thing done, and so I shall see that it is. Will you help me?"

The glow from the brazier was much fainter now, with darkness piling heavily upon us. "Yes," I finally murmured, knowing I could say nothing else. "I will help you if you wish me to."

She sat up and opened her knees, rising so that she straddled me, our faces bumping clumsily together at first, but then her lips found mine, and we kissed, tongues probing past teeth, me already hard for her, she grinding against me, me fumbling at my breeches while she drew her gown up about her waist, and all the time, Nimüe snoring somewhere behind us, and us soon grunting to a similar rhythm. We had to be quick about it, with Brigid in the next chamber, and there was some dim and remarkably charitable part of me that regretted that I was probably giving her my cold. We strove clumsily to find a workable position, the struggle ending with us lying on our sides on the hard floor, my chest to her back, her buttocks soft against my crotch, and then I was inside her, thrusting away with little enough grace, but it felt good, so very good, and she moaned softly, long fingers drumming the floor, then reaching back to rake my neck sweetly and grip the bunched fabric of my tunic, which was now hiked nearly to my chest. Sometime after that came release, glorious but much too soon, and we lay there, limp as trout, sweat gluing my hip to the floor tiles, and me to her, and for all the obvious discomfort, me wishing we wouldn't soon need to get up again.

The next afternoon, after spending most of the day attending to various administrative duties, Guinevere finally had time to meet with me and Nimüe in the courtyard grove, where the slanting sunlight was tinted gold and orange by the autumnal canopy overhead. Wrapped in a hooded cloak the color of fine ash, Nimüe sat on the roots of a dwarf oak, her hangover as plain as a bruise on her pale, pinched face, while her kitten stalked the dead leaves that skittered like lizards at her feet. "Is this how one's supposed to feel after drinking, or am I under yet another curse?" she asked in a small pained voice.

"You get used to it," I said as I leaned against the tree, ignoring the tiny orange, black, and white predator that suddenly left off chasing leaves to hurl itself upon my right foot, needle claws probing the soft leather of my buskin. "That's part of growing up."

"What, being a drunken sot?" said Gwen as she settled gracefully on the marble bench, resplendent today in a wine-colored gown with a dark purple brocade, a gold comb, and green ribbons in her hair.

I squatted on the crackling leaves and tickled the kitten's belly, unmindful of the claws that playfully tried to open up my hand. "Well, that too, but I meant that getting used to things is."

Nimüe looked at me with big bloodshot eyes. "Are you

saying I should get used to what I am now, that you can't help me?''

Ach, but she was sharp. Had I been so clever at her age? "No, I don't mean that at all. However, it is something to think about. Are you sure you would not rather be a man? As such, you'd be master of your own fate in way that few women find possible." I looked at Gwen, searching for a reaction to this mention of last night's conversation, but her face gave nothing away. Besides being royal, my love had well learned to wear the politician's mask.

Poking at the dead leaves, Nimüe found a large gray millipede, which she let twine around her finger like a ring. "I was happy like I was and want to be that way again." Raising a thin arm, she watched the millipede crawl down it. "If you won't help me, I shall have to learn how to help myself. I brought a poor little cat from the dead. Perhaps I can learn to do more than that."

"That won't be necessary," said Gwen hastily. "Mordred knows of a man who can help you."

Nimüe's face opened like a flower and, for a brief moment, was all naked hope. "Really? Who is it? Where? Please, take me to this person, or bring him here to me!"

I leaned back against the marble bench, feeling Gwen's warmth above me, but not wanting to reach out and touch her in front of her sibling. "That's the idea, yes, but I fear it won't be easy. The person of whom Guinevere speaks is someone Arthur exiled long ago. We can't bring him back to Camelot, not without the King's permission."

Nimüe set the curling millipede back down in the leaves and picked up an acorn, which she rolled between her forefinger and thumb. "Surely he will give it. Arthur is a good and just king. He would not be so cruel as to deny me this."

My father was much better at denying things than the child seemed to think, but saying that wouldn't help. "We can but wait for his return and ask him then."

Nimüe nodded. "I guess you'll also tell me that adults are used to waiting for things. Perhaps you could show me how to make a magic wind, to blow him back here from Gaul."

I smiled, though Gwen didn't. "I can show you how to whistle down the wind and rain, yes, but such tricks won't bring Arthur back, not when he hasn't yet set sail. Be patient, love. He'll return soon enough." Oh, aye, and rather too soon for me, since once he was back, there'd be no more nights like the last one, at least not for a while.

Nimüe rose, ignoring the leaves that now fringed her robe. "If I have to wait, I have to wait." She squinted up at the small patch of deep blue sky that was visible amid the rustling branches. "I thank you, Lord Mordred and dearest Gwen, for saying you'll help me. Now if you'll give me leave, I must go while it's still light, even though my head so badly aches. Lord Gawain promised to take me across the river to Caerwent, if he got back early from drilling his squadrons on the parade ground. Brigid says there are Irish merchants in the forum, selling many pretty things. I like to buy things that are pretty, since I'm not."

"That's foolish talk, Nim," said Gwen, rising and brushing the leaves off her sister as if she were a maidservant and not the Queen. "You're quite pretty now, and will be more so, as you grow older."

Nimüe reached out and took her hand. "Well, at least I hope I'll be a woman. Can the man that Mordred spoke of really lift this evil curse?"

I thought about telling her that she was not the victim of any curse or spell, but decided there was nothing to be gained by that except more confusion and unhappiness on her part. As if she sensed my thoughts, Guinevere took her golden comb and gently brushed a snarl from Nimüe's hair. "He says he can. For now, it's best not to dwell on it, and to try to live your life as you were before it happened. Trust us, sweets, we'll do what we must to have you right again."

"Oh, Gwen," said Nimüe. "You are the best and wisest Queen that ever lived, and the best sister, too." They hugged, gripping each other for a long silent moment, while I did my best to get the kitten to bite its own tail. When I looked up, the child was gone, and a tear glistened on Gwen's cheek. *My love, it would do you good to acquire a heart as tough as your head*, I thought uncharitably. Perhaps I was slightly jealous. When I first brought Guinevere back from the Kingdom of Teeth, I'd known I'd have to share her, but thought it would only be with Arthur.

THE DRUNKEN SAINT

Now drown care in wine.

Horace, *Carmina*

Eight

NOT UNTIL two days after Arthur's return were Guinevere and I able to talk to him about Nimüe. It was a dank and drizzly night, with lightning flashing through the chamber's opaque clerestory window and thunder booming so loud and close that each rumbling burst actually shook plaster from the ceiling. Despite weather which had been miserable since before he disembarked, spilling the Usk out across the cornfields and turning meadows into swamps, Arthur had spent the day in maneuvers and war games, sloggingly conducted between the three cohorts commanded by Gawain, Geraint, and I, and at nightfall we'd all trudged back to the palace mud-splattered and sopping (something which I dearly hoped would not result in my catching yet another bloody cold, as I'd had my fill of sniffles, snot, and fever, and there were no more toads to boil). Since Gwen and I had promised Nimüe that these matters were for Arthur's ears alone, Geraint and my brother had retired to the cleansing heat and steam of the bathhouse, but I had to settle for the lesser comfort of the great hearth, before which I sat on a wooden bench, my sopping cloak spread out beside me, while Arthur strode the room in damp wool and muddy leather, ignoring the thick robe that servants had brought him at Guinevere's behest. If the basement furnaces had not been stoked, warming the air rising from the fluted tile floor, he might have caught his death, for he never paused before the fire long enough to dry out, but instead paced like a caged bear waiting to be baited. Gwen

121

sat on the other side of the hearth in an oak and leather chair, long pale hands folded in her brocaded lap, the hearthlight limning her high cheekbones and adding its luster to her hair, her features lovely even in the corpse glow of intermittent lightning through the greenish yellow window.

"An appropriate night for ill omens," said Arthur, pausing to rest a hand on Gwen's shoulder. "On such a baneful evening, I find myself not half-surprised to hear that poor little Nimüe has become the victim of some vile curse."

"It began long before this evening," said Gwen, her delicate hand settling on his rough one in a way that made my teeth want to clench. "And it's no curse, but a misfortune of birth, which is worse than any spell, since those can always be lifted."

Arthur looked at me, his face unreadable behind its mask of firelight and shadow. "My son, who knows more of these matters than both of us put together, has so far remained silent." *My son*, two words that came more readily to Arthur's lips these days, but still did not sound natural there. "Mordred, I would hear what you have to say about all this, for I hope I'm less foolish than I once was. It's true that I didn't listen when you last tried to advise me in such dark matters, but I was greatly sorry for it later."

Not as sorry as your bride was, when Melwas came for her on her wedding night, I thought. Ach, still, this was not an admission I ever expected to hear. My father had indeed mellowed, but in a way I almost wanted the old inflexible Arthur back, for he'd been easier to dislike and thus to cuckold. "I'm the one who told Guinevere that it is indeed likely that the child is the victim of no magic, but of an obscure natural phenomenon. Sometimes, an apparent girl becomes a boy when adulthood draws nigh. Extremely rare though this is, it is no more magical than the fact that some children are born with hair of one shade that changes as they grow older, the way I'm told I was born as ginger-haired as you, but am now dark as any Pict. However, no matter what the cause of this change in Nimüe's nature, it will surely take magic to undo it." *Undo*, of course, was not really the correct word, for if Merlin was to be believed, she'd always been male inside, but there was no point in confusing my father.

Arthur fingered the pommel of his sword as if he yearned for a problem he could cut his way through, like Alexander with the Gordian knot. "Perhaps I'm more willing to consider such an option than I once would have been, but that does not mean it's my first choice. I should summon Bishop Gerontius and see what he says."

Suppressing a sigh, I stretched my feet out toward the crackling embers. "There's more you need to know. While in the North, I encountered Merlin."

The name hung in the air, its chill effect spreading like ripples in a pond. Arthur stiffened for a long moment, but finally relaxed again, a weary and resigned half smile spreading across his creased face. "Ach, that's a name that I am not glad to hear again. I had, of course, known that the vile little creature was still alive. Indeed, I suspect he always will be. And perhaps that's a good thing. It's useful to have a living reminder that, for all the good my father did, he was not himself a good man, that in some ways he was one of the worst. I must never forget it. If we can't rise above our birth, our surroundings, the muck we call the world, nothing is worthwhile, but if we can truly do so, then everything is."

Maybe it was just the firelight, but something in his face suggested that he did not so much believe that as dearly want to.

He walked to the table, picked up the Castorware amphora, and poured himself a cup of wine. "Did Merlin know who you are?"

A silly question, or at least a naive one. "Of course. More to the point, he also knew about Nimüe. He said he was the only one who could help her, and that he will come if you send for him."

Arthur sighed, then drew his sword and held it in front of him, seemingly entranced by the way the hearthlight played along its polished length. "He said that, did he? His ability to see the future is not infallible, then," More than ever, Arthur sounded like a man trying to convince himself of what he was saying. "Even if he could help, I would not and could not accept his offer, even if it came with no strings attached. It is an article of my faith that by God's grace no man is irredeemable, but I am not sure that is true in Merlin's case—indeed, I doubt he even has a soul. It's not just what he has done in this life that makes him what he is; his foulness is an intrinsic part of him, a taint that runs deeper than his outward sins. That wrinkled little degenerate is as much of an abomination as any demon, sprite, or goblin, and as such can never be welcome here. No, not even if the poor child were not just changed but actually dying, and he alone could save her."

Guinevere rose, eyes sharp as Arthur's blade. "I understand your feelings in this matter, my husband, but I must ask you not to be so quick to make such extreme pronouncements. Nimüe is as precious to me as though she were my own daughter. Were the Devil himself to offer me his help in curing her, I would accept it."

Arthur looked her up and down, a martyr's expression flicking briefly across his face. "I know that, Gwen. I also know it's hard on you that our union has not been blessed with children." He put his sword back in its sheath and held out his arms to her. "Wife, I would do so very much for you, but don't ask this one thing of me."

She walked toward him, me doing my best not to frown at the way her hands reached out to his. "When I was captive in the Kingdom of Teeth, would you have asked Merlin to get me out again, had Mordred not been able to do so?"

They stood facing each other, the fire a pulsing red glow between them, while I rose and poured myself more dark red and resin-tasting wine from the amphora, wondering if I should leave now, wanting to go but not wanting for them to be alone. What was it that Merlin had called love, the knife that wounds the world?

"Yes," said Arthur, his tone suggesting he was not proud of the admission. "I would have gone to him then had it been the only way to get you back."

She settled into his embrace. "If you would risk so much to have me here, would you not also have me happy? Please, my husband, I think poor Nim will take her life if we don't find a way to help her. Merlin has asked nothing of you, at least not as far as we yet know—he only wishes to live in the South again. Don't let Nimüe suffer for a point of pride. I, too, am a Christian, and have no love of the dark powers, but whatever Merlin is or does, I would not refuse his help, not in this.''

He stepped back, gently disentangling himself from a strand of her long hair that had stuck to his harness. ''Jesus have mercy upon me, and upon you, that you put me to this test. Wife, you may think you understand what you are asking of me, but I tell you that you do not.'' He reached out and stroked her cheek, his voice softening. ''Ach, I must think on this. It's been too long since I spent any real amount of time in chapel. Perhaps if I remedy that, the answer will come to me. For now, for tonight at least, do not press me on this matter, but let me meditate and pray. Maybe I've become too worldly of late, or perhaps I am still not worldly enough to be a good king. Regardless of this dilemma, I shall give you a better answer in the morning.''

She held his dark callused hand in her two pale ones, then raised it to her red lips. ''I would not trouble you with this, had I any other choice. Please know that.''

His smile had too much fond sadness in it to be a grimace, though it came close. ''I do indeed.'' Turning to me, he nodded. ''As always, Mordred, I thank you for your counsel, and for the comfort you have given both to my Queen and to the child, in this grim matter. You and I will also speak further on the morrow.''

''Of course, my lord. I am indeed sorry that these troubles have arisen to spoil your homecoming.''

He shrugged philosophically. ''Ach, but it's been a long time since we were touched by such darkness here. Perhaps I've been as foolish as the grasshopper in the fable, who basks in the summer sunlight unmindful that winter must surely come again.'' With that, he trudged from the room.

Gwen looked at me and at the fire and then again at me. Stooping to pick up Arthur's forgotten lambswool robe from where it had been warming on the hearthstones, she walked over and kissed me on the forehead. ''I had best take him this and make him wear it,'' she said softly. ''There's no heat in the chapel, and the poor man's clothes are still quite damp. With all else I've done to him, I would not have him

fall ill on my account.'' And then I was alone with the hiss
and crackle of the embers.

Sometime later, I stuck my head into the chapel to see if
Arthur was still there. He was indeed, but before I could go
in search of Gwen, something alerted him to my presence,
and he turned and motioned for me to join him.

"I don't expect you to go on bended knee with me, so
you might as well make yourself comfortable,'' he said,
pointing to the bench set against the right-hand wall. Having
originally been built to display the legion's standards and
contain a statue of the Emperor, the room was fairly small,
with actual services being conducted three blocks to the
southeast in Bishop Gerontius's church.

"Comfortable'' wasn't a word I would have readily ap-
plied to the rough-hewn pew, but the only other choice was
to stand, so I sat, almost immediately getting a splinter in
my thigh. Apparently, the Mother of God didn't appreciate
my presence here. Since Arthur wasn't looking, I bit my
thumb at her, but refrained from hiking up my tunic and
trying to extract the sliver from my flesh.

Arthur continued to kneel, but he'd stopped his low muttering. "Does it still feel like you're just going through the
motions?'' I asked idly.

He looked down at his clasped hands. "There's still this
hollowness inside that wasn't there before. When I found
out that I'd conceived you upon my own sister, I was so
stupidly ashamed that I could hardly talk to Our Lady or to
Her Son. But it never felt like they weren't listening. Indeed,
no sooner had I returned from that fateful trip to Orkney
then I spent a day and a night here on my knees, looking at
these worn tiles because I couldn't bear to meet the Virgin's
painted gaze. I'm glad that shame is gone, since it only made
me behave even more shamefully, at least in the way I
treated you, but there are times when I wish I still had such
certainty.''

I had nothing useful to say to that, so I just sat there and
watched him, wishing I were in a tavern or a brothel, or
better yet, with Gwen. Finally, he rose, shook the stiffness
from his limbs, and joined me on the bench, the set of his

face suggesting that he'd reached some solution to his dilemma.

"Tomorrow, go to Bishop Gerontius and tell him I need a very holy man, one who can work miracles. Maybe poor Nimüe and I both need such a person—she so she'll be changed back into what she was, me so I can see someone with that spark burning inside them, the spark I myself once felt."

Such talk was making my head hurt. "Merlin said you would send for such a one, and that it would be to no avail."

He looked at me with what must have been an attempted smile. "Ach, did he now? I wonder why, after so many years, that creature has decided he wants to become part of my life. Well, I could simply concede defeat and send you to Caledonia to fetch him here. However, if I did that, I would prove him wrong by not acting as he said I would, and, of course, that might mean he could be wrong about other things, too." Sighing, he brushed his short graying bangs off his brow and rubbed the bridge of his hawklike nose. "I quite preferred the sort of tactical problems I was contemplating in Gaul. The Franks are an even fiercer potential foe than the Saxons, but at least they present the kind of difficulty I'm accustomed to dealing with. Had I known what faced me here, I might not have come back."

Well, you're welcome to go away again, I thought. "So, I must seek out Bishop Gerontius in the morning." Bloody hell, why me instead of Arthur? Visits with the clergy were hardly my forte, although His Grace was certainly preferable to Merlin, since the only threat he posed was one of boredom.

Arthur rose, nodding. "I'll have to answer to Gwen if I don't do something, and I must confess I'd rather try to break a Saxon shield wall than disappoint my own Queen. She loves that child so much that at times I find myself getting foolishly jealous, though I have no right to such feelings. Ach, if only I could give her children."

Actually, the fault could hardly lie in him, as he'd proved himself fertile, whereas neither his seed nor mine had taken root in her. But it was in my father's nature to always blame himself.

"I will call on His Grace in the morning," I said, still not terribly enthusiastic at the prospect of starting my day with such a visit. Ach, I supposed that this was a less unpleasant duty than digging sewers, but only just.

Bishop Gerontius's modest brick-and-timber town house shared an adjoining wall with the colonnaded limestone church that had once been a temple of Diana. Rather than having me wait in the atrium, a pursed-mouthed, turnip-nosed servant ushered me around back to a small garden, where I was bemused to find His Grace digging on his knees in the autumnal sunlight, his sleeves rolled up and his thin white arms crusted to the elbows in sticky black soil, a battered straw hat covering his large bald head. Besides the hat and a leather gardener's apron, he was dressed in his usual plain brown robe and sandals, for like Arthur he shunned ornamentation, although he suffered fancy vestments when it was necessary to impress visiting nobility.

The servant helped him to his feet. Gerontius was one of those leathery-faced men whose youth leaves them early, but who never seem to age much after that. I had no idea how old he was, but he looked much as he had twenty-two years before, when at the age of eight I'd attended Arthur's coronation. "Ah, Lord Mordred," said the Bishop in smooth continental Latin, "I'm pleasantly surprised to see you here, though not half as pleased as I would be to see you take baptism next door, as your brother has."

I bowed, glad that he was not wearing a ring and would be unlikely to expect me to kiss his dirty knuckle. "I fear I must disappoint you in that, for I've come not for myself, but at the behest of the King. He has much need of Your Grace's wisdom." Remarkably, I managed to say the last without sounding overly unctuous or sarcastic.

The expression on his wizened and beaky face made me think of an intelligent and not unkindly turtle. "Really? I suppose I should wash my hands, then, for fond of informality as both my sovereign and myself may be, it would never do for me to visit him like this, lest he think me more interested in harvesting herbs than souls."

I shook my head. "No need. Arthur hopes you will be so

kind as to discuss certain delicate matters with me, so that I can bear your wisdom back to him.'' Indeed, it had finally occurred to me that the embarrassment of having to describe Nimüe's condition had prevented Arthur from coming himself, as would normally have been his wont.

Surprise flickered for a moment in the pale blue eyes that were the only colorful thing about him, and until he smiled I wondered if he was offended to be dealing with me instead of with my father. ''Of course, I'm sure the King is most busy since his recent return from Less Britain. I had hoped to talk to him of how the Church fares there, but I understand the need for patience. Shall we have a seat and discuss this present matter?''

I nodded and bowed again, and he motioned me to a stone bench set among ferns in an alcove in the slate wall. His servant handed him a cloth, and he wiped his hands on it. ''Forgive my untidiness, but I've grown terribly fond of my herbs, for they make even the plainest tablefare a feast, and I've never been able to forgo all pleasures the way our monastic brethren do. The servants try to tend my garden for me, but they really don't have the touch, and I feel bad about making them labor to serve my fleshly appetite. Besides, I like rooting around in the miracle of Our Lord's creation. The intricate stamen of a flower, the mold on a fallen leaf, the worm that wriggles in the rich brown earth, and the snail whose trail glistens on the stones, even these smallest things are a testament to His glory.''

I groaned inwardly at the platitude, but restrained the urge to tell him to save it for the choir. ''That's a lovely insight, but I fear I must darken your day by speaking to you of less pleasant matters than either theology or gardening.''

Gerontius nodded. ''Surely, else you'd not be here, for I know you don't share your father's enthusiasm for such talk. What is that His Highness wishes you to discuss with me?''

I told him of what had befallen Nimüe, going into a little more detail than I had with Arthur. His lips pursed, but never quite formed a frown, and to his credit I must admit that there was more of concern than horror in his eyes. ''The poor child. I shall pray for her.''

In my years at Camelot, I'd never previously had a long

enough conversation with the Bishop to form an opinion of the man, but although I now found him both sharper and more pleasant than I'd expected, I was in no mood to waste time. "More than prayers are needed here. Arthur wants a miracle."

His contemplative expression became more stern. "That sounds less like your father talking than yourself. You can't demand a miracle in the same tone of voice you'd use to tell the palace tailor to make a new royal robe. The power of the Lord is manifested at no one's beck and call, not even that of the High King of All the Britons."

I met his reproving gaze without a blink. "Fair enough. However, even though I'm a pagan, I know that some of your holy men can indeed perform a kind of Christian magic. Arthur, of course, knows this, too. His Queen wishes to see her dear little sister become truly her sister again, and along with his understandable pity at the child's plight, the King wants to keep Her Highness happy. Surely you must know of someone of your faith that can help him do that. If not, there is at least one pagan magician who claims to be able to do so. It would not help the cause of British Christianity for such a one to succeed where no Churchman could." Of course, if Guinevere had her way, Nimüe's plight was not going to become a matter of public knowledge, but there was no reason that Gerontius should know that just yet, not when the opposite possibility could prove a valuable spur.

The Bishop rested his chin on clasped hands, his sunken eyes half-shut in thought. I was beginning to wonder if he was going to answer my question when he surprised me with a low chuckle. "Ah, and here I was thinking that my oh-so-learned wisdom was needed to solve some knotty theological dilemma, when what you're really asking for is the sort of thing that a savage chieftain of yore might have demanded of his druid, a contravention of natural law to suit his personal whim. This suggests quite a change in your father and my king. In the past, he's been more interested in solving the riddle of what God wants of him than saying what he wants from God."

He reflexively fingered the polished wood of the simple cross that hung at his neck, and for a moment he looked like a very old man indeed. "However, to answer your question, yes there do seem to be those of my faith who successfully call upon the power of the Lord in a more direct way than I myself would ever presume to attempt. I've heard reliable accounts of several such holy men, and by fortunate happenstance the most convincing testimony concerns the one who is also nearest, a certain learned clerk turned hermit named Cadog. There's a fisherman in Caerwent who lost his eye to an Irish raider's spear and got it back, when Cadog gently closed the lids of his empty socket, then bade him open them again. Many itinerant holy men are said to be able to heal the blind—it's probably the most common of all alleged miracles. However, it's the rare miracle worker indeed who can replace an eye that's been skewered like an olive and plucked completely from its socket, yet that's exactly what Cadog did. I know, for I met the man who was healed, both before and after his restoration. The new orb was bluer than the old, with none of its predecessor's rheuminess, so through Cadog Our Lord actually made the fisherman better off than he was before his injury."

The certainty of his tone impressed me, for Gerontius was anything but a credulous fool. And what was it that the Bishop had said about this holy man being somewhere near? That would be good news, for I'd feared I might have to travel to some far wilderness and didn't relish the thought of another such trip after my recent sojourn in Pictdom. "So where can I find this Cadog? You implied he dwells nearby."

Gerontius rose and shook dirt off his apron, which suggested our interview was nearly done. "That is a relative term, of course. He is near as a hawk reckons distance, but maybe not so much so for the man who must traverse this earth which Our Lord saw fit to make so uneven. Last I heard, he'd set off on the high road to the upland crags, where the half-wild hillmen still languish in their paganism. No doubt he means to win them from their folly. I pray he does, for it is not good to have remnants of the old dark ways looming above the Christian capital of Britain. No offense, of course."

I smiled thinly. "None taken." There was plenty of pa-

ganism nearer at hand than that, with more than half the
population of Britain's "Christian capital" worshiping
something other than the crucified carpenter, for Arthur was
not such a fool as to try to force the conversion of either his
troops or the civilian settlement. However, by the "old dark
ways" I knew that Gerontius meant a form of belief that he
considered more sinister than the rites of Mithras or even
our own homegrown Nodens. To hear some of his fellow
clergy moan, you might think that in the decades after the
Roman withdrawal the island's more backward folk had resumed burning men in wicker. Few if any had gone that far
in their embrace of the old ways, but there's something about
a pulpit that seems to encourage exaggeration.

Nine

THE TRACK had begun as a fine road through gentle river land where cornfields nestled against each other in the sun and black cattle grazed amongst gorse bushes and the jagged outcrop of gray rocks. When the bare path veered away from the old paved route and meandered up the valley slope, the fields and grassy meads gave way to tall heather, resplendent in its autumn purple, and beyond that, crags whose pinnacles scraped cloud. As my way lay upcountry, where the hills tumbled into mountains, I rode not my usual Gallic charger, but a shaggy brown goat-nimble pony, which I'd taken at the suggestion of an experienced palace groom.

It was a good thing I'd put aside enough pride to take the advice of a toothless little peasant who smelled of hay and horseshit, for by afternoon I was alone among mountains and mad streams, grateful for the surefooted aplomb with which my uncomplaining little mare picked her way up the broken spines of ridges and down stone-toothed valleys. Not all was sky-piercing rock, of course: I passed over hollows where lush hillsides descended to buttercup meadows and salmon rivers wound their way through mountain shadow, and there was much variety in the slopes that rose up on all sides. Some were long and gentle, some sharp and rugged, some dark with trees, some green with grass, and others bare and brown, yet lit up here and there with patches of light gorse, or terraced with queer pink limestone.

As the afternoon wore on the way became dank and drear.

133

Great clouds blown inland from the coast stole slowly over peaks strewn with huge boulders that looked as though a careless foot might send them crashing down on the narrow highland path. Bare, dark, stone-ribbed cliffs rose on either side, and the wind came through the pass with a chill whistle I remembered from my boyhood. Here, so far from wave-bound Orkney, I found myself moving as one does on that island moor, through waves of rippling damp air as full of turbulent motion as the sea. The salt was missing, but not the water, for as the ridges narrowed in around me, a thin rain began to fall, rustling in the heather and shining on the dark and lichened rocks. Distantly through the drizzle, I could hear the faint bleating of mountain sheep and the rush of falling streams. Ach, but it's a melancholy feeling to be alone in the uplands when the rain sweeps over them and the wind cries like something that's been lost since the beginning of the world.

The downpour stopped, but only for a while. The path rose and twisted like a snake, and several times I rounded a bend to feel the sudden clamminess of mist on my face and hands as I ran into a cloud. Peaks and pinnacles and huge moels jutted out of the fog, partly in sword-sharp daylight, partly in deep shade that foretold the coming dark. In the space of minutes I traveled from rain to fine weather and back to rain again, and on one sopping occasion the thin drizzle gave way to that peculiarly Gwentish torrent that descends with the enthusiasm of a rival breaking bad news. While it lasted, it was a constant cataract, blotting out mountain, sky, and even the path before me. It almost seemed a separate element, one in which a man could lose himself as easily as in a sea fog, the kind of rain that runs around corners with the wind and even blows upward over the edges of high places. Such a rain finds its way up your sleeves and down your neck, and before long you feel it in the small of your back and even the crevasse of your bum. It hisses in the air and sings as it runs along the ground, a thousand minute streams that soon twine into a mountain torrent, bursting through the heather stems and tumbling over stone and down the lower passes. Such rain seems the work of some malignant god bent on drowning the world and wiping from the mind of man all memory of dry places. In that cataract, I could do nothing but take shelter beneath the nearest limestone overhang and pray I was not in the path of flood or mudslide, cursing the lost time and the way my wet wool and leather and even the unfamiliar shape of my mount had scoured my thighs with a dully throbbing rash.

Fortunately, the downpour stopped as rapidly as it had begun, and before sunset I topped a ridge that looked over a river valley where the mists of the evening lay like gray smoke, while on the bright slopes immediately below me, just above the creeping line of night, a few blue butterflies still flitted amongst the golden gorse, having somehow survived the torrent and seemingly unmindful of the lateness of the day and season. The dying sun glimmered in gold bars over the wet grass, the wind was gentle as Gwen's caress, and a thrush sang his evensong from a high stand of mountain larch. For the first time, I found myself happy to be away from Camelot, alone in this high and empty and joyfully uncomplicated place with no thought of the mission that had brought me there.

The path had either ended or I'd lost it, so I had to carefully steer my nimble pony down the darkening valley side, passing from daylight to sunshadow to actual night the way a swimmer slips from the shore and passes from the shallows to the depths. Above me, the sky deepened from sunset-stained blue to deep indigo and the shadows of the high ridges were like curtains of dark wool blotting out the stars. In stands of larch and pine the birds and beasts of night began their waking noises, and once the ghost shape of an owl drifted overhead. Luckily, there was little underbrush, and I crouched over my mount's neck as a precaution against low-hanging branches, allowing the pony to find her own way through the wood. Before long I smelled the fires of the settlement, then saw their flicker through the trees as the ground began to level out at valley bottom.

It was not the safest thing I've ever done, approaching the stronghold of wild mountain tribesmen after dark, although in a way it was safer to do so alone like this than in a company that might be taken for a raiding party and thus met with arrows before wary questions. The people of the high places had never been Romanized like the lowlanders, although the legions had cut roads through their passes and isolated them in their heights, denying them any possibility of unification. After the Eagles left, the uplands folk had not faced the Saxon terror like the other Southern kingdoms, but instead suffered invasion on another front, when the *Scotti* tribes of Ireland came not just as raiders but as settlers, cutting off the mountains from the coast and even trying to pass over them in order to attack the lowlanders on two sides. First Ambrosius and Uther had curbed the Scots' advance, then Arthur had pushed them back across the sea and even crossed it after them, giving the Irish kingdoms a taste of their own fire-and-sword medicine in a way that Rome never had. Duly impressed by this, the mountain chieftains of High Gwent now swore a loose fealty to Camelot, although it's significant that Arthur did not demand taxes of these near neighbors the way he did of other British tribes, even those as far away as Strathclyde and Gododdin. In return, the mountain silver mines went unmolested, and Arthur was able to pay his troops.

In the clearing ahead of me, I saw a bonfire burning atop a high bare mound, and beyond that, the beehive shapes of round stone-and-thatch houses not unlike the ones I'd seen in Pictdom. Above these loomed a large square-shaped timber hall, tendrils of faint white smoke curling like ghostly snakes from the holes in its roof. The wind changed, and the dogs got my scent, a yapping chorus greeting me before my pony was out of the dark wet trees, and rather than risking too close an uninvited approach, I reined in and waited.

There were shouts and grumbles and the rattle of weapons, and before long a cluster of men approached behind their shields, spearheads glittering in torchlight, their dogs running before them and snapping at my pony's heels. Fortunately, the little mare stood planted on all four hooves rather than rearing, though she snorted and showed her teeth at them with all the disdain of a true warhorse.

"Who are you and want do you want here?" demanded a baritone voice in British that was both burred and clipped, his high-country accent making him sound like he was biting off and swallowing the ends of his words.

I risked letting go of the reins to show my empty hands. "I am Prince Mordred of Camelot, Commander of the High King's Horse, and I ask nothing more than a night's lodging and a small bit of information. In the morning, I must seek a Christian holy man named Cadog, who I've heard dwells somewhere in these wild hills. Arthur has need of him."

The stocky, stoop-shouldered man who'd challenged me pushed through the shield wall, teeth gleaming beneath his drooping black mustache. "And Arthur is welcome to him, for that monk is a bloody nuisance. Were it not ill fortune to harm a madman, I'd have fed his guts to dogs by now. He jabbers like a magpie and has the manners of a spoiled and insolent child. How do the men of the Usk tolerate such insolent priests?"

I dismounted. "Not being a Christian myself, I wouldn't know. May I ask to whom I have the honor of speaking."

The warriors had stepped back well behind their lord, lowering their spears and slinging their shields over their shoulders. Several looked disappointed to realize they were unlikely to get a chance to run me through. The man who'd spoken fingered his gold torque. "I am King Rhyn," he said, puffing out his broad chest, the set of his round dark face and glitter of his darker eyes challenging me to question his use of the royal title. "In the morning, one of my men can guide you to the cave where the wretched Christ-man lairs. Until then, you're welcome to the hospitality of my hall and hearth. Be warned, though. The fire is warm, the food and mead are good, but you may dislike the company." The men behind him laughed, their grins as friendly as those of wolves.

I handed my reins to a slope-browed wide-mouthed spearman who looked as though he'd as soon eat my pony as stable her, and the way she rolled an eye at me as he led her away suggested she had similar suspicions. The other warriors moved aside to let me pass, nudging each other and chuckling, and I had the sinking feeling I was the butt of some rude joke. Well, there was nothing for it but to bluster on.

"Have no fear, King Rhyn. I was born in far Orkney, where the hills are not so high as here but life is just as raw.

I'm no soft-skinned Southerner, used only to padded beds, hot baths, and lisping Latin poetry. Give me the company of honest strong-hearted men who know what's true and good in life, and I am happy.'' Actually, even in the South few Britons still enjoyed the luxuries I'd just pretended to disdain, and, of course, I was quite content to be among that spoiled minority, but one should always try to make a good impression on one's hosts.

I was led toward the smoking hall, where I smelled roasting meat, burning wood, and something less pleasant. Surely even this unwashed lot should not stink so badly. Did they shit on the floor like their dogs and pigs did? No, that wasn't it; while there was the usual reek of sweat, piss, and excrement, I also detected a musty rankness redolent of an open grave, an unexpected reminder of my late mother's necromantic hobbies.

Rhyn, who like so many self-proclaimed British kings was really little more than a tribal chieftain with a tiny warband to his name, lived in a typical ''palace'' that consisted mainly of one huge room with a great hearth running between the central pillars like a culvert in a paved street, holes in the thatched roof letting out the smoke. As rude as Orkney had been, at least Lot's royal hall had boasted a second floor with separate apartments. That had seemed raw enough at the time, and it was now odd to find mainland nobility living in an even more elemental fashion this close to Camelot. Nor was this the isolated pocket of barbarism it might have been a century before, but something only slightly less refined than the increasing norm. Of course, that shows just how tenuous British civilization has become. We shall not have what we once had, not in my lifetime nor that of anyone I know.

There was a long table on either side of the hearth, and a shorter one against the far wall, the longer ones set with benches and the shorter with raised, high-backed chairs. Women and children moved among the seated warriors, filling their cups and drinking horns from buckets rather than anything so refined as amphorae, while a few dogs, pigs, and goats milled about, and a rather sorry excuse for a bard leaned against an oak pillar and plucked drunkenly and most unmusically at his harp. None of this was out of place or unexpected. What drew my surprised attention were the ragged figures that appeared to be standing stiffly between the benches, rigid and motionless in the smoky gloom.

As I was led nearer, I realized these figures were the source of the unpleasant odor, for on closer inspection they proved to be corpses, at least a score of them, strapped upright like scarecrows to poles that had been driven into the earthen floor. Some were little more than skeletons, held together by splints of wood and strips of cloth and cowgut, but most were leathery cadavers, the flickering shadows giving the illusion of changing expression to their ravaged gray and blue-black faces, yellow teeth grinning in the dark gashes of their mouths. Their clothes were in better repair than they were, for they'd been dressed in clean and new-looking woolen tunics and breeches, with fine plaid cloaks pinned about their bony shoulders with golden brooches, firelight glittering on the silver torques and armbands that marked their nobility.

Because of my sorcerous upbringing I had neither the Roman nor the Christian fear and horror of human remains, but it was still an unexpected and less than pleasant sight. Rhyn and his escort peered at me through the smoke, seeming disappointed that my face should register so little shock and horror. "It's that season of the year when it is our custom to feast amid our honored dead, whom we bring forth from their sacred barrow for the occasion," said Rhyn, his tone of voice daring me to express some sort of outrage. "If you find their company unwelcome, you may eat and sleep in the hall used by our women and children, or spend the night in the stables."

In truth, either would have made for more pleasant lodgings, but a stubborn part of me refused to back down from the implicit dare. "Ach, I've dined with less welcome companions, and at least these smiling folk won't bore me with tedious conversation. If they do not object to my presence, I have no complaint about theirs. Still, I'm glad you explained what they are, else I'd think your feast a poor thing, that you have such starved-looking guests at your table."

For a moment I thought I'd gone too far, and they found

my jest blasphemous, but then the warriors around me laughed and the way Rhyn's wary scowl turned over into a grin showed that rather than being offended by my levity, he was impressed with my aplomb, which was the effect intended. I was given a place at the end of one of the long tables, near the raised shorter one, where the King and his advisors sat. There was a corpse to my immediate right and another about ten feet away on my left, but at least I was not sitting where I had to look directly into their empty eye sockets.

A dark-haired moon-faced woman with a silver circlet on her head brought me a horn of mead and a bowl containing chunks of boiled pork and a porridge of lentils and mutton marrow. Several large sections of roast ox smoked and sputtered on spits set above the long hearth, but I was not offered any of that choicer meat. Instead, four adolescent girls, all with a family resemblance to the woman who'd served me, sawed off small portions with well-honed silver knives and piled them into silver bowls, then stood on stools and used the points of their knives to delicately insert the pieces into the corpses' mouths. After each cadaver had been "served" in this fashion, a young boy would then take the girl's place on the stool and pour a small quantity of mead into the grinning rictus of its mouth. From the thickness of the amber liquid that trickled down leathery chins and onto torques and tunics, it must have been so briefly brewed that it was little more than honey and water; apparently the blessings of long fermentation were considered wasted on the dead. Why my hosts were so frugal with their mead yet so generous with their best meat was a mystery, but then what religion is truly logical?

The living men around me ignored all this. Indeed, despite the fact that they were taking part in some arcane pagan custom, they seemed no different from revelers at any feast, quaffing and boasting as they filled their bellies, and if I'd held my nose and avoided looking to either side, I could have easily imagined myself back in Lot's hall or the fortress of Cuneda or even some Irish, Pict, or Saxon steading. At least the mead served to living guests was much more highly fermented than that ladled into dry dead mouths. Not only did its lack of sweetness mean less chance of a hangover, but the higher potency and generous portions would eventually leave even the hardiest warriors snoring on the floor, and thus give me a chance at undisturbed sleep.

The dangers of becoming too soon insensible became evident when the miserable excuse for a bard slid to the floor, laid his harp beside him, and passed out. This was a blessing, as he could scarcely have made more unpleasant sounds if he'd been plucking the guts of a live cat. He'd only lain there a short time when one of Rhyn's warriors rose unsteadily and pissed on him, in which activity he was soon joined by several laughing companions, but despite the veritable torrent of urine, the unconscious harpist did not stir. The men standing over him joked about dragging his feet into the fire, but the fact that they did not actually do it suggested that they'd not found his playing and singing as painful as I had. This also made it clear that I would be foolhardy to try to sleep before anyone else, no matter how much their company bored me, lest I become the butt of a similar joke.

King Rhyn himself had not engaged me in further conversation, which was also a blessing, as he did not seem nearly so sharp and interesting as Cuneda of Gododdin. At least I had a full belly and a pleasant tingle from the mead. If not for the corpse stench, I might have been reasonably content, if not so much at peace as I'd been in the high pass when the sky cleared and a rainbow arched over the crags.

I wasn't looking at the large oak-and-iron door when it swung open, so I've no idea whether the bar was somehow magically lifted or simply burst quietly asunder. All I knew was a sudden draft sent embers skittering from the hearth and guttered those few torches that still burned in brackets on the wooden pillars, and when I looked up from my mead cup the door was open and a lanky half-naked figure stood framed against the night.

"This is an abomination!" roared a deep voice with a lowlands accent and the projected articulation of a trained speaker. "Even the Saxons do not feast in such a blasphemous manner. Men of High Gwent, you shall dwell forever in a much lower place if you do not cease these filthy heathen ways."

I sat up in my chair, glad to see that Cadog, who this must surely be, had decided to come here and thus save me the effort of finding him, but not at all sure of what to do if Rhyn and his warriors tried to kill him, which seemed all too likely. Well, if that happened, it meant that I would be spared his company on the trip back to Camelot.

Several warriors were already on their feet, drawing their swords or fumbling for the spears they'd laid under their benches or set against the pillars. Rhyn had risen from his high seat, his face livid as the embers. "You damned interfering priest, how dare you burst in here unasked! I'll have your tongue cut out for this!"

In the smoky guttering light I could make out few details of Cadog's appearance beyond the fact that he was tall and lean and naked except for a loincloth and the intertangled mass of his uncut hair and beard, from which skinny and filth-encrusted arms and legs projected like the limbs of a spider. As the four nearest warriors advanced on him he clasped his hands together and muttered what I presumed to be a prayer. His would-be attackers slowed, apparently against their will if their confused cursing was any indication, then stopped their forward motion entirely, though they flailed their arms about and twisted their upper bodies like poachers caught in a mantrap. At first I thought they'd somehow grown shorter, but then saw that they'd actually sunk into the floor, as if the hard-packed sod beneath the straw had suddenly turned to deep mud, then hardened again about their knees, so they could only thrash helplessly in place, dropping their weapons and shouting for assistance. None, however, seemed forthcoming.

Cadog's eyes were still shut and his hands were still clasped, and he continued to mutter softly to himself and to his god. Nobody else made a move toward him; indeed, astonishment kept the rest of us as immobilized as the poor fools mired in the floor. What happened next was even more incredible. With a loud snapping, tearing sound, the corpses tethered in our midst broke away from their supports and stood on what was left of their legs and feet, tottering stiffly forward in the dancing firelight. At first I thought that they'd come to some magical semblance of life in angry response to Cadog's intrusion, but no, his posture and expression indicated that he'd expected this and had himself somehow called upon them to rise.

With a most unroyal yip of terror, Rhyn shrank back into his chair, while those of his warriors that could force themselves to move cowered behind pillars or took shelter beneath the tables, with several fainting dead away. As imperious as one of his fabled prophets, Cadog pointed a bony finger out the open door. "Back to your grave, you unshriven dead," he boomed. "It is not proper that you should stand over these living fools who may yet still have some small chance at avoiding damnation. Back I say, back to your heathen mound!"

Like those storied warriors reanimated by the black cauldron of Annwn, the walking corpses lurched in single file out into the night. Cadog did not watch them go, but kept his furious gaze upon the cowering living. "Fools, would you doom yourselves as they are doomed, to everlasting hellfire? Some of your deceased fellows at least had the excuse of having died before the Gospel of Our Lord was ever preached on this island. But not you, not proud and insolent Rhyn and the foolish band who would follow him into darkness, no; you've seen the light that flickers in the lowlands, yet have chosen to turn from it. Woe unto you and all your generation."

And then his searching gaze found me. "And who are you? You are not the same sort as these, yet I find you here among them. Have you given yourself over to the cleansing of the One True God, or are you simply a more civilized sort of pagan?"

I rose and bowed, too fascinated by the display of power I'd just seen to be particularly frightened. "I am Prince Mordred of Camelot, come in the service of the High King Arthur. He has much need of your holy wisdom, for someone close to him is afflicted with a sorcerous ill that he fears only the grace of God can cure."

Cadog stalked toward me, preceded by a reek worse than that of the recently departed corpses. For folk who put so much stock in ritual immersion, Christian ascetics seem to have even less use for hygiene than the average barbarian, and there's something in their diet that makes them prone to diarrhea and flatulence. Indeed, no sooner had Cadog come within a few feet of me than his arse let loose with such an explosive fart that I was surprised it didn't blow his foul, shit-stained loincloth right off his sunken, scabby hips. Perhaps it would have, had not his own crusted filth more or less glued it to his body.

He had large, deep-sunk, blue-gray eyes whose piercing glitter reminded me more than a bit of Arthur's, a high, wide forehead, and a large nose that looked like it had been broken more than once in his life. How long that life had been, there was no easy way to estimate; any gray in his hair was hidden by the dirt that turned it the color of mud, and his face seemed less wrinkled by time than turned into leather and scabs by the ravages of the elements. Here was a man who'd walked near-naked through sun and frost, swamp and thistle, leaving his body as scourged as that of any flagellant. Which I supposed was more or less the point.

His gaze became slightly less censorious as he sat down on a bench recently vacated by a corpse and two of Rhyn's warriors, the latter of whom now huddled like frightened children in the shadows between the far pillars and the wall. Peering owlishly into the misshapen clay bowl in front of him, he speared a chunk of stewed goat on one filthy fingernail, transferred it to his equally filthy mouth, and chewed vigorously on it, then surprised me by washing the tough morsel down with the contents of the nearest drinking horn. "Don't stare so," he said with a burp nearly as loud as his recent fart. "The Scriptures tell us that the Lord wishes His followers to have meat and drink. Were the men of High Gwent not too savage and debased to appreciate it, I would demonstrate the power of the True Faith by changing this poor mead of theirs into good red wine."

Nobody else spoke, although Rhyn growled and cracked his knuckles, only to stop glaring when Cadog glanced his way. Bemused to find myself less intimidated than my fierce host, I coughed to regain the holy man's attention. "As I was saying, a member of the King's family suffers a sorcerous affliction, and Arthur has need of your aid."

"Yes, yes, I heard you the first time," said Cadog. "All

my senses are quite functional, thank you, the Lord sees to that.'' Burping again, he reached for the mead horn next to him and drained it, too. ''In truth, when I find myself having to do without good wine, I wish that my sense of taste were not so keen. But this is no time to speak of such selfish matters. I must be strong, even though it unnerves me to be in a place where so many men are gathered together, even savages like this. My soul is raw, and easily wounded by sin, which is why I seek the protection of the empty places. However, the Lord's work must be done, and I must not doubt that He will give me the strength to do it.'' Clasping his hands together and resting his elbows on the table, he shut his eyes and began muttering a Latin prayer.

This went on for quite some time, and just when the warriors about us began to shift in their seats, some looking to their weapons and others to the door, he opened his eyes and stood up. ''The one you call the High King has done great things in the name of God. When still War Duke of the Britons he wore the image of the Holy Mother on his shield at Badon, and with Her protection slew over three hundred of the heathen foe with his own hand. The churches he consecrated at Caerwent and Colchester have saved nearly as many British souls as his soldiers have saved British lives. Unlike the soft Southern bishops, I and my brethren have no love for the so-called kings and great lords of this world, but this Arthur is better than many a man who's worn a crown. However, I am not his dog to be summoned when he wants me, for I go where the Lord wills, and I am needed here.''

Behind him, the four men trapped by the floor were cautiously digging the cementlike earth away from their calves and ankles with their knives, which were stained with blood where their own nervous terror had caused them to slip and stab themselves. This display of power alone, never mind the reanimated corpses, made it clear that I would be unwise to try to make Cadog do something against his will, so I could forget about my original fallback plan of tying his thin wrists together and dragging him behind my horse.

I finished the dregs of my mead horn, then set it down upon the table. ''Yes, that is what the foul wizard Merlin told me would happen. He said that none but he would be able to lift the curse that's been cast upon the Queen's sister, and that it was foolish of Arthur to seek help elsewhere. I had hoped that Merlin would be proved to be as full of lies as his hellish father, but that does not seem to be the case. Now I must journey to the Caledonian wildwood, there to tell Merlin that he was right, and that he may now come in triumph to Camelot.''

Cadog ran a gnarled hand through his beard, somehow avoiding getting it stuck in those filthy tangles. Rhyn had settled warily back into his chair, while most of the men who'd taken cover behind pillars or under the table had resumed their places, although they still regarded Cadog with eyes like those of startled deer. ''It is a dark day for Britain, that its former champion should so readily seek damnation,'' snapped the reeking holy man.

I shrugged. ''Men are often blinded by love, and he loves his wife and she loves her sister. Merlin has said that no priest, monk, or holy hermit will be able to cure the blighted child. It is best that you remain here and bring these benighted mountain folk out of darkness, rather than to attempt a task at which you will surely fail, and have news of your failure spread throughout the lowlands.''

The warriors had finally extracted themselves from the floor, some of them leaving their calfskin boots and buskins behind in the process. Now they squatted on their haunches, or sat cross-legged, while rubbing their feet and ankles to restore circulation, their terror somewhat faded now that Cadog's attention was turned fully upon me. Although he clearly knew what I was up to, Cadog surprised me by actually smiling, exposing an unpleasant mouthful of horsy gray teeth.

''You are a clever man, Mordred of Camelot, to so glibly turn your king's request for aid into a challenge directed at heaven itself. Take care that such arrogant sophistry doesn't bring you to your doom. For now, your gambit has succeeded, and it seems as though these fools must languish in their darkness while I accompany you to Camelot.'' Turning his glittering eyes upon the cowed warriors, he shook his finger at them like a schoolmaster admonishing his pupils. ''Men of High Gwent, you have been shown the power of the Lord tonight. Remember it and cast aside your heathen ways. When I am done in Camelot, I shall return here, and show you the way to salvation.''

Got you, you bastard, I thought to myself. Such holy men give the usual lip service to the sin of pride, yet often prove more vulnerable to its blandishments than to those of the other vices they devote far greater time and energy to denouncing. Even the meanest hermit in a mud hut is scarcely less humble than a palace lord.

Ten

THE USK shimmered and twisted like a gray-green snake beside brown mudflats pocked with the arrow-point tracks of stilt-legged marsh birds. Behind me, the sky over the uplands was a duller, darker version of the river's leaden hue and heavy with soggy-looking clouds, but the way ahead shone clear and sunny, with yarrow and cow parsley glimmering on the meads and the groves aflame with orange, gold, and russet leaves. I dearly wished I could smell them, rather than the stench of the man who rode beside me. Ach, but he gave new meaning to the phrase "odor of sanctity."

That smell was one of the few things about him that had not changed once we'd left the uplands behind. In the knife-cold light of early morning, he'd ridden in calm, almost arrogant silence, his knobby back straight and his hands relaxed on the reins, his impassive face giving no sign that his nearly naked body felt the mountain chill. Now, despite the warmth of the lowlands afternoon, he twitched and shivered in his saddle, his grimy fingers nervously playing with the knots of his beard as though they were rosary beads, and his gray lips quivering in a low liturgical drone that had become as annoying as the buzzing of horseflies.

"You seem distressed, Brother Cadog," I said, not sure if *Brother* was the correct form of address but not much caring, either. "Why the long face and the muttered prayers? I expect you'll find Camelot far more pleasant than Rhyn's stronghold, and as a Christian you will certainly be more welcome there.''

''Cities are sinkholes of temptation,'' he replied from where he sat astride the swaybacked mule I'd purchased from King Rhyn's steading, not wanting Cadog's reeking body any closer to mine than necessary. ''So many people having so many unholy thoughts, no matter how many times they say Mass. That's the way it is with all such places. As those who call themselves kings go, your Arthur is a good man, but he cannot change our fallen nature.''

''You make it sound as though sin is inevitable whenever and wherever men come together,'' I said idly, glad that we were almost there and I would soon no longer have to make such pointless conversation. Well, at least it was better than listening to him pray.

''Of course it is,'' said Cadog mildly. ''The combined weight of their sins increases whenever men and women congregate, for there is nothing the sinner likes better than to drag others down with him. When so many folk dwell together in close quarters, they are far likelier to lure each other into sin than to lead each other into virtue. For this reason, even the smallest town is an incipient Sodom.''

I gave up the struggle to be polite and laughed. ''Then your god might have arranged things differently, so that community was not necessary for survival, in these times more than ever. It is true that Britain has become more an island of farms than cities, but even if we all lived in rustic isolation among our crops and herds, we'd have to come together to defend ourselves from those folk you call heathen. Without a standing army, every church and monastery would be looted and burned to the ground, and armies bring more men together and give them greater occasion for this thing you call sin than cities ever could. Bishop Gildas says that the Saxons were set upon us as a punishment for our behavior, yet it seems to me that their existence ensures that we will behave in the very ways that supposedly require such punishment. Are you telling me that your lord *wants* his children to burn in hell?''

Cadog hawked up yellow phlegm and spit it out upon his grimy, pitted thigh. ''That is errant sophistry, and you know it. Just because I want nothing of the world, don't think me an uneducated fool to be caught in the snares of your empty rhetoric.''

I sighed, inwardly wishing him a protracted martyr's death for so spoiling this lovely day with his mere presence. However dangerous, at least Merlin was clean and free from odor, and rather less of a bore. Still, continued sniping was pointless, and would only make the trip seem longer. "Such was not my intention, Brother Cadog, and I am sorry if I made it appear so." For the sake of peace, I refrained from pointing out that through his scorn he'd evaded actually having to answer my question.

He ignored my mealy-mouthed apology, but stared past me down the road, his bloodshot eyes lidded like a hawk's. "Many men on horseback are approaching," he said idly. "They will spill blood before this day is done."

Whatever Cadog's age, his eyes were better than mine, if those eyes were what he'd used to see ahead of us. For my part, I heard the riders before I saw them, as the recent rain made the road too damp for telltale dust. I halted my pony and motioned for Cadog to do the same with his mule, wondering if we should take cover in a nearby stand of trees, for even in as safe a part of Britain as the Severn heartland, one is a fool not to take caution at the approach of strangers.

The superior smirk on Cadog's face sorely tempted me to slap him. "It is because you live solely in and for the world that you fear its dangers so," he said blandly. "With no trust in the Lord to protect you, you are ready to hide like a rabbit at the approach of your own brother."

I laid my bow across the front right horn of my four-cornered saddle and opened the flap over my quiver. "My brother? Do you mean that literally, or are you now going to start preaching to me about the fraternity of man?" Not that he struck me as the sort to spout such uplifting rhetoric.

"The one who rides at their head came from the same sorcerous womb as yourself," he intoned, "although he has walked a straighter path."

I looked at him sharply. "Gawain is coming?"

A man as filthy and pocked as Cadog should not look so smug. "If that is his name, yes."

I was too intrigued to simmer long. "Tell me more, Brother Cadog, about this gift of yours. I find it interesting that your power can tell you what Gawain and I are to each other, and what our mother was, yet not his actual name. Can you read thoughts? See at a distance and into the future? Is this faculty always in you, or does the Holy Spirit just occasionally deign to whisper tidbits in your ear?"

His frown was no less sanctimonious than his smile. "The very way you phrase that question demonstrates that you are beyond understanding. You seek to comprehend what you have seen and heard by pretending I'm just another sorcerer. You should give more consideration to where this power comes from and less to how it is manifested through the humble vessel that is myself."

Humble vessel, my blistered arse, but before I could yield to the temptation to say as much, the curve of road and hill had brought the riders into sight, and their orderly formation and the gleam of sunlight on mail and lance point meant they could only have come from Camelot. A stocky figure rode at their head, and from the way he sat his horse I knew it was indeed Gawain.

I dismounted, taking my pony and Cadog's mule by the reins and leading them off to the side of the road. It wasn't a long wait, and Gawain's hawk's gaze must have recognized me at some distance, for his company reined in a dozen yards away, leaving him to come on alone.

"Well met, brother," he boomed at me. "It is good to see you, though I fear I can't tarry long. There's been a slave uprising at Dolau Cothni, and I must get there before nightfall." The expression on his face made it clear that he did not like the assignment, for all its obvious necessity. Dolau Cothni was where condemned criminals and the most dangerous of Arthur's captured foes worked the restored silver mines, without which Arthur could not finance his army and thus retain the semblance of a Roman-style urban economy.

"I have just come from the mountains," I said, "though somewhat east of where you are bound. Had I known, I might have prevailed upon our ally Rhyn to help us."

Gawain nodded, giving Cadog a curious once-over. "Aye, I'd heard you were off on some mission of Arthur's. I'm glad to see him put such trust in you these days; I always told you it was just a matter of time.'' The wind shifted, and he caught the full effect of Cadog's miasma. ''Christ's wounds, who is this fragrant scarecrow?''

Cadog stuck out his neck and gave Gawain a look of scowling disapproval. ''Don't take the Savior's name in vain, for you at least have some small hope of salvation,'' he intoned. ''My name is Cadog, and I am bound for Camelot at the request of Arthur and Bishop Gerontius, to invoke the power of Our Lord in curing the Queen's sister of some sorcerous ill, the nature of which Prince Mordred has not seen fit to tell me. Not that it matters, for the Lord's will shall be done.''

Gawain blanched. ''It bloody well does matter, if I understand you right!'' He turned his furrowed gaze back to me. ''Does this man mean Nimüe? She seemed fine enough yesterday, though still with something of the sadness she's suffered of late. What's the matter with the poor child, and why has nobody told me about it?''

Oh bloody hell, this was what I'd promised to avoid. ''It may all be over before you're back from Dolau Cothni. There's no time to go into it now, not if you're needed up at the mines. I would say more, but I promised Nimüe herself not to speak of it. She's not in any physical danger, you have my word on that.''

I was rather surprised by the conflicted look on his face, for my brother didn't put much ahead of duty. Biting his lip, he glanced back at his men. ''If not for my mission, I wouldn't leave until you told me more. For whatever reason it is that Nim needs this fellow's help, God be with him and her.''

''He is with me, at least,'' intoned Cadog with pompous certainty. Gawain said nothing, but bent from the saddle to give my shoulder a brief squeeze, then he signaled his troops to follow him, and in another moment all were clattering down the ancient pavement.

I looked at Cadog and wondered if his god's lightning would smite me if I dragged him from his saddle and thrashed him like a slave. ''The child and her sister the Queen had both requested that Gawain not know of her condition. Thanks to you, I have broken my promise.''

Cadog looked genuinely puzzled. ''If your brother is a Christian, why would you deny him knowledge of the Lord's benevolent power?''

I climbed back up into the saddle. ''Never mind. At least we shall be there soon.'' Indeed, that was a good thing, for if I rode much longer in the company of this holy ass, the temptation to throw him in the river would become overpowering. Of course, with my bloody luck he wouldn't sink, but would stand atop the water and preach at me like his Jesus.

We rode in silence beside the sighing water, and at length Camelot appeared amid the gleaming meadows, the gabled strip houses of the civilian settlement sprawling from the shadow of the high walls to the wooden docks, the whitewashed slab of the palace just visible beyond the turreted battlements. ''There she is,'' I said with more civility than I felt. ''Have you ever seen her equal?''

Cadog stared for a long time before speaking. ''No, I have not,'' he said with less enunciation than usual. ''I've already told you why I don't like cities. For that reason, I have never set foot in one.''

That surprised me. ''Yet you are an educated man, surely. Gerontius said you were a former clerk. I assumed you had apprenticed at some bishopric before taking the word of your god to the wild places.''

He shook his head. ''My youth was spent in foolish indolence in my father's country villa. One afternoon the Lord's purpose was revealed to me while I was drowsing in the orchard. From that day I wandered the countryside, avoiding sinful luxury and seeking further revelation in the empty places. When I spoke to the people of the towns and cured them of their ills, it was usually because they left their teeming hives of sin behind to seek me in the unpeopled wastes, although sometimes I visited their smaller steadings and settlements. I have spent decades refining my spirit, melting away the impurities, and for this reason I must be careful what I expose it to.'' He reined in his mule. ''We must bide a moment before we go farther.''

Before I could ask why, he'd already scrambled from the

saddle and was on his knees, his hands clasped in prayer, affording me a most unwanted view of his unwashed and unwiped bum. Too surprised to be angry, I could only wait until he'd finished groveling.

"What on earth was that about?" I asked when he finally stood up, his face flushed and sweat tracing rivulets in the dirt of his brow. "I've seen you raise the dead and make those who would attack you sink into the earth. You marched right into a stronghold of pagan warriors and set them to trembling like whipped dogs. Why should a citadel of Christian Britain now give you such pause?"

He fumbled awkwardly at his beard. "Christian? Your father would like to think it so, I'm sure, and I will grant that it is a better place than it once was. Still, it is a city."

I watched him get slowly and awkwardly back up on the mule, intrigued despite my irritation. "Yes, yes, a sinkhole of depravity and all that. What, does the Lord's Champion fear for his own purity?"

His eyes were fixed on Camelot's eighteen-foot ramparts, pointed with white mortar and picked out by lines of red paint, the crimson dragon of Arthur's united Britain writhing above the turreted gatehouse, underneath which some fishermen were taking a cartload of dried mackerel.

Cadog said nothing, just stared on ahead, each step of our mounts' trotting pace making him look less and less like a Prophet of the Lord and more and more like someone who desperately wanted to be going somewhere else. At first, such a complete and unexpected change in his demeanor had been amusing, but now it was getting on my nerves.

"By your bloody Jesus," I snapped, "I think you'd balk at the gates of the heavenly city itself! When I went in search of a holy man, I hardly expected to find such a cringing and timorous one. Who was it who just told me that the man who wants nothing from the world needs fear no part of it? It could be construed as an insult to my King and father, that one who so boldly invaded a den of pagan barbarism should cower here."

That broke his glum reverie, and his eyes had some of their former commanding fury. "You know nothing about it! Be not so ready with your blasphemous mockery, Prince

Mordred. You saw what I did, back in that unholy sanctum in the Black Mountains. Do you wish me to call the Lord's wrath down upon you?''

I was in no mood to be threatened, no matter what his power. "I don't think you can, Cadog, at least not for what I've just said. Yes, I've seen the power you call upon halt the advance of men who would do you harm and thus keep you from spreading the message of your faith, and I've seen that power raise the dead to a semblance of life. Somehow, though, I don't think it is quite so easily used for such a petty purpose as a salve for your wounded pride. I mocked you and your hesitation, not your god. Indeed, by bringing you through those gates, I will be offering you a chance to demonstrate his glory. Now, shall we go on, or do we continue this foolish bickering?''

He looked at me steadily, with no trace of smugness, but also no cringing indecision. "Are you my personal tempter, then? But no, you're right, as even the Devil tells the truth when it serves his need. I have been too long afraid of crowded places. Now, in order properly to serve my Lord, I must master such fear. Let us go on in.''

I nodded, almost but not quite feeling an unexpected sympathy for the man. "Perhaps it's good that you shall soon meet Arthur. His faith is strong and has enabled him to work his own sort of secular miracles, yet he wrestles every day with what he perceives as his failings." Of course, my father's faith was actually not so strong as it had once been, but there was no point in getting into that.

I continued to watch Cadog's face as we approached the northwest gate, fascinated despite my contempt by the feelings I saw played out on that grimy stage. We passed crumbling grave monuments decorated with cracked marble vases, for the Roman fashion had been to bury their dead along the roads just outside of town. Next was the perimeter earthwork, which the road rose to mount, and then a ditch spanned by a plank-and-timber bridge. Farther on was a double row of limestone outer barracks, mostly empty at this time of day, although a circle of convalescing or malingering soldiers played dice in the shadow of one wall, while a mixed group of wives, servants, and whores beat laundry against the side of another one, and children played in the dirt between the long low buildings. Then the gatehouse was looming above us, sentries nodding to me from the scaffolding. A gang of Silure laborers parted before us, several of them tugging their mustaches respectfully at the sight of my finely woven tunic and gold-pinned cloak, while several more grimaced at Cadog's stench. The hoofbeats of his mule and my pony echoed for a moment in the darkness beneath the thick wall, then we emerged onto the crowded main avenue. There was a flicker of actual terror in Cadog's eyes as they scanned the milling crowds of soldiers and workmen, slaves and servants, merchants and messengers, that thronged the regular grid of culverted, slate-paved streets. Looking at him, I knew that he'd never seen so many people in his life, not just all at once but perhaps not even cumulatively.

He coughed and crossed himself, then gazed intently down at the scuffed pavement and the stone-built drains, like someone who's just stared over the edge of a vertiginous height and now has to look away. "Everything is so very clean here," he said at last. "Even the people, or at least many of them. I remember the bathhouse of my father's villa. The pipes broke when I was still a boy, and the artisans could never repair them properly. My father became very profane and angry about it. That's a lesson of this world, that the playthings of man's vanity don't last, but he refused to learn it. My father was like so many in that regard. He wanted our bodies and our clothes to be clean, but didn't care about our souls. Only souls last, of course. They're all that matters. You forget that, when you're in a place like this."

Which brought up a subject I'd been meaning to address. "I see no reason why a clean soul should preclude a clean body, Brother Cadog, and I don't understand why baptism has to be the last time some of you Christians immerse yourselves. It is not fit that a representative of your faith should stink more of filth and excrement than the pagan wildmen he's been preaching to. I think we need to stop at the bathhouse before we go on to the palace. If you are enamored of your filth, I'm sure you'll acquire a fresh coat of it in little enough time, but for the present there's no harm in catering to the prejudices of those folk who can't see beyond the material world. You made a blatant show of power to impress the wild hillmen. Here, we've seen power, many kinds of it. Impress us by seeming civilized."

To my surprise, there was no protest. "Yes, it would be good to get out of this crowded space," he muttered, peering wildly from the tangled thicket of his hair. "So many people here. So many bodies. So many souls. So many sins. It's like a great weight pressing down on me. Can't you feel it?"

I looked into his eyes, which were redder and wetter now. They did not look like the eyes of a man who could command the earth to open or the dead to walk. Instead, they looked like those of one who could scarcely control his own bladder. "Get ahold of yourself, man," I said with exasperation. "Do you need to get down and pray again? If so, do it and be done."

He half toppled from his saddle and knelt on the paving stones. I slipped down beside him and held his reins and mine, not wanting to get too close but trying to keep him from being trampled, while exasperated traffic made its way around us, cursing in British, Gaulish, Irish, and some Latin. A big freckle-faced Ordovici in regulation harness snarled and drew back his hobnailed sandal for a kick, but I stepped forward with my hand on my sword hilt. "I know he's a nuisance, soldier, but let him be. He's a very holy man, even though he doesn't smell like one, and he's under my protection."

Fortunately, recognition dawned in his eyes before his lips could form a hostile retort. "Ach, sorry, Lord Mordred, I didn't realize you were with him."

"I almost wish I wasn't," I said, looking down at Cadog, who was on his forearms and knees, his left cheek and ear pressed against the pavement. "So many sins," he muttered, "and I can hear them whispering to each other. They whisper so loudly that I cannot hear the Lord."

I wanted to kick him square in his scrawny, filthy bum, and was more than a little sorry that I'd prevented the big, florid Ordovici from doing the same thing. "Well I'm sure he can hear *you*, so call on him to give you strength. Right now, you're not setting a very good example for us heathen.

You almost had me converted last night, do you know that?'' That wasn't true, of course, but such a lie would be a cheap price to get him moving. ''The way you are now, though, I could find men acting like this in any tavern at closing time, mewling drunkards suddenly afraid to go home to their wives. Get up, Cadog, and show Camelot you're made of sterner stuff than this. On your feet, man.''

The soldier looked like he was about to slink off. ''Wait a minute, you,'' I said grimly. ''I can use your help.''

His ruddy face darkened. ''Sir, I'm on leave.'' From his expression, I could tell that even this hard-looking and less than clean lout was disgusted by Cadog and afraid that he might be asked to touch him.

I handed him the reins of both the horse and mule. ''Argue with me, and you'll be mucking out places that smell worse than our friend here. Give me your cloak—you can have this mule in exchange—come on, the trade is in your favor.'' Still frowning, he unfastened his patched and rather threadbare orange mantle and handed the garment to me, although he took off his enameled brooch first, and pinned it to his tunic. ''And take my horse back to the palace stables,'' I added. ''See now, that's not so terrible, is it? Be glad I don't make you carry this fellow to the bathhouse for me.''

The expression on his face indicated that he was very glad indeed, and he hurried off as if he was afraid I might change my mind and ask him to do just that. Turning back to Cadog, I draped the cloak over his still-prostrate form. ''Now, your holiness, if we can just get you on your feet and to the bathhouse, your ears will get cleaned out, along with much else, and *then* you'll be better able to hear your god. Also, it's quiet there, and as you say, less crowded. Come on, time to stand up again.'' Gripping his upper arms through the fabric, which spared me having to touch his pocked flesh, I finally managed to get him to a standing position, and was relieved that he seemed steady enough once he was up, for even with the cloak between us I would not have wanted to put my arm around him.

The baths were just beyond the southwest gate, and Cadog's steps became noticeably lighter once we were back outside the walls. About a dozen soldiers and merchants were in the courtyard, several exercising with lead weights or tossing a leather ball against the sandstone wall, the others sitting on oaken stools and benches and drinking wine from red clay cups. All made sour faces at the sight of Cadog, which became even more sour at the scent of him, and a pair of Silure captains whom I recognized from Geraint's cohort apparently changed their minds about going inside, once they saw that was where we were bound. I motioned to one of the merchants, showing him the coin in my hand, and he sent his small son trotting over with a jug of cheap wine. The boy was the only one who did not seem repulsed by Cadog, but instead stared at him in big-eyed fascination.

"My father's bathhouse was much smaller than this," said Cadog, who eyed the wine as if he wanted some, too, while I sipped from the jug.

"The one at Caerwent is even larger," I said, "although the folk there don't use it as much as Arthur would like. Do you want some of this wine?"

He didn't answer, but his hands leapt at the jug like hungry spiders. "It's not very good," I said, bemused by his eagerness, "but potent enough, and our journey has made me so thirty I could drink mule piss. Now let us go inside and wash off all the grime."

"The real dirt never comes off," he said, tucking the jug protectively under his arm. The contrast between the selfish gesture and the sanctimonious words amused me so much that I allowed him to keep the wine. Looking around, I spotted one of the bath attendants, a plump, pink-skinned young man named Marcus, and motioned him over. He did not actually hold his nose when he came close enough to smell Cadog, but his expression suggested that he wanted to.

I shook the last three coins out of my purse. "Here," I said. "I don't care where you get it, but I need a reasonably clean robe or tunic for Brother Cadog here. Doesn't have to be anything fancy, just something that will keep him covered after we get him washed off. Think you can do that?"

He nodded, though his sour expression made it clear that the idea of Cadog polluting his bathhouse gave him no pleasure, and if our relative stations had allowed it, he would likely have told me to shove off. "No problem, my lord. I expect I can find something suitable in the storeroom. From time to time our patrons accidentally leave things behind, you know.''

I gave him a knowing smile. "You mean, sometimes they get so drunk that they don't notice the attendants stealing their possessions.''

Marcus's frown was so theatrical it might have been painted on an actor's mask. "On, no, Lord Mordred, none of the staff would dream of doing such a thing.''

Right, I thought, *and you never sell your bungholes to those soldiers too drunk, lazy, or undiscriminating to go and find a whore, either.* "Whatever you say, Marcus. Just have something ready when we finish our baths, because my companion is supposed to be a guest at the palace, and I can't very well take him in there in his filthy loincloth. That's one personal belonging your boys are welcome to steal.''

Marcus's expression of horror at that thought was far more sincere than his previous outrage, but he didn't say anything, just went padding back inside the building, presumably to fetch the requested garment. I turned back to Cadog, who was sitting on the nearest bench, the first smile I'd ever seen on his face and red droplets glittering in his beard, while his gnarled fingers absentmindedly stroked the jug's unglazed surface. I motioned for him to get up and follow me, but he shook his head. "I think I'll just wait here in the warm sunlight while you clean yourself. I was glad to get out of the crowded street, but the superficial cleansing that goes inside that building is just another kind of fleshly pleasure, a distraction from spiritual concerns. My grime marks me as being free from those.''

I gave him a cold stare. "Then it's just another kind of ostentation, a badge of your sinful vanity. And what of that container you're caressing like a whore's tit? Are its contents not also a fleshly pleasure?''

He wiped his mouth on the back of his hand and took another gulp, burping in mid-swallow, and the thought of his backwash made me sure that I didn't want the jug returned. "Our Lord drank wine. Indeed, He liked it enough to turn water into it. The Scriptures do not, however, mention him or any of the disciples disporting themselves in a bath-house.''

I walked to him and took hold of the wine jug. Since he refused to let go, my attempt to wrest it from him pulled him to his feet. ''Be that as it may, I've had quite enough of your most unholy stench. If you want to keep the wine, you're going to have to come inside with me.''

Last night, I'd not have dared order him around, but the power he called the Holy Spirit almost certainly was not moving in him now, and my theory that he could not use it for petty or selfish ends seemed correct. I let go of the wine jug and hooked my thumb toward the door. ''Now, come with me and it will soon be over.'' After a moment's hesitation, he silently followed me inside, sipping from the jug as he walked.

The floor of the changing room was decorated with an intricate mosaic depicting a beardless youth on the back of a wild bull. Some latter-day artisan had attempted to Christianize it by giving the boy a halo emblazoned with the Chi-Ro monogram, but from the expression on Cadog's face, he was not fooled by such a transparent attempt to disguise an icon of pagan idolatry. The plastered wall contained niches for our clothing and belongings. I stripped off my cloak, harness, tunic, undertunic, breeches, and shoes, and motioned for Cadog to disrobe as well. I stored the cloak I'd bought for him beside my things, but left the nasty loincloth on the floor. Cadog's genitals, I noticed with distaste, were scarred in a way that suggested he regularly scourged himself down there. Ach, it's human nature for us to attempt to screw each other over, so I've never been surprised by what people do to *others* in the name of religion, but the things they do to themselves in that regard continue to amaze me.

Marble steps led down to a plunge bath. I made Cadog precede me, and when I slipped into the bracingly cold water, I pressed myself against the far side of the tank, trying to avoid the skim of filth that floated around his pale, distended belly and lean, scabby hips. ''Immerse yourself all the way,'' I said, holding my nose and ducking underwater to show him how, but he simply stood there in the shallow part of the pool, clutching the wine jug to his sunken chest, so in disgust I finally splashed to him, took the jug away from him (easier now that the unglazed red clay was slippery with condensation), and, putting a most reluctant hand atop his head, shoved him bodily underwater. He came up outraged and sputtering, but I simply laughed and climbed out of the pool. "Come on," I said, holding out the wine jug. "You'll have to follow me to the tepid room if you want this back!"

The bait worked, and he padded after me to the next pool, this one of lukewarm water. Only after he reluctantly ducked under its surface did I give the jug back to him. After our immersion, we lay stretched out on wooden benches while two attendants rubbed us down with hot oil. Cadog had about half emptied his clay vessel by this point, and the wine seemed to make him increasingly relaxed and cooperative, which was a blessing. After the attendants gave us wooden sandals, I led my now much more quiet and docile companion to the hot room, which was located just over the furnace, heating the floor so much that it would have burned our feet if they'd remained bare. Steam roiled around us, as pale and opaque as mountain mist, but warm and soothing rather than clammy, and the expression on Cadog's face, at least as near as I could make it out, suggested that he was enjoying the sensation despite himself. After we'd been basted for a sufficient period in our own sweat, we clacked back to the tepid room, where the attendants scraped the perspiration, oil, and dirt from our bodies with blunt bronze hooks. After that came a bracing plunge back into the cold bath, and I at least felt like a new man.

A small bundle waited for us in the changing room. Marcus had found not only a decent brown woolen robe for Cadog, but also a pair of worn but quite functional leather sandals, which seemed to fit him well enough. Maybe it was the effect of the wine, which appeared to be almost all consumed now, but Cadog seemed pleased with these. "Such useless vanity," he said with a hiccup as he adjusted the sleeves of his tunic, his smile belying his scorn. "Still, when in Rome, one should do as the Romans. I must admit that I feel better, for all that it's an illusion." He raised the jug and drained the last of its contents. "Christ's mercy, but is there any more wine to be had?"

He looked much better than before, though the damp tangles of his beard and hair would have benefited from a barber's scissors and comb. At least the combined effects of steaming and soaking had removed the worst of the crusted filth, and his oiled and scraped flesh no longer smelled of pus, sweat, and excrement.

"No more wine for you," I said, "at least not for now. I can't bring you before the King stinking drunk." Actually, it was too late to prevent the drunk part, for he was already far more inebriated than I'd realized, and I had to steady his arm and lead him outside, such closeness being easier to tolerate than it would have been before his bath.

Eleven

ARTHUR STOOD in the chapel doorway, arms crossed and a look of mild concern on his face. "This holy man you've brought me seems quite in his cups. Did you stop at a couple of taverns before coming here?"

I sighed and looked in at Cadog, who had been incoherently praying on his hands and knees in front of the figure of the Virgin, but now appeared to have stretched out on the chapel floor and gone to sleep. "No, just the bathhouse, and if not for the wine jug I bought him, I don't think I could have ever gotten him inside it. You should be glad I did. I hadn't known a living man could smell so bad."

Arthur rubbed the bridge of his once broken nose with a callused thumb. "Well, I'll take your word for that, but I'm not entirely sure that this is an improvement. And you used no trickery to get him into this state? I know you too well to think you wouldn't enjoy seeing a Christian holy man debase himself."

I leaned against a column, surprised to find myself feeling slightly offended. "No, not unless you call buying a jug of wine and offering him a sip of it a trick. It was like holding a piece of raw meat in front of a mastiff. Also, the fellow apparently has a problem with towns. The sight and sound of so many people brought so close together distresses him in a manner which I'm not sure I can adequately describe. For a moment or two I actually feared he might collapse from apoplexy in the street. No doubt this anxiety contributed to the eagerness with which he drank. I have no idea

164

when he last ate, and I expect the wine was particularly
potent on an empty stomach.''

Arthur turned from the doorway and looked out across the
colonnaded courtyard. "And yet you say he can work miracles.''

I again told Arthur what I'd seen Cadog do, in more detail
this time. "Truth to tell, I find it hard to credit that this is
the same man, but really, none of us are just one thing. We
both know that, I think. Where is Nimüe?''

Arthur paced a moment before speaking. Clearly, this
wasn't what he had expected when he sent me after a holy
man. "She is with Bishop Gerontius and Gwen. They are
due to come here shortly. You better wake up our guest.''

I walked into the chapel and gave Cadog a gentle kick.
"Arise, good sir. The Bishop is coming soon, and with him
the child I brought you here to cure. The King is already
here.''

Cadog wiped his mouth and rubbed his eyes. "King and
bishop are just words, hollow ornaments for man's vanity.
High and low, we all remain little better than worms in a
dunghill. Worms, worms, worms.'' He sat up, rocking back
and forth and holding his head in his hands. "Even me;
despite the power that Our Creator sometimes sees fit to
grant me, I am no better, and must never forget I, too, writhe
in the muck of this fallen world. Look at me now. I thought
I was strong enough to face this place, but no, I stand revealed as a poor weak vessel, not worthy to bear His heavenly standard. I should have remained in the pagan
wilderness. Things are so much simpler in those barbarian
wastes.''

Arthur, who'd been listening in the doorway, now came
forward. "Brother Cadog, I am King of this place, and as
such I must ask you what is so terrible about Camelot, that
one who marches under the banner of Our Lord into the den
of the wild hillmen finds it daunting. We are many of us
Christian here, and I should certainly hope we are no worse
a folk than those to whom you are accustomed to preaching.''

Cadog rose unsteadily to his feet and stumbled to the
bench along the wall without bowing or otherwise acknowl-

edging Arthur's station, which irked me. "But there are so many more of you," he said, "with so many everyday sins, all rubbing against each other and multiplying like a nest of spiders. I can hear their incessant whispers in my head. All towns and cities are like this. Why do you think I chose to live in the wild places? There was nothing for me to fear in that pagan hall, nothing to tempt me or sway me from my purpose. For all the physical danger they posed me, their vileness was of a different kind than mine and yours; I saw no reflection of myself in them, and in their dark dens I was no more tempted to stray from the true path than I would be if I were preaching to dogs in a kennel. Here it's different, and the Christian veneer you've given this place only makes it worse. So many folk cannot live together in righteousness. It is not in our fallen nature. Wherever men band together there will be sin, and it increases exponentially with their numbers." He buried his face in his hands, his voice trailing off into low mumbling. Arthur and I looked at each other, neither of us having any idea what to say.

Fortunately, the uncomfortable tableau didn't last long. There were soft footsteps on the paved walkway outside, and then Bishop Gerontius appeared, followed by Guinevere in a simple blue linen gown and Nimüe in a plain hooded gray robe. I made the necessary introductions. Gerontius nodded to Arthur and me, then knelt before Cadog.

"Welcome to Camelot, good sir. I have heard many inspiring stories of the wonders you have wrought in the name of the Lord. Would that I were able to do the same, to feel and know His glory as you do."

Cadog looked at Gerontius with bleary, red-rimmed eyes, his head bobbing like that of a pigeon. "Do you now? Would you really give up your fine house, your servants, your good food and wine?" His eyes got all dreamy when he pronounced that last word, and his face softened for a moment. "I do not think I could, had I ever allowed myself such things. Indeed, I speak so harshly of them because I despise my own weakness. It is true that I have sometimes wished I was a bishop, but that is not the path that God chose for me."

"Indeed," said Gerontius with a wry smile, "for my part,

I rise each day hoping I am living the life that He intended for me, and there's always that nagging doubt that I may have gotten too comfortable, too caught in all the traps of the world. Perhaps that's why His glory does not manifest itself directly through me, the way it does through you." Gerontius's glittering eyes didn't miss much, so surely he noticed Cadog's condition, but he gave no sign of concern or disapproval.

Nimüe surprised me by speaking next. "Can you help me, good sir? Surely you can, for God's power knows no limits." Gwen stood behind her, one long-fingered hand protectively on her shoulder, saying nothing.

A bead of sweat left a train down Cadog's flushed face like that of a snail on red brick. "So this is the accursed child. You are no older than my sister Livia. She died when I was still a boy on my father's farm. That's how it is with pretty things, they all die."

"And I will, too, though I'm not pretty," said Nimüe calmly, "but I want to live my life as a woman. Please make me female again. They say you can do all sorts of miracles. Surely this is not the greatest of them."

Cadog chewed on the worn ball of his right thumb with crooked gray teeth, rheumy eyes widening in surprise and skepticism. "What do you mean, live your life as a woman?" he said at last, taking his finger out of his mouth and wiping spittle on his beard. "You are a woman, or at least becoming one. I do not understand. What is the nature of your affliction?"

Nimüe turned to me, the angry glint in her eyes again reminding me of Gwen. "You haven't told him? Surely you could have done that by now!"

Oh, fuck. "I apologize, Lady. I was so occupied by the business of fetching the good brother here that I never got around to describing the details of your misfortune. This is inexcusable, I know."

I hung my head, not wanting to see Nimüe's disapproval mirrored in Guinevere's eyes. "It is a most unusual situation," said Gerontius in a tone of voice that suggested he hoped to be spared actually having to describe it. "Very unusual indeed. The child's physiognomy has suffered a sorcerous change, altering her very nature.''

"No," said Guinevere with steely calm, "her 'very nature' is the same, absolutely the same; it is only her outward form that has been altered. Good sir, this is difficult to talk about in front of my sister, and these men are likely to be no help. Walk with me outside for a moment and I shall tell you all you need to know."

Cadog made a sound like a cat coughing up a furball. "Your Majesty, I cannot be alone with a woman, not even one so highborn as yourself. Your very sex invites corruption!''

I looked up at that, waiting for Gwen's blistering retort. However, before she could say anything, Nimüe stepped forward, strong chin stuck out in defiance. "Perhaps so, but I want it back. I can spare us all some time, I think." Saying this, she bent down and grasped the hem of her gown and pulled it to her chest, revealing herself to Cadog.

This time his sound of outrage was more doglike than catlike, a startled yip, as he clasped his hands over his eyes and collapsed back onto the bench. "This is indecent!" he sputtered. "You are far too young to be damning yourself this way."

Gerontius came and sat by Cadog on the bench, a slight trace of exasperation twitching across his wise turtle's face before the studied calm returned. "Good sir, the child is rash, but she means well. As she is transformed in her most private regions, she can hardly show you the affliction without so revealing herself. Had you not closed your eyes so quickly, you would have seen that she now has the male generative organs, although she was born to all appearances female, and this change has only come upon her since her last birthday."

"You can stop covering your eyes," said Nimüe in a calm, soft voice that bore only the slightest flavor of contempt. "I'm covered up again."

Cadog clasped spidery hands in front of his face and sucked for a moment on his extended black-nailed forefingers, his eyes half-shut and his body swaying slightly on the bench. "I need some wine. Somebody fetch me some wine."

Arthur had watched all this in silence, his weathered face giving no hint at his thoughts, but the circular movement of his right thumb on the pommel of his sword suggesting his irritation. "Not now," he said in a deceptively gentle voice, the one that made troops who knew him quake. "I think you've had enough for now. You should not need wine before calling upon the power Our Lord has given you."

"What do you know of it!" snapped Cadog. "What do you know of anything, any of you? I am doing nothing until I have some more wine."

Gerontius rose and stood over him. "I have fine wine in my cellar," he said in a voice full of practiced soothing. "And you are welcome to as much of it as you would like, but only after we are done here. I have seen a little of what you can do, good Cadog. I would very much like to see more. Please help the child, if you are able."

Nimüe knelt before Cadog. "Yes, please help me. Make me into what I was born to be. Am I no less deserving of healing than the blind and the lame?"

Cadog straightened his shoulders, his head extended and his hands gripping his knees, and gave her his most formidable stare. "We are none of us deserving, child, none of us. Never forget that. Perhaps it is God's will that you remain this way. Indeed, it may be a blessing. Men, I think, have an easier way into heaven than women do. Perhaps this increases your slim chances at salvation."

I was obscurely proud to see that Nimüe did not flinch from his rheumy gaze. "You are saying you cannot do it, then, that the power that you claim comes from God is no match for this curse that's been placed on me. Is that what you really mean? Please tell me that it is not. I need a miracle. I think I will die if I do not have one." For just a moment, the adult mask slipped, and one could see the former little girl beneath. "Please help me, good sir. If you do, I shall serve God all my days. I know you can work miracles. I beg you not to deny me one."

Neither of them blinked for several long moments, and finally it was Cadog who looked away. "I work no miracles," he said, cracking his knuckles and stretching out his arms like a laborer preparing to attempt a feat of strength.

"However, sometimes God chooses to work them through me. Come, kneel before me."

Nimüe did so. Cadog raised his hands above her bowed head, the robe's wide sleeves falling away from arms as thin and brown and rough as sticks, traced here and there with the pale scars of thorn and bramble. His hands flexed in the air, his eyelids fluttered, and he began to mutter softly, spittle collecting on his vibrating lower lip. His mumbling became louder, but the wet syllables formed by his quivering mouth were not recognizable words, just something that sounded like "*buh-buh-buh-buh-buh-buh.*" His body was shaking all over now, his bony hips rattling against the bench, the heels of his sandaled feet drumming on the tile floor. His hands snaked out, each grasping a clump of Nimüe's hair. Nimüe grimaced as Cadog's convulsive vibrations jerked her head from side to side. Cadog's eyes were white slits, and a blue vein pulsed on his sweaty forehead. The sounds he was making became an explosion of air and spittle as he jerked forward, rising off the bench and collapsing almost on top of Nimüe, who lurched awkwardly back in surprise and terror, nearly colliding with Gwen.

"Ach, make him let go of me!" she cried, Cadog's grip on her hair pulling her head down toward the floor, his convulsions whipping it from side to side. "He's hurting me! Please, make him let go." Her large hands closed on Cadog's thin wrists, her nails raking his leathery skin, but his fingers simply became more tightly entwined in her hair, and as he lurched from side to side, he began cuffing the sides of her head with his palms, a low *thump-thump-thump* in rhythm with the wordless sounds his wet mouth was making.

Arthur and Gerontius both seemed paralyzed by this, and I was bloody little help myself, but Guinevere lunged forward and grabbed a finger on each of Cadog's hands, bending them back until he reflexively let go of her sibling's hair. I don't think she actually broke either of his fingers, although I'm sure she would have if she needed to. The man made a high, keening sound and pitched forward on his face, writhing on the chapel floor like a snake that's been run over by an oxcart, while Guinevere bodily picked up Nimüe and carried her a dozen paces away. Gerontius and Arthur both crossed themselves, and I could only gape in astonishment.

Finally, Cadog lay relatively still, his mumbling turned to gasping sobs, a pathetic trickle of urine spreading from the hem of his bunched robe. "There is too much sin here," he said in a small choked voice. "I can do nothing. I *am* nothing—at least, in this place. What an unworthy fool I was, to think to call upon His heavenly power while in such a state." With that, he began to weep.

Gerontius softly cleared his throat. "Lords and ladies, perhaps we should step outside and allow Brother Cadog some time alone, to pray and hope for Our Lord's guidance."

"Bring me wine," said Cadog, rising to squat in his own piss. "I've said I need more wine!"

"And I've said that's the last thing you need or are going to get, you besotted fool!" said Arthur, real anger burning on his face for the first time I could remember since his marriage. "You condition and behavior are indeed a disgrace, both to yourself and to His Majesty in heaven. You need to spend some time sobering up. After you've done that, it would behoove you to pray to Him for guidance and forgiveness."

Arthur turned back to us, his face still livid. "Mordred, my good Bishop, forgive my temper, for I hold neither of you responsible for this. But surely this man is a fraud. Perhaps he does wield a certain kind of power, if what Mordred saw really happened, and was not just a conjurer's illusion, but I cannot bring myself to believe that Our Savior would work through such a crazed and unworthy wretch."

"Those are rash words indeed, you who call yourself King of All the Britons and dare to think that such a title means anything," snapped Cadog from behind us. All heads turned to see him rise, more steady on his feet than he'd been so far. "Are you yourself not a flawed vessel, and yet did the Lord of Hosts not work through you at Badon, when your arm blazed with His fury and you slew over six hundred of the foe by your own hand? You were no less a sinner than myself, yet the holy power was in you. When you took office and the petty bauble that is the crown of Britain was placed upon your head, did you not find the power to face down Merlin, that unholy creature who is half a demon? Like me, you've had your failures, your weaknesses, but do these mean that everything you've achieved in His name is nothing? Oh, rash, imprudent man, to speak so of this servant of the Lord, who suffered so much to come here at your bidding!''

Suffered so much, my arse, I thought; I'm not the world's best company at times, but a day's journey in my presence, with a good bath and a jug of wine at the end of it, hardly constituted suffering. However, there were more important matters at hand than my offended dignity. Stepping back beside Guinevere, I whispered in her ear, "Get Nimüe out of here.''

She embraced the child tighter. "Is he dangerous?''

"Now, he is,'' I said softly. "Just go, please. Quickly.''

"No,'' said Nimüe, somehow slipping from Gwen's grasp and walking to stand by Arthur. "I will not leave. This man can't hurt me. I don't believe he can do anything!''

Gerontius stepped between them, clucking like a schoolmaster. "Your Majesty, good sir, gracious lady, we will gain nothing by this, I fear. Brother Cadog has expressed a desire for wine. I think we all might be best served if he returns to my house with me, to drink as much of it as he likes. The King himself can testify that it is very good wine, perhaps the best in Britain.''

"I don't care about that!'' snapped Cadog in a tone of voice that suggested someone rather younger than Nimüe. "I want wine now, and I want this rash and prideful king to bring it to me. The Lord's servant is not to be abused in such a manner.''

I think Arthur would have drawn his sword and cut Cadog down in the next instant, and I for one would have been glad to see him do it, but Nimüe seemed to know what he was going to do, and the touch of her hand stayed his, although he rocked on the balls of his feet with the fury raging inside him. "Does not the Lord provide to his servants?'' she asked, mockingly. "Oh you who call yourself a man of God, if you would truly have wine, why don't you make some? That is no greater a miracle than raising the dead or restoring sight to the blind. Or is it possible that the Lord doesn't want you to have any?''

He cocked his head and stared at her like a rooster. "The Lord provides. All my life, He has provided. I could make wine if I wanted to."

Her smile was that of one who senses a winning gambit. "Or so you say. I've heard that you can do a lot of things, but have seen precious little proof. Show me what you can do, or slink off like a dog, I don't care which, but I am tired of empty boasts."

Cadog shook himself, ran his hands through his hair, and straightened his posture, as if dignity was still possible. His face softened, his eyes lost their watery gleam, and his hands stopped shaking. "I haven't been myself since coming here, it is true, and perhaps you cannot be blamed for doubting me. Be that as it may, I would like some wine. Since it will demonstrate Our Lord's power, I will indeed make some now, loath as I am to use my abilities for selfish ends. Watch, and know His glory."

Saying this, he knelt by the puddle of his own urine and stuck a finger into it, stirring the yellow liquid that was drying on the pale blue tiles, his eyes shut and his lips silently quivering. The small trickle darkened in color and seemed to grow, becoming a crimson pool spreading across the floor, as if an invisible jug was being emptied into it. I no longer smelled piss, but something sweeter. Cadog bent down and actually began to lap at it like a dog. Still the pool continued to grow, gushing out as though there were some hidden spring beneath the tiles. It surged past our shoes, lapping at the edges of the altar, and then the far walls, in a few seconds obscuring the entire surface of the floor.

"That's a very impressive demonstration, good Brother," said Gerontius nervously. "But I really think you can stop it now."

He made no reply but gulping noises, his long, snarled hair trailing out around his head, floating off the surface of the floor, its tips turning from gray to purple to crimson. The wine had penetrated my shoes, where it felt cool and sticky between my toes, the alcohol in it burning in the fresh blister on the ball of my left foot. I looked down to see that it nearly covered the tops of my buskins. "I'm not sure he can," I said.

Everyone else was staring at Cadog and the rising flood, but I glanced over at Nimüe. She stood stiff and still, her eyes hooded, upper teeth gleaming in her mouth where she was biting her lip, her hands clasped and clenched before her. Did she have something to do with this? Was her own latent power being added to that which Cadog thought he commanded? As I watched, her body quivered and she seemed to come to her senses, her eyes opening wide and her wide mouth curling up into a smile.

The wine was splashing loudly out into the colonnaded walkway. Faces appeared in the doorway. "Are you all right in there?" asked one helmeted captain of the palace, rather inanely. Further shouts could be heard echoing down the corridor, and there was the clatter of hobnailed sandals on tile, which became a wet smacking noise as it drew closer. The wine, which was gushing from the floor faster than it could empty out of the room, was now at the level of our calves.

"Make him stop, or we'll all be drowned!" shouted Guinevere, pulling Nimüe toward the doorway. Arthur had his sword out, but he seemed less certain about using it than he had been a moment ago. Gerontius grabbed Cadog by the shoulder. "Enough of this, I say! Good Brother, you must stop!"

Cadog looked up, his beard and hair now a mass of limp magenta tendrils, his face pale where it wasn't smeared with more wine, his eyes very round. "I can't," he said in a choked voice. "Perhaps it will never stop. Perhaps this is the second flood. Woe to you who didn't believe me!"

Arthur raised his sword. "I am warning you for the last time. End it now, or face your own end."

Cadog laughed, splashing like a child in a fountain. "Go ahead, cut me down, it won't stop with my death. Indeed, I hope it never does! Praise Him, praise His glory, now and forever, amen. This is His blood. Drink of it, so that you may live. Come, take Communion with me, before it is too late."

Arthur turned to me, his face wracked more with frustration than fear, and I knew that was the thing he hated most of all, a danger he could not fight. "Mordred, can you do nothing to stop this? Shall I kill him? Will that help?''

I shook my head. ''There's nothing I can do. And no, killing him won't help. Whatever power has been set in motion here, it's no longer his. We better get outside.'' Indeed, the ruddy torrent had almost reached the level of our knees, and rather than abating, seemed to be increasing in force, speed and volume.

Guinevere had already pulled Nimüe out into the courtyard, slogging through the colonnade and into the open square, where wine was already gushing down the central storm drain in a carmine whirlpool, and amazed soldiers and servants stood about with open mouths, some bending to scoop up the liquid with cupped hands, others rushing off in search of drinking vessels or even buckets. ''Come, sir, it is not safe to remain here,'' I said, taking Gerontius by the arm and pulling him after me, the soaked lower portions of his robe threatening to trip us both. Only when we were past the columned walkway did I realize that Arthur was still inside. Looking back, I saw wine gushing out of the chapel in a surging wave over two feet high. In the long instant while I debated going back after my King and father, its force and volume more than doubled, for when he appeared in the doorway, it was at the level of his waist, and he stumbled in the ruby flood, falling to his knees when the torrent wrapped his cloak about his legs, great carmine gouts splattering off his back and shoulders as he pitched forward on his hands, to come half-swimming, half-scrambling out of the room on all fours.

Both Guinevere and I ran to him, but he'd already unpinned his cloak and, free from that wet burden, made it to his feet again. He gently shook off our helping hands. ''Put those cups and buckets down,'' he said to his captains. ''We must get everyone out of the palace, and quickly. This is as dangerous as a fire, if not more so.'' Behind him, the russet deluge continued unabated, the smell so strong I felt drunk from the fumes. I started to ask where Cadog was, but a soggy bundle appeared in the doorway, borne on the crest of the flood, and was bashed limply against the doorframe until the current chanced to turn it so that it could burst free. Cadog's corpse splashed out onto the colonnaded walkway, his red-stained face turned up and wine running from his open mouth.

"Did you kill him?" I asked.

Arthur shook his head. "No, although I certainly wanted to. He either passed out from the wine he'd swallowed or simply swooned from his own ecstasy, and his soaked robe held him under. There will be more dead if we don't hurry and get people out of here."

By this time, the entire door to the chapel was filled by the bacchic torrent, which came roaring out at the height of a man, churning down the walkway and crashing through the columns, and at this rate it was clear that the entire court-yard would soon be as flooded as that room had been. I was apparently not the only one made giddy by the fumes, judg-ing from the way those around me stumbled and staggered through the front gate. "Get trumpeters—we must sound a general alarm!" yelled Arthur, I have no idea at who, for I was too busy fleeing toward the Via Principalia, Guinevere ahead of me, her long legs making excellent time despite the hindrance of her soaked gown, pulling Nimüe after her.

Out in the slate-paved street, everything was confusion, with horses and mules rearing and whinnying, men shouting, sentries gesticulating from the fortress wall, and behind us a low rumble that may be the most terrifying sound I've ever heard. The wine created a not-so-miniature waterfall as it surged after us, overflowing the gutters and spreading down the Via Principalia like a giant's bloodstain. Through this cataract plunged terrified servants and swearing guards, but there was no sign of Arthur.

"He's still inside," said Guinevere beside me as if she knew my thought. "We must get him out of there. He's likely to drown while waiting to see everyone else out safely."

The flood must have reached the royal stables, which were attached to the wing of the palace that lay around the corner to our right, for there was a growing chorus of neighs and whinnies, the clatter of hooves on slate, and then several dozen horses, donkeys, and oxen came charging into view, following the natural pathway of the central square and head-ing for the main avenue. The first of them reared as they drew abreast of the front gate, no doubt balking at sight of yet more wine pouring forth into the street in front of them. I shoved Gwen and Nimüe out of the way of a bucking milk white gelding, then slipped on the wet pave stones and found myself unable to avoid a glancing blow from a vermilion-stained hoof, which knocked me facedown into the rushing red gutter. My last sensation was the smell and taste of wine, heavy with grit from the street. *Too much sediment in this vintage*, I thought absurdly, as the world behind my eyes went from a churning purple-red to a choking darkness that seemed to be made of wet black wool.

I was in the eternal forest, that domain of ancient trees, the wild wild wood that once enshrouded half the world. At first there was no particular sense of myself, just a butterfly flittering of disembodied perception, scattered impressions of sight and sound and smell, of wrinkled trunks that plunged from thick, shadow-swathed, mossy-girdled roots up and up and upward still, through endless shafts of gold-green light to the olive, copper, and russet canopy that never revealed the smallest patch of sky. For a moment my dreaming unself floated high like a windblown feather, then plummeted down with growing weight to fern and mold and the skeletons of leaves, rising more heavily to weave from tangled track to tangled track, achieving corporeality as it stumbled through clutching brambles and over the twisting serpent-shapes of roots, gathering size and solidity as it went, until I seemed to be plunging through the thickets as massive and heedless as a stag, only to shrink again, into something small and scurrying, a mouse or shrew or even mole, that could wriggle into and through the loam of the forest floor, a rich dark blanket that smelled as musky and inviting as the pussy of the world. And so the thing that was me and yet not me raced ever onward, leaping and crawling and wriggling and flying toward the very heart of the forest, and all around me the trees whispered, whispered, whispered; this island once belonged to us, the wildwood that spread from sea to sea, from lowlands to the foundations of the mountains, before the cutting and clearing and furrowing, before Roman, Pict, or Gaul or even the very old folk of mound and monolith, the wood that only slowly and reluctantly gave way to the relentless tramp of man. We were here before you, and will be here after you are gone. Already you tire, your body failing, the brief years wearing away your insect life span. Confess the failure of your transient flesh; let yourself fall back into the heady loam of the forest floor, the sweet rot that feeds the roots. Rest, for now and ever.

But I did not rest, for something in the unknowing, un-formed me still knew that I was dreaming, and that if I heeded the sighing treesong I would not wake again. Instead, I pressed onward, onward, onward, my dreamself again los-ing its apparent corporeality and the entire world seeming to tilt upon its axis, so that rather than flying I was now falling through the forest. Then, with a vertiginous lurch, the world righted itself again, and I was once more solid and standing, perhaps on two legs, perhaps on four, at the edge of a clearing, although despite the open space in front of me, the air was no brighter, the sunlight no less filtered and obstructed.

Looking up, I saw why. In the midst of the clearing was a tree, a single massive oak, as sky-reaching as the world-tree of the Saxons, its trunk as big around as any tower, its branches an entire forest in themselves. There, a tiny blemish on the vast whorled wall of the tree base, something small and wizened peered out at me from within a moss-fringed fold in the wrinkled bark, like a mummified infant emerging from a gnarled dry womb. "You will have to come for me now," said Merlin in a voice like wind in the high branches, the rustle of dead leaves among the roots. "No one else can teach her to harness that power. Or would you like to see it grow unchecked as she matures into frustrated unwoman-hood, trapped in a body she despises? What will the power do, if that happens? Tell him this, that you must come to me."

I woke up to an aching head and the smell of wine, but at least I was in a dry place, lying on a makeshift blanket of cloaks spread over wooden planks, a low crenellated wall of stone and mortar encircling me, and over that, a round roof of thatch and timber, with a cold band of sky visible between roof and wall. To my left, coals glowed in a small brazier, while to my right Guinevere and Nimüe huddled together against the battlement, Gwen's hand holding mine, Nimüe's eyes shut and her head in Gwen's lap, Gwen's eyes open and focused on my own. The wine smell seemed to be coming from our soaked clothing; there was no other immediate evidence of the supernatural flood.

My tongue was furry and swollen, and it took me several coughing attempts to spit out three comprehensible words. "Where are we?"

Gwen squeezed my hand more tightly. "A guard tower on the southeast gate. Arthur carried you here. He wasn't sure how high the flood would reach. Indeed, we feared it would drown the entire city before it subsided."

Ach, he was alive, then. As ungrateful as it sounds, seeing that he'd saved my life, I felt almost as much disappointment as relief. Even though I was as fond of him as I'd ever been since my pre-disillusioned boyhood, his drowning would at least have made my life simpler. *No, not really*, whispered a voice inside my aching head, *you are used to living this way, and cannot imagine what changes may come when he is gone.* Though that was true enough, I looked at Gwen, lovely as ever despite sopping clothes and snarled, maroon-colored hair, and silently cursed the fact that I would not be able to embrace her once my head stopped its vertiginous throbbing, if indeed it ever did.

"She helped Cadog find his death," I said in an attempted whisper that was more of a croak, tilting my head ever so slightly toward the sleeping Nimüe and instantly regretting the queasy motion.

Guinevere's eyes narrowed, and the ball of her thumb pressed into the back of my hand. "You can't mean that, Mordred. Whether an act of God or magic, this calamity wasn't her doing."

That she immediately knew what I was talking about suggested that she had suspicions similar to my own, despite her stern denial. "Sadly, I do mean it, though I wish that I didn't," I said, trying in vain to make my voice softer and more soothing. "I don't think she *meant* to do it, or even really knows what she did. But remember how she brought the cat back to life, something the trinket I gave her could not have done by itself? Likewise Cadog, whatever his power, could not have done this alone." I shut my eyes and saw a wizened-yet-boyish face grinning at me from the darkness inside my head. "By all the gods, I fear that we have to accept Merlin's offer of help, for with Mother long dead I can think of no one else who could teach her to harness such abilities. She will certainly use them again—she's stumbling toward adulthood in a body that she doesn't want, that isn't the one she was born into or raised for. Worse will happen, I fear, unless you either send her away or we seek someone who can help."

Guinevere's eyes looked past me and through the wall as she gently stroked my sticky red knuckles with her equally stained fingertips. "I won't send her away, or let anyone else do so," she said, resolve sheathed like steel in the velvet of her soft whisper.

"And only Merlin can help," I murmured, my own attempt coming out more like a bleat. "Not the best of choices." Indeed, were we ever offered any alternatives better than bad and worse?

"We shouldn't talk about this right now, love," said Guinevere, searching Nimüe's face for any trace of waking. "It would not be good for her to hear it."

"No, probably not," I agreed, "although she certainly seems stronger and more capable than she did a few months ago, or even a few weeks. Poor child; it's her fault least of all." I surprised myself by actually feeling that as I said it, rather than just mouthing it as a sop to Guinevere.

Gwen reached out and stroked my brow, rolling up her soggy sleeve to keep it from slapping me wetly in the face. The hairs on her pale forearm were stained pink and plastered to her skin, and despite my aching head and newfound aversion to the taste of wine, I wanted to run my tongue along the exposed flesh of her slender wrist. "Poor Mordred," she said in that voice that was the music of my heart, "now you've got one more difficult woman in your life. Will you never be rid of them?"

Before I could think of a suitable answer, footsteps sounded on stone and planking somewhere below us, then a trapdoor that I hadn't previously noticed was thrown back, and Arthur's head appeared a few feet from my own. His hair was wet and a rather appropriately royal purple, while his leather gambeson was stained the darker hue of an old bruise. In his hand he held a clay bowl of steaming broth.

Guinevere, who'd already let go of my hand, gave him a tired smile. "Husband, you must have more important things to do than to look after us. Servants could have brought that."

Arthur set the bowl on the planks and heaved himself up into the small room, leaving the trapdoor open. "True enough, but I wanted to see how you are doing, and it's crowded enough up here as it is. At least the flood's subsided enough that we shall soon be able to go back down." He looked down at me, his expression guarded but not unfond. "I'm glad to see you awake, Mordred. I'm not in the mood to praise God right now, but if anything could make me do it, it would be that."

The throbbing had subsided a bit, and I managed to sit up, although I immediately wished I hadn't. "It would have been a ridiculous death, kicked by a horse in the middle of a torrent of wine, although perhaps not as absurd as drowning in it."

Arthur held the steaming bowl out to Guinevere, who took it and sipped gingerly, though her expression suggested she appreciated the warmth more than the taste. "Absurd or not, plenty died that way," he said, his tone more rueful than chiding. "We can talk of that later. For now, be glad that the torrent stopped before the whole city was drowned, although in truth it was a near enough thing. Here, drink this. You need something in your stomach besides wine."

My hands were not steady, and he had to hold the bowl to my lips. "What is it?" I asked between sips of warm, rather oily broth.

"Soup boiled from the tail of a drowned ox," said Arthur. "It's likely to be bland, but at least it shouldn't taste too strongly of wine. I ordered the servants to boil all liquid from the pot, then pour fresh water into it three times, as I was afraid you wouldn't be able to stand it, otherwise."

The thought of the King of All the Britons supervising

such emergency provisions was rather comic, but only in an abstract way that did little to cheer me. Putting the bowl down where Guinevere could give some to Nimüe, I lay back upon the spread cloaks. "Pardon me," I said, "I just want to shut my eyes for a few moments. If I don't wake up again, just bury me with all the rest, I don't want anything special."

Sleep not being the best idea when one has a head injury, Arthur made me sit up again, and although I protested, pulled me gently to my very unsteady feet. "I know the world is spinning, lad, and your stomach wants to turn itself inside out, but you need to walk a while in fresh air. Come, I'll help you." At first, I could only sag against the crenellated battlement, not daring to look out and over, but after a time the dizziness subsided and I was able to follow him down the ladder to a walkway atop the southeast wall, where the cool breeze on my face made me feel some small portion of myself again, although he held my arm at first, lest I slip or stumble.

Below us, Camelot's cunningly engineered drains had done their work, and unimaginable gallons of wine had flowed through pipes and stone-lined ditches to pour out finally into the Usk, where the water seemed to have turned a muddy ocher hue, although that may have been a trick of the setting sun. Within the walls, the crimson-stained, debris-strewn streets looked like the site of some unimaginable slaughter, and if you held your nose, it was all too easy to imagine the smell of blood rather than that of wine. Most of the human dead had been removed, but here and there groups of soldiers and townsfolk could be seen cutting up the drowned bodies of mules and oxen, which they'd doubtlessly be eating later on tonight.

"We got most of the horses out, at least," said Arthur grimly, "but in some places the flood briefly got high enough to enter the raised storehouses, and I don't yet know how much of the grain and hay we'll be able to salvage. I'd pray for a mild winter, if I had it in me to pray at all right now."

I looked to the growing corpse mound outside the gates. "How many dead?"

Arthur rested his sinewy forearms on the crenellation. "A

hundred and eighty-seven was the last count, although I expect the final figure will be almost twice that many. Far more might have lived, but instead made no real attempt to save themselves, as they were too busy trying to scoop up what they imagined to be their newfound bounty by the bucket-load, or even diving into the growing flood to drink until they were too stupefied to swim." He looked up at the slate-and-charcoal sky, wind ruffling his salt-and-ginger hair, his face a map of the provinces of sorrow.

I remembered that I hadn't seen Gerontius after pulling him out of the chapel and into the courtyard. "What happened to the Bishop?" It would be darkly amusing if this calamity had claimed two wine-loving holy men, even if Gerontius's affection for the grape, like his variety of faith, had been more moderate and reasoned than Cadog's.

"He's fine," said Arthur in a low voice. "Indeed, I envy him for the way his faith seems less shaken than my own." Reflexively crossing himself, he continued speaking, not so much to me as to the darkening sky. "Why did You let this happen? This was not some natural accident or an act of godless malice, but the careless result of power wielded in Your name. Was it a judgment on me and what I've built here, or are You that indifferent to the suffering of Your creatures? What do You want of me, of any of us? All my life I've tried to do Your work. Bishop Gerontius tells me I should think of Job, but I find no solace there. Should I be glad that You've not yet tested me and those I love with boils and locusts? The world we've inherited is hard enough; if You are going to show Your hand so directly, why do so simply to make things worse? If nothing else, grant me understanding."

There was no answer but the sigh of wind on worn stone. *Not every death and disaster is a test or judgment meant solely for you*, I thought but did not say. *There's a world outside your self and soul, one in which you possibly matter not at all.* Of course, unlike me, Arthur could never find comfort in such a thought.

Perhaps he sensed my musing, for he turned back to me, his rueful smile doing little to belie the sorrow and confusion in his eyes. "No doubt I sound quite the fool, especially to you. Men have asked such questions since the Flood, and gotten no satisfactory answer. Why should a miracle gone calamitously wrong dismay me more than fire and famine and pestilence and the ravages of evil men?''

Smelling the fumes wafting up from the crimson-stained, debris-choked streets, I wondered that I'd ever found plea-sure in a wine jug. Still, things could have been worse. "We're lucky that Cadog wasn't drinking mead. Imagine how sticky and nasty *that* would have been.''

Arthur smiled again, but there was even more pain behind it this time. "Speaking of sticky messes, I can't help but wonder if Merlin knows of this and is laughing at us in his Caledonian lair.''

I coughed, not wanting to bring this up, but not able to imagine a better time. "We must talk further about that mat-ter, you, I, and Guinevere. Nimüe, too, I suppose, since it concerns her most of all, and she seems more adult than child these days.''

The sun was a copper coin melting over the edge of the dark blue uplands, turning the clouds the color of the wine-stained streets. Waiting for Arthur to reply, I shivered in my wet wool and leather, although he in his equally soaked clothes seemed oblivious to the chill autumn wind. "We're all of us getting older fast,'' he said finally. "Whatever hap-pened to the me that had such conviction burning bright inside him? The me who had no need of magicians, but no fear of them, either? I've mislaid him somewhere, down the long years.'' He looked to the guard tower, squinting as if he could see Guinevere through the stone and timber. "Of course, the me that once had such conviction didn't have a queen, and maybe that's a fair trade, though like my old one, this new adoration has a price. She would have me do the thing I would not do, had I any choice, but I have no choice, for it is what she would have me do.''

Just as I once had no choice but to go beyond the world to get her back, even though I thought there was little hope of success, and certainly knew that she would not be mine once we returned. What was it about Guinevere that made her what Helen must have been, the sort of woman for whom one might willingly throw away every other thing that one once cared about? I wondered if there were some secret self-ish part of Gwen that relished having such awful power, not just over one man but two. But no, she was seldom capri-cious in her mastery of our hearts, and only pressed the mat-ter of Nimüe because she, too, was ruled by the stern tyranny of love.

"So you will be sending me to bring Merlin here, just as he said you would." The shadows of the distant hills were lengthening over the darkling meadows, and the way the wind off the river pressed my clammy tunic against my back and buttocks made me wish for one of the cloaks I'd been lying on in the guard tower, but my usual reluctance to admit weakness in front of Arthur kept me from complaining.

Arthur bit down on his thumb for a moment, then looked at it, as if he expected to read an omen in the faint inden-tations his teeth had made in his callused, purple-stained flesh. "As you said, we shall discuss it. For the moment, there are more pressing matters. Night is coming on, and there's not much dry wood or charcoal left in Camelot. Ge-raint's cohort is out gathering fuel, while I sent your man Colwyn with a squad to Caerwent to see what could be req-uisitioned there."

I squatted, then rose again, testing my balance. My skull felt like it contained nothing but one enormous bruise, but my legs were steady enough, and the earth and sky remained in their proper places. "I can help, if need be."

Arthur reached out and squeezed my shoulder. "No, not after that close call you had. There will be plenty of work for all of us tomorrow, once we set about making the town and palace habitable again. For now, you should rest."

For once, I was in no mood to argue with his judgment, and so I let him lead me back to the shelter of the guard tower. The wind changed direction, blowing from the city rather than the river, and the night air smelled like a cellar full of ruptured wine casks. Gagging, I wondered how long it would be before I could stand to get drunk again.

The actual damage to the city proved minimal, although for weeks afterward the cobbled streets and stone-built drains were streaked a dark purple unpleasantly reminiscent of dried heart's blood, the lower portions of once whitewashed walls stained a dull pinkish red that made every shopfront look like the entrance to a bawdy house. At least the smell went away fairly quickly. I did not drink again for some time, and when I did it was always mead or ale.

Cadog was originally buried with most of the other victims of the wine-flood in a mass grave a few hundred yards from the southeast gate. However, someone dug him up again, and his remains finally ended up under a small shrine at Caerwent, faithfully tended by the now-senile fisherman whose sight (and eye) he'd once restored. Indeed, despite a death toll exceeding those of all but the worst Irish raids of past decades, he seemed well on his way to sainthood, and a rumor got about that the botched "miracle" was actually a judgment called down by the late worthy upon the King of All the Britons for having so lapsed from the faith that had once sustained him against the Saxons, the wine pouring forth from Cadog's severed neck after Arthur smote off his head in a fit of rage. Not one of the many who asked me if this story was true had any real idea why a longtime defender of the Church would have been so angry at such a renowned servant of the Lord, but a disconcerting majority seemed unconvinced when I told them what had really happened, and eventually the story became so widespread that Bishop Gerontius had to denounce it from the pulpit, although I also heard that Archbishop Gildas supported its veracity in a sermon he preached at Glastonbury, that ancient seat of religious power that had never been overly fond of Britain's secular government, no matter how Christian. None of this helped Arthur's mood. His melancholy deepened as autumn crept toward winter, and he spent much of his time in his chambers, poring over maps of Armorica and Greater Gaul, for he'd not forgotten his dream of liberating the Continent from the Franks.

Needless to say, the problem of Nimüe remained. Arthur brooded and Gwen pleaded and Arthur brooded some more, and, of course, the end was never in doubt, although he held out longer against her than I ever could have. Perhaps she would not have pressed him so if Gawain hadn't returned, the slave uprising at Dolau Cothni dealt with and our roadside conversation still weighing on his mind. Nimüe managed to avoid him for a day or two, but eventually he confronted her, and she met his gentle and halting questions with rather less fortitude than she'd shown when hiking up her gown for Cadog. Despite her tearful evasions and the lack of a visual demonstration, he came away with some sense of what had happened to her, for I remember his rage in the bathhouse courtyard afterward.

"It's monstrous," he said, swinging his lead weight like a weapon through air less chilly than usual for this time of year. "Merlin says he can help her, but how do we know he didn't cast this spell on her to begin with? By God, Arthur should allow me to go after him; I'd drag him from his burrow like a badger and shake the truth out of him soon enough."

Looking at his wide weathered face, as well-known and dearly loved as Gwen's softer-contoured one, I shuddered to think what would happen to him if he tried that. "Merlin says this was no doing of his, and I believe him. He's not the sort to refuse credit for his handiwork."

I thought about trying to explain to Gawain how boys are sometimes born as apparent girls, the same way a calf might be born with an extra leg, but decided such knowledge might make him regard Nimüe with horror rather than pity, something which could only make matters worse. Hoping to change the subject, I dropped my own weight and sat puffing on a cracked marble bench, sweat running down my bare arms. "I must confess that Arthur's anxiety at the thought of bringing Merlin here does not exactly give me confidence, should he give in to Guinevere's request and actually send me to do it. I don't think I've ever seen him scared of anything before." Well, not except for the knowledge of who and what I was, but Arthur seemed to have long since learned to live with that, and it had been years since Gawain and I had spoken of it.

Gawain sat beside me on the bench and called for a cup of wine, ignoring my expression of distaste. "He's a different man, right enough. I remember when he first became King and sent the horrid creature packing. Merlin stood before the throne, glowing like a marsh flame and muttering creatively obscene threats in that refined accent of his, but when Arthur looked him in the eye and slid the sword of Maximus a half inch from its scabbard, the fire went out of him and he slunk off like a kicked terrier, his magic as useless as a maidservant's protestations. I don't know what's happened to Arthur, that he no longer has such fierce resolve.''

I happened to him, I thought about saying, but that was giving myself too much credit, and, besides, my rescue of Guinevere from the Otherworld had at least partially healed those old self-inflicted wounds. No, this was something less tangible and more gradual. Never having believed in much of anything, I found it hard to imagine what it must be like to have that belief slipping away from you as the years march onward. ''Maybe that's why he's mentioned seeking fresh battles on the Continent,'' I said. ''War and God were all he knew in his youth, and maybe he thinks that if he seeks out one, he will find the other. It's not Gaul he wants to save, but himself.''

The intensity with which Gawain stared into his red clay cup made me think of our long-dead mother and the way she searched everything for omens, although he would not have been pleased by such a comparison. ''I love Arthur with the love due him as both my King and my uncle and rather more besides, but right now it's poor Nimüe whom I would save. I felt so cruel, pressing her for her secret, her face wilting like a flower. She cannot bear this much longer, I fear.''

Not for the first time, I wondered why he should care so much. Even if she'd not grown a cock, she'd be scarcely out of her girlhood, and it's not as if she seemed on the point of blossoming into such a beauty as her sister. Gawain was both a royal nephew and a Commander of the King's Horse, and as such could have his pick of the daughters of town magisters, tribal chieftains, and petty kings, not to mention the lesser nobility; why did he care so much for this ragamuffin child? Ach, but I might as well ask the same question of Gwen. We do not always choose where to love, or know the why of it, and the wisdom of the heart can be more obscure than that of the Delphic Oracle. Ironically, I suspected that Gawain's concern for Nimüe's condition only made her feel worse, but saw no point in saying something that could only make him more unhappy.

My suspicions were proved correct two days later, when Guinevere found Nimüe at the edge of a fourth-floor parapet with the glazed look of one getting ready to jump off. Gwen pulled her back inside, and Nimüe claimed she'd only been staring out into space while daydreaming and had no thought of leaping to her death, but the incident proved the final spur, and that night the King and Queen of Britain talked well into the dawn, with me pacing in my tower room above them, ironically Merlin's old sanctum, hearing the faintest echo of their voices up the stairwell and brooding on what was said, or more specifically, on what she was saying to him and what means of persuasion she might be bringing to bear. When I saw Arthur the next day, his face was almost as stricken as it had been that day in Orkney, when he first found out what we were to each other, and though that was long ago, it was so bloody odd to see him look like that and me not be the cause of it.

He paced for a long time without speaking, shivering slightly in the fine woolen robe that I knew Guinevere must have made him wear, his normally shaven face stubbly with several days' growth of salt-and-pepper beard. He coughed and blew his nose on his sleeve, not for the first time judging from the greenish stains there, and I wondered if he was catching a cold, a rare ailment for him no matter how many hours he spent in cold weather and wet harness. When he spoke, his voice was hoarse, and if I'd not heard him yelling orders all day on the battlefield, I would have thought it was just from him having been up all night talking.

"Go seek out Merlin in the wildwood. God be with you. I find it hard to pray for myself these days, but I can still do so for others."

And that was that. I would not have obeyed him, had I any real idea of what was to come, but prophecy was Merlin's gift, not mine.

THE WIZARD
IN THE WOOD

Wisdom is the conqueror of fortune.

Juvenal, *Satires*

Twelve

NLIKE THE temperate Severn valley, the North was already feeling the bite of winter, and I sat on a cushioned bench with a wolfskin on my shoulders and a sheepskin on my knees, glad for the fire in King Cuneda's hearth. Smoke stung my eyes as it curled up toward the roof hole, and the hangings on the ravaged walls were black with soot. A girl with a flat, rather Pictish-looking face and a bruise under her left eye brought me a horn of mulled ale, while Cuneda talked with his royal huntsmen, the combination of their accents and low voices making it difficult to decipher what they were saying, although I heard the words "Myrddin-Man" once or twice. I'd come North with an escort of fifty horse, but they were bunking in the outbuildings, and would likely remain a strain on Gododdin's hospitality while I journeyed on to the wildwood with no companion but a local guide, for I could travel faster without them. Swords could not protect me from Merlin, and there would be no danger from anyone but him, once I entered his domain.

At length, Cuneda joined me by the fire. "I did not expect to see you again so soon," he said, sipping from a finely wrought copper goblet of blood red wine, the sight of which made my stomach kick like a mule. "I am still in your debt, of course, and will aid you any way I can, although if I send you to the one who dwells in the Caledonian wood, I fear I'm doing you no favor. That man, if he truly is a man, has not troubled me, not in all the years he's dwelt there, but his presence on the edge of my kingdom unnerves me more than all of the Picts who live beyond the Antonine border and all the Irish who settle on the Western coast. Why go poking around in his hole? If you rouse him, he may wish to meddle in the affairs of men once more.''

There was no point in telling Cuneda that he owned nothing that Merlin could want and thus should have no fear of him. Besides, I wasn't entirely sure what Merlin *did* want, or even if his whims and desires and actions could be judged by the same yardstick as those of a rational man. "I come on behalf of Arthur, who needs Merlin's craft but does not fear his spite.'' Would that last part were true.

Cuneda stretched out his bowed legs, clad in green-and-black plaid trousers gartered at the calves with strips of hide, warming his bare brown feet above the flames. When he sighed in pleasure, I heard the breath whistle through the open tip of his nose. "I should not expect Arthur to need any sort of magic except that of his carpenter god. But then I've been told that Christ is the Prince of Peace, not war, although that never stopped his followers from cutting each other up. I am wondering if Arthur seeks Merlin's help against the Franks, the way the forest wizard once aided his father against the Saxons.''

"Arthur has no present plans for a Continental campaign,'' I said. Either Cuneda had good intelligence of doings in the South or, Lugh forbid, I'd become less adept at lying than I used to be, for the King of Gododdin snorted wine out the end of his nose and smiled at me with crooked yellow teeth. "I certainly hope not. Britain would not stay long united in his absence, and if he upped his taxes to pay for such foreign wars, there'd likely be rebellion before he ever left.''

"This is, of course, treasonous talk,'' I said idly, not really caring, as the turmoils of state seemed a tiny thing compared to what might await me in the wildwood.

My host hooked a horny thumbnail into the inside of his hollow-tipped nose and scratched the ancient scar tissue. "Maybe so, but we both know it for the truth. For my own part, I would remain loyal to Camelot, should someone else come to power in Arthur's foolish absence. Someone to whom I owed a debt, and who would not crush the North with taxes. Think on that, if the time ever comes.''

I looked him in his goblin face and smiled. ''This is all idle foolishness, for the High Kingship of Britain is as secure as ever, and Arthur would not throw away all he's built by seeking after foreign glory. I will *not* think on it, nor shall we talk further on the matter.''

He laughed a phlegmy laugh, then drained his goblet and threw it in the fire, where its inner surface hissed and sputtered. ''See, men throw valuable things away all the time, depending on their mood. However, as you have asked me not to speak further on this subject, I can only respect your wishes, and if you tell me that you will not think on it, I can but believe you.''

I met his snaggle-toothed grin with what I hoped was a wolfish one of my own. ''I trust you will. It is no courtesy to the man who brought your son back from Pictdom to think or do otherwise. Speaking of that, how fares Prince Teged? Does he still shit blood?''

Cuneda did not stop smiling. ''Ach, my gentle lord, I could truly learn manners at your knee. Teged is indeed fine, although it is fortunate that he is out hunting, for it would not be good for him to hear what you just said. Soon he shall be married, and Strathclyde will be united with Gododdin.''

Meaning that, were Cuneda true to his hints, I might have the entire North as my ally should I ever want to rebel against Arthur. *There'd be no sharing her then*, I thought; *Guinevere would be mine and mine alone.* I brushed those thoughts from my mind like cobwebs, for there were more immediate concerns. ''Can your huntsman take me to Merlin?''

Cuneda continued to probe the interior of his tipless nose. ''Dumglys can take you to the part of the forest where the wizard lairs, but after that, you'll be on your own. Finding him should be easy enough, if he wants you to find him.''

I no longer saw a pink, grinning, faintly wrinkled face when I shut my eyes, but I remembered it well enough. ''Ach, I'm sure enough he wants me to. Be glad that he likes

the game of having me seek him out, or else he would likely
have come to meet me here.''

Cuneda shuddered, something I couldn't imagine him doing very often, and called for more wine. I stared into the
glowing embers and wished I were South again, and in
Gwen's arms.

The southeastern tip of the Great Caledonian Wood was
little more than a half-day's ride from Din Eidyn, a proximity which made me appreciate how even the phlegmatic
Cuneda might be discomfited by the thought of my disturb-
ing what dwelt within its gloomy fastness. Dumglys, the
tense little huntsman who served as my noticeably reluctant
guide, reigned in his nervous mare and pointed at the winding dark perimeter of oak and ash and the occasional holly,
their bare branches a black latticework against the newfallen
snow. "Here it is," he said, his breath a misty veil across
his walnut-colored face. "The Myrddin-Man lives here, so I
will come no farther." Clearly, he thought I should not either, were I not a foolish Southman eager to find my own
death.

My roan gelding seemed calmer than his dappled mare,
but I dismounted anyway, my fur-and-leather-booted feet
crunching through snow and frozen grass. I wore cowhide
leggings over woolen trousers and a leather tunic over two
woolen ones, and my hooded cloak was lined with fox and
otter fur. On the trip North I'd begun to grow a beard, but
it was not yet heavy enough to provide much protection for
my face, so I'd brought a scarf of rather smelly black goats-
wool, which I now pulled down so I could speak.

"Is there a path?"

Dumglys shrugged. "Maybe, from before he came to live
here. Deer trails, at least. I'm going back now. Come with
me or go on by yourself." With that, he turned his mare
around and cantered off, leaving me alone with the snorting
of my gelding's breath and the dwindling sound of his
mount's hooves in the snow.

I looked at my horse, who rolled an eye at me. "It's just
us, then," I said inanely. "I better lead you, lest you get so
nervous you try to scrape me off on a branch.''

The forest loomed ahead, frost glistening on the picket line of stark gray trunks, their naked boughs clawing at the colorless sky. There was a clear demarcation between tree line and moor, the boundary marked by an ancient turf ditch, indicating that some tribal lord's property had once ended here, but beyond the far bank it looked like few if any trees had felt the woodsman's ax since before the Romans came, for this was all old growth, with no sign of coppicing. My horse snorted mist, balking slightly as we traversed the gentle dip-and-rise of the ditch and mound, and then we were among twisting serpent trunks with scales of bark and ice, under a canopy of glittering, skeleton-finger branches that chimed gently with our passage. In my dream, this had all been muted green, crisp brown, and flaming orange, the blended hues of summer and autumn, and the trees had spoken to me. Somehow, the monochromatic silence made this stark landscape even less real than my dreaming one, which made me wonder if I were truly awake, and I found myself wishing that I drowsed someplace far from winter or magicians, Gwen's head a gentle weight on my chest, my face veiled by her flaming hair.

The fancy passed, leaving the grim business at hand. "Ho, Merlin!" I said rather less loudly than I'd intended. "Will you appear now, or must I tramp all day in search of you?" There was no answer but the echo of my voice flitting like a ghost through the frost-scaled trees. I pulled my spear from its saddle-horn socket and used its haft to start breaking a way through the brittle, ice-shrouded undergrowth, leading my reluctant horse after me. The commotion of our passage occasionally made overhanging branches disgorge their canopy of snow, but I managed to sidestep most of these. Through luck, or perhaps something more than luck, the path I was beating soon intersected an old trail, which widened as it wound its way into the wood, so that eventually there was room for me to climb back into the saddle. Having open space ahead of him seemed to calm my gelding, but I still kept him to a slow trot. After that, I have no idea how far or how long I rode through a universe of snow and bark, the rhythmic crunch-crunch of my mount's hoofbeats lulling me into a drowsy reverie as the chill crept languidly into my bones.

That is not the safest state of mind to be in when one is alone in the icebound wildwood, even when there's little danger from wolves or robbers. I was about to rein in and make myself alert by rubbing a palmful of soft snow into my face when the path before me curved and widened, opening into a huge clearing. The air about me grew suddenly darker and colder, and I wondered if I'd so lost track of the hours while traversing this crunching black-and-white void as to be unprepared for falling night, but no, I had simply ridden into the shadow of the tree from my dream.

That cyclopean oak was perhaps the biggest thing I'd ever seen, at least in this world, with a trunk so thick at the base that a squadron could not have linked hands around it, and of such sky-stabbing height that it would have dwarfed Arthur's palace or any other building this side of Byzantium. I craned my neck, tracing its challenge to the sky, but the sight was dizzying, and I slipped out of the saddle lest I fall. Trying to regain my equilibrium by looking down at the snow, I saw the tracks of fox and badger and stoat, and there, a little farther away, bare human feet that, had I encountered their prints anywhere else, I would have assumed belonged to a child. "I am here, Merlin," I said softly. "Will you appear to me now, or must I follow your spoor?"

Apparently, it was to be the latter. Tying my horse to a sapling at the edge of the clearing, I tramped after the small footprints, which traced such a giddy, weaving course around the base of the tree that I wondered if the person who'd made them had been skipping, or even dancing. I didn't follow in each step, else I would have doubled back on myself a dozen times, but marked their general bearing, and eventually they led me to the opposite side of that towerlike trunk. There, at the junction of two gigantic roots, each far bigger around than the bole of any normal tree, was a vast hollow in the oak's base, higher than my head and as wide as my arm span. "Ah, so this is your front door," I said more bravely than I felt, my voice echoing down into that dark recess. Gaping between the two huge roots, fringed with tendrils of smaller root and lined with moss that re-

mained wet and dripping despite the freezing cold, the opening reminded me of nothing so much as a huge cunt.
"Bloody hell, do you truly expect me to follow you in
there?"

There was no answer. Feeling foolish, but having no desire to stumble blindly into that darkness, I made a snowball
and threw it, hearing it impact some distance within. How
far back, and more importantly, how far down did the passage go?

"You just awakened my guardian," whispered a familiar
voice from somewhere far down inside the moss-fringed
void. "I would welcome you to my abode, but now you shall
have to get past him before you can enter. This should be
fun."

There was a low scraping sound, then the rising echo of
heavy footsteps, like those of a large slow man climbing the
stairs leading up from a deep cellar. I had plenty of time to
draw my sword, the iron pommel bracingly cold even
through my horsehide glove, then unsling my creaking shield
from my back and unfasten my heavy cloak. The air was
darker now with more than just the great tree's shadow, and
fresh snow had begun to fall, sighing through the branches
in large downy flakes. There's something peculiarly unnerv-
ing about waiting in the cold for an attack, for as each pale
breath unfolds before your face, you find yourself wondering
how many more such misty exhalations you have left.

The thing that came slowly clumping out into the snow
was slightly shorter than me (and I am not tall) but at least
twice as broad, with gnarled tree-limb arms bigger than my
thighs and tree-trunk legs the diameter of my waist. Its wrinkled skin was much like bark, and gray-green moss grew in
clumps on its neckless head and broad misshapen shoulders,
while its face was little more than a whorled knot in which
something like dried sap glistened from two unequally sized
eye slits. Its feet were rough ovals with no toes, and there
was a gall-like swelling at its crotch. A thick tendril trailed
behind it, connecting to either the small of its back or its
buttocks, the rootlike tether disappearing into the darkness.
In its mitten-shaped right hand it held a knobbed oaken club,

the texture of which was almost indistinguishable from the arm that hefted it.

"Christ's balls, Merlin," I said in a voice that sounded distressingly like a bleat, "call off your servant, pet, or whatever this bloody thing is! You wanted me to come here, and so I've come. This is no time for games."

There was no answer from the oak's dark hollow, and the creature continued to stalk stiffly forward, raising its heavy club. Seeking to preempt that blow, I shrugged off my cloak and slashed at its face. The resulting impact was quite like that of striking a wooden practice post. My sword bit into what, had it more distinct features, I would have called its cheek and forehead, the edge penetrating less than a half inch and numb shock running up my arm. A milky, saplike fluid glistened in the cut, but was too thick actually to run out onto my blade. I drove my foot into its stomach, more to lever my sword out of its face than with any hope of hurting it, kicking myself backwards just in time to avoid the club that whisked past my head, one of its knots scraping skin from my nose. Landing on my back in the cold but cushioning snow, I rolled to avoid another blow, leaving my shield behind and nearly cutting myself on my own sword. *Gawain would be proud of me for not dropping my weapon*, I thought inanely. *Indeed, I wish I'd brought him with me to see my tumbling skills, for I sorely need his help.*

I scrambled to my feet, panting, my own misty breath momentarily obscuring my vision. The creature had nearly overbalanced while trying to strike at me as I rolled on the ground, and was still steadying itself when I closed with it. Seeing an opportunity, I lunged forward, driving my point into the lump that was at least its symbolic genitalia. The swelling splintered like the oak gall it resembled, leaking more sap, but the creature didn't seem to notice, and I had to dance back from another swing of the club. A stab at its left eye produced no better result, but simply gave the illusion that my opponent was simultaneously winking at me and weeping sap. Dodging past it, I bent to retrieve my shield, and before it turned after me I got a good view of its gnarled arse. Yes, it did indeed have two lumpy buttocks, with the root or vine that trailed behind it disappearing into the crack between them.

It's drawing its strength from the tree, I thought, and that realization was nearly my undoing, for perhaps sensing that I'd discovered a point of vulnerability, it whirled with un- expected speed, and although I got my shield raised in time, the blow from the monster's club split it clean in two, leav- ing half my body numb. Reeling back, I shook off the frag- ments of my shield and dodged clumsily around my opponent, hobbled by a left leg that was nearly as unrespon- sive as my left arm. As I went past it, the creature swiped at me with its empty hand, the glancing blow knocking me face forward into the snow. No time to look behind me, I scrambled to my knees like a crippled beggar, frantically brushing snow out of my eyes, and there was the trailing root in front of me. This time I *had* dropped my sword, and now I fumbled madly for it, at any moment expecting a crushing blow from the monster's club, then the icy pommel was in my hand and I hacked once, twice, three times at that wrist-thick tendril, my hysterical strength severing it on the third blow. Not daring to look back to see the result, I wrig- gled through the snow on my elbows, sword slipping from clumsy fingers and me cursing my inability to rise as blood pounded in my ears and urine ran hotly down my leg.

In my panic I nearly scrambled headlong into the base of the great oak. Using roots and knots as handholds, I pulled myself to my feet, then set my back against it, panting like a bellows and sparks dancing in my vision. Fifteen feet away, the creature lay facedown in the snow, as motionless as the fallen tree trunk it resembled. I coughed and sneezed and rubbed at my eyes, and when my vision cleared, and I saw it was still immobile, I managed a grunt of triumph. Yes, my inspiration had been correct; this roughly man- shaped mass of wood and bark and moss had indeed drawn its strength, its animating essence, from the umbilical-like tendril that protruded from its arsehole, connecting it to the oak from which it had emerged.

Somebody was clapping. Painfully, I turned my head, to see Merlin sitting on one of the huge roots that flanked the entrance to his lair. As usual, he was wearing nothing but a short woolen tunic, and his bare limbs seemed very pink against the dark wrinkled texture of the tree, the snow that was as white as his curly hair. "Oh well done!" he said, giggling, "well done indeed. Mind you, it was a close thing, and for a moment there I thought I was actually wrong about what was going to happen." He looked wistful and even more childlike than usual. "It would be rather nice to be wrong just once, but after so many unsurprising decades you stop hoping."

"Fuck you, Merlin," I said, rubbing my numb arm.

He laughed again. "That's the very thing I mean. I could indeed make you do that—fuck me, that is—but I shan't. I shan't because I won't; it's simply not what's going to happen, and that's that. Knowing the future makes it as unbending as the past. Mind you, I don't see everything, not clearly, which allows me some saving ambiguity in my daily life. I'm not always sure whether my next bowel movement will come out firm or runny, or what the weather will be like in the morning, or what I will have for dinner, but the big things like sex and death, I see those a mile off. Not that there aren't times when I forget what's going to happen, just like you don't remember every minor detail of your past, but really, I rather think that if you and I were going to be fucking anytime soon, I would probably remember it. I envy you, you know. It must be lovely to think one has choices."

Sighing, I found my sword and sheathed it, then shook snow out of my cloak. "All right then, what does happen next? Please don't tell me that we continue to stand here in the cold and discuss philosophy. I'm not entirely sure that's preferable to being sodomized."

He leapt nimbly down from the great root, his bare feet apparently causing him no discomfort, and bowed. "That's an easy one. You enter my abode and dine with me, enjoying my hospitality for the night. On the morrow, we go to rejoin your escort at Din Eidyn, where my brief visit will make Cuneda nearly shit himself, and then on to Camelot."

If there was one thing I absolutely could not imagine myself enjoying, it was Merlin's "hospitality." Still, there was no point in baiting him. "Why don't we just go back to Din

Eidyn now? My horse is right over there." At least, I hoped
he still was, not having checked.

Merlin seemed to have read my thought. "Oh, yes, your
steed is fine, and will be just as fine in the morning, I can
assure you that, for my arts will protect the beast and keep
him warm. Since you live in a world where effect seems to
follow cause, I will speak in terms you can understand, rather
than tell you that we will not return to Din Eidyn until tomorrow because that is simply what we will do, an outcome
as set in stone as anything that happened yesterday. Instead,
look around you. It's getting dark, and the snow is falling
more heavily, and it will not be a night for traveling. Be
sensible and take shelter at my hearth, where I assure you
that no harm will come to you. Do me this favor. I've not
had a guest since my last boy, and you offer a more cerebral,
if less tactile, sort of companionship. Really, would you prefer I forced you to come inside? You know a bit of hedge
magic, but surely you don't think you can resist my will."

It was indeed getting quite dark. Merlin was a shadow
against the snow, ghost-shrouded in his own breath. I was
debating what to do when light flared from the opening at
the base of the great oak. It was not a pale sorcerous sort of
illumination, but a hearty yellow glow, radiating warmth.
Don't be a stubborn git, I told myself. *You went crawling
like a mole into the Kingdom of Teeth; you can do this. If
he meant you harm, he'd take great pleasure in telling you
so, knowing there was nothing you could do about it.*

"All right then," I said, fastening my cloak and flipping
it back with a bold gesture. "Lead on."

Merlin skipped ahead of me, his small feet almost silent
on the snow, and motioned me to follow him through the
fringed and dripping opening. The sourceless yellow light
glimmered on oily gnarled steps that looked more like they'd
somehow grown out of the wood than been carved from it.
Ducking under the curving, moss- and root-hung ceiling, I
followed Merlin's surefooted lead, the passage winding
downward into the bowels of the tree. Down and down and
down we went, the opening long since having disappeared
behind us, and nothing visible ahead but the damp twisting
stairs, the wetter low-hanging roots. It was no longer cold,

and in a few minutes I was actually sweating in my cloak and heavy tunics, although Merlin seemed no more affected by this bathhouse warmth than he'd been by the outer chill. Still we descended, my ears actually popping from the change in pressure, my spirit recoiling from the feeling of entombed confinement, the crushing weight of tree and soil above us. I smelled earth and mold and moss and sap and wood rot, and a faint drip-drip sound whispered up and down the winding stair. "Quite a cozy place you have here," I said with what was intended as light irony, but my voice was a small, distant thing. Merlin quickened his pace, and I was forced to speed up, too, lest he get ahead of me and disappear around a bend, for I had a sudden irrational fear that if that happened, the sourceless light would go out, and I'd be trapped here alone, while his triumphant laughter echoed away from me in the closing dark.

And then, just when I wondered how much longer I could stand it, the stairway leveled out and the fringed overhanging ceiling disappeared, the warm yellow light flaring up ahead of us to reveal a large, unevenly shaped chamber, with high-domed roof and curving walls of wrinkled bare oak. Impossibly, there was a huge oval brick hearth set in the wood of the far wall, a hissing, crackling fire burning there, and Merlin skipped ahead through its dancing light, then spun on the ball of his pink left foot, his slender arms outstretched, his shadow spilling out before him. "Welcome, son of Arthur and Morgawse and grandson of the man I loved more than food or drink, shelter or warmth, or even soft-skinned boys. This is my wildwood villa, if you will, where I have lived these twenty-two years. It's not much, perhaps, but I call it home."

There were wicker chairs and padded couches, a long oaken table with finely carved legs, and an impressive collection of freestanding, variously sized amphorae, some taller than me, their red, orange, and black glazed surfaces shining in the hearth light. Ornate tapestries hung on shining brass rods suspended from the whorled ceiling, partitioning off the interior space. These were decorated not with designs or figures, but carefully woven and brightly colored verses. I read the one nearest me.

Arthur falters in his faith,
  and dreams of foreign glory
While I live like a badger
  under oak and holly.
Winter chills the wildwood
  and Uther's bones are dust
But I remember what will happen
  in that city by the Usk.

That one, at least, was ambiguous, but the next seemed more ominous.

The hated fire that burned within
  my beloved's pious son
Meant I could not harm him,
  but now that fire is gone.
With its ashes no protection from
  the vengeance of the wronged.

''Pay no attention to my clumsy doggerel,'' said Merlin lightly, standing on the other side of the long oaken table, which was now laden with food, although it had looked bare a moment ago. ''Come eat, for I know you must be starved.''

True enough, my stomach was in knots, a condition which was much less easy to ignore now that food was laid out before me. A fat, herb-crusted dormouse the size of a small rabbit steamed succulently in a clay pot, while a savory trencher of garlic-scented bread was piled high with leeks, buttered onions, dark spongy mushrooms, roasted chestnuts, and pale chunks of blue-veined cheese, with a Castorware mug of mulled ale set nearby. For a brief moment I hesitated, wondering if Merlin's den was like a fairy hill, into which I would be lost forever should I eat or drink anything offered me. But no, that could not be my host's purpose, for he had plenty of other ways of making me stay, were that what he truly wanted. Casting aside all caution, I sat on a three-legged stool, drained the cup in a single swallow, then drew my knife and dug in with the fatalistic eagerness of a condemned prisoner offered an unexpected meal.

Merlin poured me more ale while I sucked juicy dark

flesh, as tender as that of a steamed squab, from the dormouse's plump haunch. Such a creature might not be hard to find in the vicinity of Merlin's lair, hibernating in its warm hole and still fat so early in its winter slumber, but I wondered about the leeks, which were not dried or pickled, but fresh enough to have been picked that day. The fact that Merlin, who'd seated himself opposite me, had no food of his own laid out before him made me more suspicious. Had I been thinking with my brain or my empty stomach when I decided no harm could come to me at his table?

"What am I really eating?" I said, swallowing my last bite with sudden difficulty.

Merlin smiled, the fire behind him tinting his bleached hair. "Whatever do you mean?"

I started to take another swig of ale, then wondered about that, too. "Don't take me for a fool. I doubt you wish to poison me, or bind me to this place like one who eats fairy food, but you're not above your little jokes. I wonder how delightful I'd find your table were you to show me this meal as it truly is, rather than as you've made it appear."

Merlin's hands slid together, his supple fingers entwining, his smile unperturbed. "You underestimate me. Not my generosity or goodwill, which can indeed be capricious, but my power. What you see before you is what your food now is, truly and completely, just as Nimüe will be a true and complete woman when I am through with her, although that's a much stronger magic. Yes, I can indeed show it to you as it used to be, but I doubt you'd like it. Isn't it better to accept it as it is? Few men have the stomach for the truth."

I shook my head, more from a stubborn refusal to appear weak in front of him than anything else. "I am the son of a sorceress, and have done enough grim magic of my own. Go ahead. It won't bother me if you lift the veil."

Merlin's dimpled smile spread wider, almost to his translucent, delicately lobed ears. "Always the bold one, aren't you. Very well. Just remember, I won't use my magic to clean you off if you vomit on yourself."

He made a languid motion in the air, where a ghostly afterimage of his spidery hand lingered for an instant, as the light changed from orange-yellow to a pale green. Looking down, I saw that my trencher of bread was now a strip of slug-streaked bark, crawling with writhing grubs and scuttling beetles, and although the centerpiece was still a dormouse, it was no longer freshly killed, skinned, cleaned, and cooked in a clay pot, but a bloated, moldy-furred carcass, with more grubs writhing amid its burst viscera. Turning away in disgust, I saw the room was no longer lit by the now nonexistent hearth. Instead, a clammy light issued from dozens of glowing wall nooks, in which were set crude bowl-shaped lamps made from human skullcaps, most so small they could only have come from children, and all filled with a suddenly reeking oil that I knew must have been rendered from their late owners' fat. Instead of tapestries, the raw skins of those dead boys hung glistening in the putrescent light, the verses on them not woven, but scrawled in blood and semen.

Merlin waved his hand in the other direction and the room was as it had been before. My stomach had indeed turned over, but I'd not vomited, and now I looked him steadily in the eye. "I told you I was used to such things," I said, reaching for a slice of cheese and trying not to wonder if it had recently been a grub or beetle. It tasted fine, but was still just a bit difficult to swallow, and I washed it down with ale, glad that I'd not noticed what had originally filled my cup. Despite my bravado, I didn't eat any more dormouse, although it continued to smell delicious.

Merlin put his hands behind his head and leaned back, looking rather impressed. "I am genuinely surprised. As I said outside, I can't always remember the details of what will happen, and I really didn't recall how you would react. Minor surprises are better than none at all, at least."

I wiped my knife on my sleeve and put it away, wishing I could stretch out before the fire, but not feeling that relaxed. "And do you remember what happens next?"

Merlin clasped his delicate hands again and smiled at me over them. "Oh yes, quite well. The egoist in me would hardly let me forget. You will sit there and drink more ale, wondering all the while what it was before it was ale, while I tell you the story of my life, or at least a much condensed version of it. I have to, you see, for my own authorial gift is very slight. I will tell you how I came to be what I am, and before you die, you will write it down, even though you will turn my history into a minor footnote to yours and Arthur's. I should be cross with you for that, but I am not, for I long since learned to stop to looking for justice in this sad world."

I sipped more ale and stared into the hearth flames, which were the color of Gwen's hair. Not the best way to spend the night, but I'd endured worse. "All right, Merlin; tell me your story."

Thirteen

"**I** WAS born with a full set of teeth and the hazy knowledge of my death," said Merlin, "the latter a memory which seems sweeter as I tumble toward it, for from the cradle onward I knew there'd be scant joy in my life, and one does get tired of knowing everything important that will come to pass. I didn't have the true gift of prophecy then, in that I could not have foretold anyone else's fate, but I came out of the womb knowing who I was and, somewhat less distinctly, how and when I would die. The latter certainty kept me from feeling any fear when the men of my mother's household made their first fumbling attempt on my young life, trying to drown me in a barrel like an unwanted kitten, only to find I breathed water as easily as air. And really, who could blame them? I was not what could be called a cuddly and endearing child. Besides the teeth, which caused my mother's milk to be flavored with her blood, and the fact that I could speak British by the time I was two months old and Latin six months later, the circumstances of my birth would have been enough to earn me fear and suspicion.

"Like any well-to-do townsman's fair-faced daughter, my mother had her share of suitors, and as is sometimes the case, the one she favored above all others was not the best of prospects. When her father forbade the union, they conspired to run away together. The night of my conception, she slipped out of her father's house, planning to meet her lover at the stone ring just outside of town. He, however, was thrown by the horse that he'd stolen for the purpose of carrying her off, and died about the time of their planned assignation, gasping his last in a muddy ditch four miles away. She, of course, did not know this, and so waited for hours in the shadow of the weathered menhirs. When the moon arose, and shone upon the standing stones, another suitor came to her in her lover's stead. He was not of mortal flesh, but of the Otherworld, and his caresses were not so gentle as she was accustomed to. When her father and his hired men tracked her to the stone ring, they found her disheveled and delirious, babbling of the burning eyes and ice-cold member of the one who had come to her by moonlight.

"The details of my preternaturally brief infancy don't matter. Suffice to say I was weaned quite early, but not early enough to save my mother's health, which had been bad since my conception and worsened once I emerged from her swollen belly to drain her of blood as well as milk. Her father might have tried harder to destroy me as an abomination, but greed stayed his hand. His fortunes had been failing during the economic turmoil that followed the first Saxon revolt, and he found himself unable to refuse the coin offered for me by a scholar named Blwys, who fancied himself a wizard. And thus, when I was less than two years old, although with the stature, bearing, and wits of a child of six or seven, this Blwys became my master.

"However paltry his power, it was enough to dominate what I was then, and I spent the next decade as his slave, with him calling me to his bed almost every night. Unlike my later and much happier bondage to your grandfather, I found no pleasure there, for Master Blwys was a crude bumbler at such matters, with a crushing sweaty belly and a huge, blue-veined penis that he rammed home like a Jute driving in a tent peg. Still, I submitted to his advances, and although it was not his intention to teach me, I soon learned everything there was to learn of his meager arts, reading his books and scrolls with more understanding than he'd ever possessed. Yet despite my new learning, I was still unable to free myself from his subjugation.

"Until one day, when Blwys had the sort of mad inspiration that is so often the undoing of second-rate men. He'd found a spell for calling up the Myrddin, that prophetic spirit that rides a man like a lathered horse, driving him to madness while temporarily investing him with divinatory gifts. In such turbulent times, there's always a booming market in soothsayers, the future being most important when it seems most uncertain. Blwys thought he could cast this immaterial being into me, and because he was my master, he would be its as well, profiting from my frenzied prophecies until the inevitable time came when it wore out my mortal flesh. But I was only half-mortal, and that was his mistake. Rather than it mastering me, I mastered it, absorbing its power and essence completely into my own, and with this transformation, Blwys no longer had the slightest control over me. I paid him well for his harsh treatment, killing him half a dozen times, each more painful and sexually inventive than the last. I was now eleven years old.

"After that, I made my own way in the world for a time, in what folk now call the dark days of Vortigern the traitor. Not that I cared anything about the ongoing ruin of Britain, for I was in no danger from Saxon, Pict, or Irishman, nor from the native brigands who preyed upon the dispossessed. Untouched and rather amused by the bloody turbulence around me, I idly wandered from dying town to dying town, working small magics and great ones, acclaimed sometimes for what I did, at others scorned and feared. There's a small village in Gwynnedd where they still revere me as a saint, and there were several other ones that did not exist once I was through with them and their inhabitants. My callow vagabond days were pleasant enough while they lasted, but boredom set in soon enough, and I was ready for a change.

"Rather garbled word of me and what I was reached Vortigern, by now hard-pressed in his battles with Uther Pendragon and Uther's brother Ambrosius, who were seeking to restore what they saw as the legitimate government of Britain. Vortigern's own wizards had told him that, if he wanted to defeat Uther and Ambrosius, he should sacrifice a boy without a human father. And so for this foolish purpose I was brought to his fortress in Cornwall, much to the consternation of his wizards, who'd thought they could distract him from their own inadequacy by telling him that their magic required the blood of someone who didn't exist. I made short work of them all, conjuring a dragon which devoured the fraudulent soothsayers and destroyed the central tower of the fortress, although Vortigern himself survived. The next day, Ambrosius and Uther arrived and laid siege to his stronghold. His men had little heart left in them after my spectacular conjuration, and I expect that my prophecy that he would die in that day's battle didn't help matters. Indeed, Uther later called me the real victor of the day.

"Ah, Uther, what shall I say of him? Can one really map the heart's oblique geography? The fact that I knew who I would love before I ever met him, and could foretell the course of our passion in advance, makes me no better able to explain the why of it. I could say that his hands were gentle for such a big man, as skilled with caresses as sword cuts, or that his eyes were the color of the sky reflected in winter ice, or that his deep chest-shaking laughter seemed to absolve the gods of all the sad iniquities of this world. None of those glib phrases catch his essence, or what he made me feel. Oh, I had no illusions, and won't pretend that he cared half as much for me as I did for him. Uther dearly wanted to be as Roman as his brother, and sticking his dick in me while engaging me in brittle Latin conversation allowed him to play at being something more than a barbarian warlord. I was an advisor, of course, an exotic pet, and something of a trophy, but I didn't mind, or at least pretended I did not.

"He eventually tired of me, as I'd have known he would even without the gift of prophecy. In my boredom I turned to slave boys, as well as the occasional girl, using them in somewhat drastic ways that would hardly have pleased Uther, had he known of it, but I had quite a bit of autonomy by this time, and he didn't meddle in my affairs. I know you find me abominable in my pleasures, but really, what is the foundation of society but slavery, and are not slaves ultimately expendable, to be used as their master wishes? Your mother certainly used up more than her share, and even Arthur, with his delusions of Christian kindness, could not rule long without those who toil in the uplands silver mines or on the great plantation farms to the south, minting the coin and reaping the corn that funds and feeds his army. I simply use them up sooner and make no pretense that I'm serving anything but my own fleshly appetite. You may think me a monster, the physical opposite but spiritual image of the giant you slew on that fateful day when Arthur discovered your paternity, and in that you might be right. You may also think me completely unlike yourself or Arthur or any of the folk who don't disgust you so much as I, and in that you are wrong. Every man who can do so consumes his fellows in some way, each to his particular need. My need is my delight.

"And so the decades passed, Uther growing distant from me as he lost the adventurous tastes of his youth. Despite his becoming older and less interesting, I could deny him nothing, even to the foreknown wounding of my heart. When, late in life, he became foolishly obsessed with the dull and cowlike wife of one of his loyal allies, nearly destroying the hard-won unity of Britain in pursuit of her smelly cunt, I not only aided his coming to her in sorcerous disguise, but made him a potion that lent his failing cock the stiffness necessary for that night of puerile pleasure, even though I knew this would also give him the potency to sire the son who would one day exile me. Later, I taught his daughter something of my art, scraps of which she'd already learned from her Breton mother, laughing sourly to myself as I thought of how she would one day use these skills to seduce the brother I'd helped create. I've watched these preordained events unfold with all the delicious anticipation of an aficionado of Plautus, whose knowledge of the well-loved play only increases his enjoyment of the performance.

"Think on that, Mordred son of Arthur. As repellent as you may find me, I'm the reason you exist. Amusingly enough, that's the same argument I used to forgive whatever deity truly rule this unhappy world, back when my own existence seemed less tiresome. Here, let me refill your cup. Don't frown; it was nothing but rainwater before I turned it into ale, not piss or blood. You might want to think about getting some sleep, actually. Despite all my power, I cannot speed the passing of the night, nor lessen the miles once tomorrow comes and we begin our trip to Camelot."

With those words, my host was gone, I didn't know

where, leaving me blessedly alone before the crackling hearth. Either some subtle magic or my own exhaustion finally overcame my unease, and eventually I did indeed stretch out before the fire, which I told myself really was a fire, no matter what it had once been, and fitfully slept, dreaming of the time Guinevere and I lay together in the warm dry hay after I rescued her from the Otherworld, with the sound of rain on the barn roof whispering of the world's sweet possibilities.

Fourteen

FEW OF the royal guard had served when Merlin still dwelt in Camelot, but they all seemed to know who he was and practically fell over themselves getting out of our way. Gawain pushed through their cowering mass and hugged me hard enough to make my ribs creak. "Welcome home, laddybuck," he growled warmly in my ear. "Would I could have gone with you, for I doubt you had a pleasant trip." Turning to my companion, he glowered fearlessly down at him. "Merlin, my brother assures me that you are not responsible for Nimüe's transformation. Mordred got the brains in our family, and I believe what he tells me, or at least I try to. That's the only reason why your head is still on your shoulders." Saying that, he crossed himself, his twitching fingers looking like they'd be more comfortable closing on his sword hilt.

Merlin cocked his head and grinned sardonically, his sharp little teeth very white against his red lips and pink skin, the faint tracery of wrinkles around his small mouth spreading into dimples. "Ah yes, the renowned Prince Gawain, fiercest of Arthur's dragons, and just as charming as when I was last in Camelot, if more grizzled. I'm sure you mean what you say, but so do most fools. My head is still on my shoulders because it's not yet time for it to come off them, and your bearish threats can't change that, so you needn't waste your breath. Now are we going to stand here at the gate and continue these pleasantries, or shall we go inside? I'm sure Arthur is very eager to see me."

Gawain's hand squeezed empty air that I knew he wished
was Merlin's throat. *Don't try it, brother*, I thought silently;
please, let's not have everything end in disaster just yet. Oh
yes, I was in quite an optimistic mood.

"You're not seeing Arthur," said my brother in a low
voice. "Not now, maybe not ever. Instead, the Queen wishes
to speak to you in the inner courtyard."

Merlin clapped his small hands together and bounced on
the balls of his bare feet, the beam of sunlight that shafted
through the colonnade making his tousled hair look more
gold than silver. "Ah, yes, the lovely Guinevere. It will be
a pleasure finally to meet her. Knowing things from a distance and ahead of time is not quite the same as experiencing
them firsthand, and I've been curious to see the woman who
won Arthur's pious heart."

No, I wasn't liking this at all. Bloody buggering hell, why
had I ever let Gwen persuade Arthur to send me after this
creature? Me, who understood the danger better than anyone!
That's love for you, sending one off on mad and destructive
errands; the heart is always a more capricious master than
the cock. There was a part of me that didn't care what might
happen when Merlin met Arthur, that was even amused to
contemplate all the possible calamities, but Merlin meeting
Guinevere was quite another matter.

"Listen to me, Merlin," I said with strained gentleness.
"It is because of the Queen that you are here. Do not be
insolent with her, and do not threaten her in any way. If you
do, I will try to kill you. You can tell me that I won't succeed
and that may even be the truth, but I will try nonetheless.
Whatever your game is, whatever you intend to do here, I
don't think it will be helped if I die trying to kill you, at
least not just yet. So do behave. I ask you nicely, and even
say please. There is nothing to be gained in baiting her, or
in causing her harm. Do we understand each other?"

Merlin looked at me with eyes hooded by translucent blue-
veined lids framed by a delicate tracery of wrinkles. "Better
than you might think, actually. Your threat is somewhat
more compelling than your brother's. When you look at me
like that, I see the Arthur who was able to drive me from
this place. You have more of him within you than you re-

alize. If I didn't know what was going to happen, I might be wary of you. At any rate, yes, I shall be on my best behavior, so shall we go inside?''

With no more excuse for delay, I let Gawain lead us to the inner courtyard, Merlin padding catlike on the paving stones, his red-flecked eyes noting the wine stains on the once whitewashed walls and the bases of the colonnade. "Christian mystics are such amusing fellows," he giggled. "They sometimes wield incredible power, but have no idea what to do with it. I confess that I don't understand why one would make oneself a vessel for such capricious forces. Always doubting themselves, always worrying about this nonsense they call sin. At least I've been spared that, thank you very much."

"But you admit that the Lord has power over you," growled Gawain.

Merlin stuck his tongue out at a maidservant and leered at a scrub boy, both of whom quailed against the pink-stained wall. "I admit that those few who manage to worship him with an extreme amount of single-minded rigor do have some power over me, which is not the same thing. As for the Christian father spirit, his carpenter son, and his consort-mother, they don't affect me in the least. Once, in Colchester, I saw quite a lovingly carved and painted life-size sculpture of the Crucifixion. I was out of sorts that day, and tried to annoy Uther by briefly bringing the silly figure on the cross to life and making it piss on the fat bishop mouthing platitudes below it. Had the fool's faith been stronger, I couldn't have done that, but it's a question of the power of the worshipers, not the worshiped."

Why was he telling us this, confessing to such chinks in his sorcerous armor? Clearly, Merlin thought (no, I would not use the word *knew*) that something irrevocable was at hand, the final checkmate, the chorus's last chant. More than ever, I wanted to lash out at him with my sword or simply turn and run away, anything to show I was not a pawn in his obscure game. Damn you, Gwen, damn your wit; your warm words; your burning hair; your lopsided smile; your big feet and hands; the long-legged, cream-skinned, golden-fuzzed body that I've mapped with fingertip and tongue; the wide green eyes that have stared so deeply into mine; the fierce unbending spirit guarded from pomposity by sardonic humor; the sharp and grasping mind; the all-inclusive *you*. *Damn you for loving Nimüe so much and me not more.*

And then we turned the corner into the inner courtyard, and there she was, waiting for us, the sight of her evaporating all my silent imprecations like the dew from tall, sun-dappled grass. She wore green ribbons in her unbound hair, gold slippers on her feet, and a gown somewhere in color between pale ash and winter ice. There was a gold circlet at her long white throat, but no crown. Four conical-helmeted men-at-arms glowered on either side of her, brandishing polished spears, and Bishop Gerontius stood behind her with a scroll of Scripture in one hand and a crucifix in the other, but her eyes were those of a woman who would not have been afraid to meet Merlin alone on an empty moor at midnight.

He gave a little laugh at the sight of her, a childlike yip with no apparent malice in it, and skipped forward past me and Gawain, only to halt at the last respectful moment. "Lovely, you are so very lovely," he said, bowing so low his white hair brushed the dead leaves scattered at his feet. "Arthur doesn't deserve you."

Guinevere crossed her arms, her face impassive. "That's not for you or anyone to say, Merlin. It may be true, if you mean that he deserves better, but your opinion of the royal marriage is not asked for. Not that I'm going to waste much effort expecting courtesy from you."

Gawain and I stepped up on either side of Merlin as he bowed again. "Then you shall be surprised by having it, Your Most Fair and Royal Majesty," he said in a more sincere voice than I'd have imagined he was capable of. "Courtesy, like many desired things, is more graciously given when not demanded, but you should have it in any case, and I apologize for my gauche outburst."

"That's a pretty enough speech," said Guinevere, smiling her best politician's smile, a gift her husband never mastered. "For my part, I thank you for offering to help my sister, if that is why you are truly here."

"I will do that, and quite soon," said Merlin, clasping his

hands behind his back and turning his head languidly from side to side like a cat stretching its neck muscles. Noticing Gerontius, he nodded the Bishop's way. "Greetings, Holy Father. I remember when you were an apple-cheeked altar boy."

Gerontius's eyes were stern and unafraid, but there was a hint of fatalistic resignation in them, and I knew that his faith was too tempered with worldliness to be of any use here. "While you are much as you've always been, Merlin. That you are pagan is not such a great matter, for it is a sad commonplace that many deny themselves salvation. That you are a sorcerer is less forgivable, but that alone does not make you an abomination. That you are a defiler of children, and perhaps worse than a defiler of them, is your darkest stain. Still, it is possible you will indeed do good while you are here, in the way that even the best men and women sometimes do evil. I pray for that small crumb."

Merlin stuck one thumb in the belt of his tunic and sucked idly on the other. "Oh, be more ambitious than *that*. Why not pray for me, while you're at it? Thank of the glory, if you could win my soul for Christ! Or do you believe me irredeemable?"

Gerontius shook his head. "No man, or even half-a-man, is irredeemable, and if you were sincere in asking me to pray for you, my heart would be overjoyed. As it is, your mockery is cheap and ill becoming. Get thee behind me."

Merlin snickered. "Too bad you never said that to me when you were a boy. I would have quite enjoyed getting behind you then."

Gerontius did not blanch, and there was more sadness than anger in his frown. "Your Majesty," he said to Guinevere without taking his eyes off Merlin, "I am here at your request, but I do not see how I can aid you, at least not in dealing with this creature. You have already heard my counsel and made your own decisions. Such is your prerogative, of course, but now there seems to be little I can do for you but pray. Forgive me if I do not speak further with Merlin, but there is nothing to be gained by it. I would say a few more words to him, were I able to command him as the King once did, but in the absence of such power I shall be silent."

Merlin clapped with ironic theatricality. "It seems a day for pretty speeches! And speaking of the King, where is he? He did not fear me, once. Can it be he does so now?"

"I insisted on seeing you first," said Guinevere in a low uninflected voice that only I knew meant that she was biting back her anger.

Merlin nodded. "Because you wanted to know what my intentions toward him are, although you did not tell him this was your reason," he said. "Oh, yes, he fears me right enough. Our Arthur is not the shining paladin he once was. When he saw his faith injure himself and others, he began to let go of it, and has not been able to get it in his grip again."

"That is true enough," said a deep voice from behind us, "although it does me no credit to confess it. However, I pray it was a passing weakness."

We all turned to see Arthur standing in the entrance to the colonnaded walkway, wearing his usual scuffed leather but with a golden circlet on his brow and a bronze cross hanging at his neck, the ruby-hilted sword of Maximus glinting at his belt. Beside him, holding his hand, was Nimüe, clad in a simple white gown, her feet bare and a crown of holly on her brow. There was no fear in either his eyes or hers.

Merlin again bowed low. "Ah, Your Royal Highness, I'm delighted you could come after all. And this, of course, is the child who is the principal reason why I am here, or at least why you summoned me."

"I think I am a child no longer," said Nimüe in a steady voice. "What I would be is a woman, and must ask your help in that."

Merlin glided toward them, bare feet making no sound despite the plethora of dead leaves. Arthur put his hand on his hilt, but the aged boy paid it no heed, concentrating instead on Nimüe, who held her strong-jawed head erect and did not shrink from his approach. "But you know the one thing I cannot know, and that is change. You were a child, and now you're not. You were a girl, or at least appeared to be, and now you're not that, either. You do not ask for your childhood back; why your seeming sex? It's not such a dreadful thing to have a penis. Aside from the power it gives you in this world, I find it a most delightful organ.'' He brushed his fingertips against her crotch, causing her to shrink against Arthur's side.

''Don't you touch her!'' said Gwen. Gawain and I both started forward, along with several of the guards, but Arthur already had his sword out. He waved us back with his empty hand, while thrusting the blade like a barrier between Merlin and Nimüe.

''No, wizard, you offered help, not this. Have a care what you do now.'' His voice was deceptively calm, but I could read the tension in his face.

Merlin ran a fingertip down the length of Arthur's sword, his eyes half-shut. ''I have given much thought to what I'm doing, so much that I can almost pretend it was the decision of one who believed in choices.'' His hand closed around the blade without injury and pulled it gently to his mouth, where he touched it briefly with his tongue, leaving a dab of saliva on the polished steel. ''Had I done that when I was last here, you would have taken off my head, and felt yourself the instrument of your god in doing so. Whose instrument are you now, oh King of All the Britons?'' Arthur said nothing, but there was a drop of sweat on his brow, and his shoulders shook as though he was straining against a terrific weight.

Gawain's sword was also out. ''If we rush him, he surely can't stop us all,'' he whispered to me.

''Oh, but I can,'' said Merlin without turning around. ''However, I shan't have to.'' Gawain made a low growling sound, and I turned to see him also straining forward, muscles corded in his thick neck and bulging in his forearms. For my part, I didn't even try to move.

Letting go of Arthur's sword, Merlin stepped back and turned to Nimüe, falling on one knee. ''My lady, your wish is my command. But is that wish truly to be a woman?''

''Yes,'' said Nimüe, straightening up with something of Gwen's majesty. ''Can you make me one?''

Merlin sat cross-legged on the flagstones, his right hand idly stirring the leaves. ''I can do things you can't imagine. That's why I'm here.''

Whatever force had held Arthur immobile now released

its grip, and he swayed for a moment, leaning on his sword like a cane. "What is your price?" he said grimly.

Merlin crumbled a leaf and scattered the pieces across his own lap. "To come here one last time, to look you in the face and know you no longer have any power over me, and see that you know this, too. A small thing, really."

"Husband, I'm sorry," said Guinevere softly, her head bent so low that her green eyes were veiled by her crimson hair.

Pointedly not looking at Merlin, Arthur walked stiffly toward her, pausing for a moment to squeeze the shoulder of the still-straining Gawain. "As am I," he said with equal softness as he took her in his arms. Just once, my heart did not clench at the sight. "Sorry that I'm not stronger."

If you were, I thought, *he never would have come. Jesus, Mary, Mithras, Lugh, and all the rest, please let this farce be over soon, with no more calamity than this.*

Merlin rose again, shaking leaf fragments out of his tunic. "We shall need the figure of the Virgin that stands in the old Chapel of Standards. Have it brought here, please."

"Sacrilege," said Arthur.

"It's just painted wood," said Merlin. "I believe you've said so yourself, even though you once gladly wore her image on your shield. Have your men fetch it, and we shall soon be done here. And when we're done, you will be done with me. Now, isn't that a tempting inducement?"

It was for me. "I'll get it."

Arthur put out his hand to stop me, while Gerontius prayed softly. "No. He presumes too much."

"Father," I said, using the word for its effect, "this is his game, and we must let him play, for there's nothing else to do. You had me bring him here. If you can send him away again, do so now, but if not, give him what he wants."

I didn't like looking at the turmoil on his face and was glad when he turned to the guards. "Go with Mordred and help him. Two of you can carry the statue back here, while the rest wait outside the courtyard. You needn't see this."

We were back with it in a few minutes, and Merlin bade us set it down within the miniature grove, in front of one of the marble benches. Arthur then thanked the guards who'd helped me and told them to leave us. "You too, Gawain. Sadly, you can do nothing here."

"I won't leave her alone with that creature," growled my brother, shaking his head like a baited bear.

Nimüe, who'd been talking softly to Guinevere while I was away, now met Gawain's eye for the first time since entering the courtyard. "Please go," she said in the voice of the little girl she used to be. "I know you care, and want to protect me, but you can't right now, and it's harder for me with you here. Please, Gawain. I promise you I'll be all right."

He took her hand and kissed it. "I'll be just outside, if you should need me."

Her face was nearly as red as her hair. "I know, and thank you."

I feared he'd say something else to Merlin, but instead he simply squeezed my shoulder, much as Arthur had squeezed his earlier, and walked away from us. Bishop Gerontius met Arthur's gaze for a moment, shook his head sadly, then trudged after him. That left me, Arthur, Gwen, Nimüe, and, of course, Merlin. The latter grinned at us with sardonic amusement, then rising lithely to his feet, stretched and cracked his knuckles as prosaically as a peasant getting ready to lift a heavy stone.

"Such a touching display," said the magician. "Now, those of you who would remain, come stand within the cluster of these small trees. Yes, that's right. Nimüe, you lie upon the bench. The rest of you, reach out and touch the nearest trunk. You too, Arthur. There, that's good. It is a measure of my power that I can do this here, in an artificial grove of dwarf transplants. Of course, most of those who call themselves magicians could not do it if they stood within the very heart of the ancient wood. Now, all of you, shut your eyes. Just for a moment. I know this makes you feel vulnerable, but believe me, the transition will be easier on you if they're closed."

"Do as he tells you," I said, closing mine. Merlin began to chant, not in Greek or Latin or any dialect of British, but the older tongue that my mother had used when working her strongest magic, and that I'd never learned. The air around us grew colder, there was a dizzying lurch, and my ears popped. The distant sounds of the palace ceased, replaced by a familiar sighing rustle, and I smelled bark and moss and mold.

When I opened my eyes, we were no longer standing in the tiny grove, but among much older taller trees, amid frost-bitten underbrush. The towering mossy boles were the only things visible around us, while overhead bare branches swayed against a lowering sky. Arthur said one short prayer. Gwen muttered an unladylike curse, and Nimüe gasped softly. "You've brought us to the wildwood," I said in awe, wondering if we'd ever get out of it again.

"More impressive than that, actually," chuckled Merlin. "We are still in the courtyard, at least in a sense, but I have brought the wildwood here." He pointed to the statue of the Virgin, which stood in a kind of archway formed by two bending oaks, with Nimüe still lying on the marble bench in front of it, which now looked rather like an altar. "Listen. She is coming."

There was a flapping noise and a shadow fell upon the chill ground as a huge raven came gliding through the trees, to perch on top of the icon's painted head and regard us with one glittering button eye. It spread its black wings wider than those of any hawk or eagle, and a deeper blackness spilled beneath them, pouring like ink over the figure and into the ground. I blinked, not sure what I was seeing, as the bird seemed to fold itself into the wood. The Virgin's painted features darkened, rippling like a reflection in a stirred pool.

Nimüe was trembling all over, her eyes unfocused and half-shut, and I could hear her chattering teeth. "Jesus save us all," said Arthur. Gwen was praying into her clenched hands, muttering the name of Mary over and over again.

"Even me?" said Merlin. "No, I don't think he'll do that. And it's no use calling on his mother, for this is not her icon anymore." He pointed at the carved figure. It was indeed no longer the Virgin. The face was birdlike, predatory, with a long curved nose and hair swept back like folded wings. Instead of the robe, she seemed to be clothed in black feathers. "Mórrígán, Mother of Ravens," chanted Merlin, stepping forward to stand over Nimüe, who was panting now, face flushed and eyes rolling in her head. "Grant me the power to do this in your name. When I tear away this child's sex, change wound to womb!"

He pulled her gown up around her waist with little ceremony but some gentleness, exposing the tiny pale penis and mushroomlike testicles that poked from her nest of copper pubic hair. Grinning back at us, flashing his small, sharp white teeth, he ducked his head and lightly kissed her crotch, then bit down hard, jerking his head back and spitting something bloody at the statue's feet. More blood welled from Nimüe's groin. Her back arched, her contorted face went white, and her mouth opened in a piercing scream.

Guinevere screamed, too, although hers was more battle cry than banshee wail, and when I looked her way I saw that roots and vines had twined like shackles around her feet, holding her fast in their tangled grip. Arthur was also trying to charge forward. He managed to draw his sword and hack away at the lashing tendrils, but more sprang forth like Hydra heads, and in an instant he was bound as tight as a snake-caught mouse. To either my shame or credit, take your pick, I'd not moved, but only watched, although my heart was in my mouth, more for fear of what would happen now that Guinevere had seen Nimüe apparently mutilated than anything else.

But was she truly harmed? She was sitting up, her white face a mask of sweat, her eyes wide but focused, her gown still bunched around her waist. Although blood gleamed on her white thighs and the whiter marble, none welled from her crotch, where the only colors were pale skin and copper pubic hair. She looked down, touching herself with one tentative finger, and I had a brief glimpse of a labial fold before she pulled her gown back over herself. "I'm not hurt," she said in a hoarse unbelieving voice as she rose on unsteady feet, standing on the bench. "Sister, Arthur, it's done, and I'm a woman!" There was something different about her face, a new delicacy, and perhaps her hips were slightly wider, her waist more narrow, although that might have been my imagination. "And the power, oh, the power!" She shut her eyes and stretched out her arms, big hands more graceful than ever before. "Can you not feel it rushing in like the tide? It's coming into me, or out of me, or both at once. Is this what being born is like, or what the butterfly feels when it bursts from its chrysalis? Oh Raven Mother, for this boon I am ever in your debt!''

Merlin licked his lips and coughed wetly. "Oh, yes, thank the goddess but not me who called down her power. That's all right. I don't mind.''

Arthur had stopped thrashing against his vegetative bonds. Ignoring Nimüe, Merlin padded to him, eyes gleaming as he smiled his dripping red smile. "See how easily I did that? The child is fine. She may even be more powerful than me, and if she finds the future opaque and believes that she has choices, at least she'll have the possibility of happiness.'' Clearing his throat, he spat blood and phlegm on Arthur's chest. "And now, King of All the Britons, there is one more thing to do.''

"No!'' shouted Gwen, who no longer struggled, but stood tall and straight in her thorny shackles, ignoring the places where they cut her gown and tore her flesh. "Merlin, you've done what you said you would. Now take us from this place. If my sister is truly whole and unharmed, you can have anything you want.''

Merlin wiped his mouth on the back of his hand and shook his head. "Anything, lady? Can you bring Uther to life again and make him love me? Can you change the world so that I do *not* know what will happen next? No, there's only one thing I want now, and I will get it soon enough.''

"Damn you, Merlin,'' said Arthur. "At least have the courage to face me when I'm free instead of trussed like a pig.''

"But I like you that way,'' said Merlin, "and damnation is either inevitable or an empty threat.'' He reached out and caressed Arthur's crotch. "Now what do you suppose would happen if I kissed you as I just kissed Nimüe? How would Guinevere feel about you, if you had a cunt? It would amuse Mordred, I rather think, as then he'd no longer have to share the Queen's favors with his father.'' Turning to Gwen, he shook his head in mock sadness. "Now there I go, being ungracious again. I really wish you no ill, but that was just too tempting.''

"Don't add lies to your sins," said Arthur through clenched teeth.

Merlin stroked his cheek. "Oh, I never do. I don't always tell the complete truth, but I never lie. Nor do I really think I could change you, not the way I changed her, as you don't have the necessary essence. Still, it would make you quite an amusing monster, wouldn't it? Imagine, summoning priests to heal that wound! They wouldn't be able to, of course, and one can only guess what the Saxons would start saying, as well as the petty kings of Britain. You keep encountering humiliations in your life, but you never seem to learn anything from them. It may be pointless, but it's fun to think of giving you another one. Shall I kiss you? I quite want to."

"Get away from him, Merlin."

The voice was familiar but different, and a new power echoed in it. It came from Nimüe, who still stood atop the marble bench, arms outstretched, her hair flapping around her head in the breeze that seemed to blow between the trees that arched above the transformed statue. "Enough of this," she said softly, making one simple motion with her hands.

My stomach lurched, my ears popped again, the world spun or rippled, I'm not sure which, and we were back in the courtyard, on the edge of the tiny grove, sere leaves scuttling over flagstones, while my vision blurred and I tried my damnedest not to vomit. Somewhere, someone was shouting.

It was Arthur. Free now, he lunged at Merlin, the ruby-hilted sword flashing in the pale afternoon light, and there was a butcher's block sound and something round and white and pink bounced on the pavement, leaving a red trail. I've remarked before on how hard it is to cut a head off with one blow, how it's almost never done in battle, but Merlin had a small, slender neck, and Nimüe's magic may well have aided Arthur's arm, just as it surely made Merlin vulnerable to the blow. Arthur stood there panting, his eyes wild and empty of any knowledge but hurt and hate. Nimüe ran to Guinevere, who hugged her tight, murmuring something low and soothing, fear and relief struggling in her eyes. There was the tramp of hobnailed boots, the clatter of arms, and

Gawain came running into the courtyard, the guards somewhat reluctantly behind him. "Bloody Jesus," he said when he saw Merlin's body slumped before the bench.

Arthur walked where the head lay, faceup and eyes open. I shouted hoarsely at him to leave it alone, but there was no listening in him, at least not to me. He gazed down at it and it up at him, for it was not dead, not yet. Merlin blinked, and although he had no lungs and his vocal cords were severed, words bubbled from his red mouth.

"Yes, now it's over, at least for me, and as far as I'm concerned that's all that matters. It's not easy for one such as me to die, and I needed help, both from you and from her whose power I freed. I had no intention of changing you, at least not physically, but the threat was necessary. Not that I bear you any goodwill. Live now, knowing what you know, that your son has been fucking your wife ever since he brought her back from the Kingdom of Teeth. Much happiness to you and yours, King of all the Britons."

Arthur snarled and hacked at the head, sending it rolling over the flagstones, then stomped on it with his boot, repeatedly, until it was too soft and shapeless to roll farther. Again and again he cut at it, grunting, growling, none of us daring to stop him, his blade chopping into pulped flesh, crunching through bone, and sometimes ringing dully on the stones underneath. Seemingly done at last, he lurched back to the grove and hacked at the statue, which was the image of the Virgin again, and at the small trees around her, chopping like a clumsy woodsman, blunting his sword of office. Gawain and Guinevere both ran to him, pulling at his arms, while the rest of us stared helplessly.

He shook off Gwen, but didn't struggle when Gawain threw thick arms around him. "Damn them, damn them all," said my father to nobody in particular. "Damn them all to hell, and me with them." Lowering his sword and leaning stiffly into Gawain's embrace, he sobbed briefly. I wanted to run to Gwen, but that wouldn't be safe, if anything was safe now.

"You can't believe what that thing said," murmured Gawain. "There is no reason for it."

Arthur pulled away from him and sat on the bloody bench.

"Oh, no reason at all, except that he liked to wound with the truth, and I am wounded sore. Where is my son? Where is my bloody son?"

I walked warily to him. "Right here."

"Have you been fucking her?" He said it low and tonelessly, then allowed himself a bitter smile. "I just said 'fucking.' Well, why not? I've done worse in my life than curse. I don't want to live in a world where nothing is wrong, because if I do, then nothing is right, either, but that's how it seems right now. Nothing is wrong, or everything is. Answer my question."

"Arthur, please," said Guinevere. "Let us talk inside."

"I am not speaking to you, wife," said Arthur. "I do not hate you, and I will not harm you, nor him either, but I am not speaking to you now, and I do not wish you to speak to me. Can you really believe that I've not suspected, during all these years? Why do you think I've struggled so with my faith? Still, I never truly knew, nor wished to know. I shrank from the truth as much as I shrank from Merlin. After such knowledge, what's left? Prayer, perhaps. I wish I could pray. I wish for many things. So do you, I'm sure. Mordred, I will have an answer. Let me phrase it with more gentleness, although I do not feel gentle, not now and maybe never. Have you and the Queen been lovers?"

I looked at Gawain, all naked confusion, and then at Gwen, who was tense but resigned, her hands clasped, her eyes unknowable. Would they ever be knowable again? Would anything? Finally, I turned my gaze back to Arthur, and said what I had to say, my liar's gift all fled.

"Yes."

Arthur stood up. He still had his sword in hand, but did not raise it. One small shiver ran through him, he blinked and swallowed and ran his other hand through his blood-splattered hair. "How often?"

I could not look at him, could not look away. "Since I brought her back from the Kingdom of Teeth, although I loved her before that. Her virginity bound her there, in the realm of Melwas. When we made love, the spell was broken and she was free."

He shut his eyes then. "And you didn't tell me? I would

have forgiven you, would have wished the two of you happiness, even, despite my hurt. She and I were not yet married.''

Guinevere came forward. ''He wanted to. But you know you could not have let him marry me and remain at court, and I didn't want to be bundled off to my father, like some expensive houseware tucked away until the next market. All my life I've been pawn and trophy, I told him; now I want something for myself. That was greedy of me, yes. But I also loved you. I loved him, and still do, but I also loved you.''

Arthur did not open his eyes. ''Guinevere, step away from me please. I never gave you cause for this hurt.'' She stepped back. Nimüe came forward, her face all hair and eyes, and wrapped her thin arms around Gwen. I continued standing there, waiting for Arthur to open his eyes. Finally, he did.

This time, he seemed to look through all of us, staring back into the past, as Merlin had looked into the future. ''Mordred, I wish I could say I never gave you cause either, but we both know that's not true. I once thought my sin was in siring you, and later decided it was in shunning you when I learned the truth. I don't really know anymore. Can it be that you still hate me, and this has been your revenge for that day in Orkney? If so, it's been long in coming.''

I shook my head. ''I love her because of her, not because of you or anything else.''

Arthur looked at his sword for another moment, then sheathed it without wiping off Merlin's blood. ''Perhaps that's to your credit.'' He walked to the hacked statue of the Virgin. ''I am sorry, Lady, for I've done you no honor today. How can I, with no honor in me? Perhaps, before I die, I will get some small portion of it back, even if I have to cross the Channel to find it. Things were simpler, when all I knew was war. Maybe they need to be that way again.''

He pulled himself up straighter, but did not turn around. ''Listen to me, all of you. I am going to find Bishop Gerontius and confess myself to him. My faith was a weak and pitiful thing today, but there was a time when it was strong, when I knew what I was doing and why. Perhaps the Lord will listen to my prayers, if I again serve Him the way I once did. It's been a long time since I was a soldier, firm of purpose, fighting an evil I understood.''

He turned then, an expression on his face I'd not seen since that day in Orkney when he found out who I truly was. He was not looking at us, but at some image of himself, falling yet again from grace. *Not the martyr's mask*, I thought; *honest rage would be preferable to this*. ''Mordred, Guinevere, after I have left this courtyard, you can say your good-byes. Take as long as you like, but say them. Gawain, I charge you this. Make sure your brother leaves Camelot on the morrow. Give him a retinue of fifty horse and sufficient coin to pay them for a year, but make sure he goes. Where, I do not care, as long as it's beyond Gwent's borders. For yourself, I need you, first here and then in Gaul, if you will stay with me. And Guinevere must stay, too. I feel no love for her, but we were married before God and I will not part with her yet, not until the Lord has told me what I should do. Once, she would have ruled in my stead while I strove to free the Continent from the Franks, but it seems I must find another for that office. I'd give it to you, Gawain, if I didn't need you with me when I go. That is all for now.''

Without looking at any of us, he trudged out of the courtyard, his boots echoing hollowly down the columned walkway.

In less than an hour, everything had changed. You'd think I'd be used to having my life turned upside down by now, but a decade of relative contentment makes a man complacent. Perhaps this day had been inevitable ever since Gwen and I first coupled upon a floor of teeth, but it had not seemed that way. Unlike Merlin, we'd been stumbling in the dark. A selfish whining part of me wanted to curse the gods, Arthur, even Guinevere, but in the end it was me who was to blame, just me, nobody but me.

Gawain cleared his throat softly, interrupting my reverie. ''He'll change his mind, surely. In time, I mean.''

''No,'' I said, for once feeling as sure of the future as Merlin had been. ''I don't think so. Are you going to stay with him? Join him on his mad quest to find absolution on the battlefield?''

Gawain walked to me, looked me sternly in the eye, then

hugged me. As he pressed me close, I heard a muffled sob. "I must, brother, as much as I love you. Here is all I know. I've served him since I was fourteen, turning my back on my father and my kingdom. I can't leave now. He won't forbid me to visit you, I think, but at present I must remain at his side. He needs me. He has no one else."

"Yes," I said with some bitterness. "Poor Arthur."

He pulled back. "You have a right to be angry, maybe, but you must have known this would happen someday. It was your choice."

I looked up at the sky, darkening now on its edges. It would be night soon. "Choice? Merlin would have found that possibility a comfort. I do not. Gawain, I love you dearly, but you are not the one I would talk to just now. Since I'll see you again, I must ask you to leave us."

He turned on his heel and bowed to Guinevere. "I'm sorry, Your Highness."

She nodded, her arm around Nimüe, whose lip was quivering. "As am I. Try to forgive us both."

He looked down, scuffing leaves with his booted toe. "Ach, I already have. Would that I could make others do so." Then he left without looking at us again.

Nimüe gently extricated herself from Gwen's embrace. "All my newfound magic, yet I don't know any way to make this right. Oh, sister, I wish I could help you."

Gwen brushed a crimson curl out of Nimüe's flushed face. "It's beyond magic, I fear. Despite all this, I'm happy to see you changed. Maybe you can make something for yourself that I never had. Now leave us, sweets. I will have need of your comfort later, but leave us now."

Nimüe walked to me with uncustomary grace, looking more than ever like her sister. I hugged her briefly, neither of us saying anything, and then she, too, was gone.

I walked to where Guinevere stood among the blowing leaves, hair in her eyes, her gown torn and blood on her bare arms. She came to me, kissed me, pressed herself against me, held me tight. Neither of us seemed to have any words left. Throwing my cloak around her, I led her past Merlin's body, into the tiny grove, wishing that it was the wildwood again, and that we could walk away through it forever. Too soon, we reached its other side, the ivied courtyard wall looming close. There, as far away from anyone else as we could be, we sat down on the cold loam, my back to a tree and hers resting on my chest, my arms tight around her, my face in her hair. Wind blew through the bare branches overhead and leaves rattled out upon the flagstones. She tilted back her head, her face pressed against mine, her eyes shut. Our hands clasped over her warm breast.

The words came clumsily, as if I'd half forgotten language. "I will come back for you. With an army, if need be." I remembered Cuneda's ambitions, and the debt he owed me.

A quiver ran through her. "You'd war against Arthur?"

Well, we'd thrown so much away, why not Britain, too? "If necessary."

She sighed. "Mordred, think of what you say. I'm no Helen, surely."

"You are to me," I murmured. "If Arthur stays here, and is content with Britain, I won't come against him, but you know he won't do that. Long before this, he was talking of what he wanted to do in Gaul. Maybe it's no longer glory he seeks there, but martyrdom. Either way, I don't care. If he goes, I will come and make you a true queen again."

It was darker now, stars twinkling on the border of the sky, cold dampness creeping out of the earth. Could I have just kept on holding her, I would have happily stayed in that chilly gloom forever.

Farewells

The fates lead the willing, drag the rest.

Seneca, *Ad Lucilium*

Fifteen

IME IS short, and I've spent too much of it already with this testament. Still, it's given me necessary respite. If you are clever (and I hope you are, for my story should be read by clever people, if only as a caution) you will have deduced the tragedy's final act. I went, of course, to Gododdin, where Cuneda received me with sardonic hospitality, wolfishly eager for news of Arthur's plans abroad. I told him what I knew and waited dully for the numbness to pass. It didn't, but eventually the winter did, and with summer came word of Arthur mustering his forces for a campaign in Gaul.

According to Cuneda's spies, my father did not approach the matter like a practical commander, but as a zealot on a holy mission, scourging himself in front of Gerontius's small church, declaring that he needed to prove himself once more worthy of God's grace, that he would compel no one to go with him, but would attack the Franks by himself alone if necessary. This sounded like a man grasping at the straws of faith because he has nothing left. Naturally, the petty kings of Britain watched and waited and licked their lips, and there must have been much unease among the cohorts.

The whole campaign was madness, but with me gone and Guinevere no longer trusted, there was no one to tell him that, unless Gawain tried to do so. Cuneda refused to send any portion of the Northern warband, citing the increased Saxon presence in the Orkneys, once my homeland but now ruled by Beortric and his band of pirates. Cador of Cornwall,

Guinevere's father, contributed only token levies. That left the five cohorts that comprised the Warband of Camelot. Arthur ended up taking three with him across the Channel; his own personal one, that commanded by Gawain, and one more. Two were left behind. One of these belonged to Geraint, Arthur's most seasoned and trusted commander other than my brother, now appointed Duke of Britain in Arthur's absence. The other was in the hands of Colwyn, my former captain. I wondered idly what he thought of my Northern exile, not realizing that I'd soon find out.

For my part, I drank too much ale and mead, spent evenings staring into the fire, and pretended to pay attention when Cuneda muttered of his plans. "I could never rule the South," he said, "but you could. Old Cador of Cornwall, Guinevere's father, he might be on your side. If I led an army down to Camelot, I would be seen as an invader, no better than a Pict or Irishman, but what if you rode at its head?"

"The time's not right," was all I could think to say.

"But it will be, eventually," was his sly answer.

Yes it would, and soon. *I will come back for you. With an army, if need be.* I'd told Guinevere that, and meant it more than anything. But did I still mean it, when the actuality was at hand? I still wanted her, of course, would always want her, ached with her absence and woke reaching for her in the empty night. But did I truly want war and all it meant? What I saw when I slept deepened my ambivalence.

For on most nights, I dreamed of slaughter and disaster, of Saxon cookfires on broken British pavements, of Camelot an empty shell, of blood running in the Usk like Cadog's wine. When Merlin died, the Myrddin-spirit within him must have been released. Had some small part of it entered into me? Was I now seeing the fixed future, or a warning? Would going to war against Arthur hasten this calamity, or prevent it? Ach, no, there was madness in such speculation. I tried to force myself to dream instead of Guinevere, but although she was always in my waking mind, when sleep crept up on me the red tide washed such fond thoughts away. And so I spent idle days in hunting and evenings brooding by the fire, pretending to pay attention when Cuneda received fresh news of Camelot and muttered of his plans.

One evening half a year after my exile began, I feasted dourly in Din Eidyn, at a place of honor not far from Prince Teged and his new bride, whose name I never learned. I'd just started on my fourth cup of ale when a strange white bird came flapping through the smoke hole, narrowly missing the fire and landing on the table, its pale quivering wings singed and blackened with soot. A moment later, a naked red-haired girl shivered on her knees, her small breasts heaving, coughing as she brushed ashes off her pale, freckled arms. "Your cloak, please," she gasped in a familiar voice.

I handed it to her. "Hello, Nimüe."

The revelers around me were muttering in astonishment, some crossing themselves, others making pagan signs against evil spells. Prince Teged shouted for weapons, but the ever-imperturbable Cuneda waved the spear bearer back. "I think Prince Mordred knows the lady," he said dryly. "Someone bring her a robe."

I helped Nimüe down off the table. When she hugged me, I noted that she was several inches taller, although still not her sister's height. "You've learned much," I said gently, "although this isn't the safest magic for one so young."

"The news couldn't wait," she said. "Guinevere says the time is ripe, if you wish to return to Camelot and can bring any sort of army with you." She paused for a moment, looking at me with the old Nimüe's eyes. "Would you really do that? I scarce believed it when Gwen said it."

At the other end of the table, Cuneda smiled and scratched his hollow nose.

There was so much of Gwen in Nimüe, although she'd never be as breathtakingly lovely. My arms tightened involuntarily around her and she gasped softly. "I told your sister I would go to war for her if need be," I said, my heart echoing in my head. "How does she fare?"

Nimüe pulled away from me and sat down at the table, shooting a hungry glance at my stewed mutton. "She's fine, more or less, although chafing at being confined to the palace, and of course she misses what she had, and you more than that. She doesn't cry much, not Gwen, she was never one to cry, but you can see it tearing at her from within. As for war, it needn't come to that. Your old captain, Lord Colwyn, came to see her the other day, and spoke to her out of Lord Geraint's earshot. The men don't like this war that's brewing in Gaul; they fear they'll be called away, too, and don't wish to give up their easy lives here to pursue a battle that it's whispered can't be won. It was different when they were fighting the Saxons, trying to keep what was theirs. Colwyn said to tell you that if you bring an army to the field, your old cohort will declare for you. That will just leave Geraint and his men, who surely must surrender when they see half their strength gone over to the other side. I only hope she's right about that, that grief hasn't driven her to folly. Poor Gwen, she misses you so much.''

"And I her," I said softly. "And yes, her plan seems sound.''

Nimüe snatched a piece of meat from my bowl and wolfed it down without asking. That was understandable, as such magic makes one famished. "I was afraid, when she first told me to bring you this news, but I had to come," she said when she'd swallowed. "I owe the both of you so much. You lost everything for me.''

I hadn't done it for her, but there was no reason to say that. "Everything's not truly lost if it can be won again," I said, again meeting Cuneda's gaze across the table. *Here it is, you old goblin, the opportunity you wished for. For myself, I wish I had so little to lose as you.*

A serving girl with frightened codfish eyes brought a woolen robe, holding it out with a trembling hand. I politely averted my eyes while Nimüe pulled it over her head, although not everyone did, and I glowered at those warriors of Gododdin who were crude enough to lick their lips. "She's under my protection," I said.

"I can protect myself, actually," said Nimüe, grabbing another piece of meat and wiping her hand on the robe. Lugh and Jesus, but she'd so changed greatly in the year since she collided with me while chasing her injured cat. But then, so had my complacent world.

"What of Gawain?" I asked. "Is he still with Arthur?"

There was a touch of the familiar wistfulness in her long,

strong face. "Yes. They are at Tours, last I heard." She paused, staring owlishly at me through her tangled hair, and I briefly saw the little girl again, not the young woman who flew with a bird's wings and her sister's forthright confidence. "Oh, Mordred, that's what frightens me most of all. I owe so much to Gwen, I have no choice but to help you, but I fear Gawain won't forgive me for it. You've known him so much longer than I have; please tell me he will. I only wish I could see the future like Merlin did."

The real question was, would he forgive me? "Believe me, child, you don't want Merlin's gift, not if what it made of him is any indication. At least my brother shall be out of harm's way. By the time word reaches Tours, Camelot will be ours. Once it is, all the kings of Britain will support us, knowing it means an end to being taxed for Arthur's war. With such a united kingdom behind us and him stranded on foreign shores, surely he won't seek battle. Even Arthur's not that mad." Oh yes, I very much wanted to believe that.

When I first met him, Cuneda had boasted of being able to bring some twelve hundred men to the field. Now, with his son's marriage uniting Strathclyde and Gododdin, the total forces he commanded numbered over two thousand, a huge army by British reckoning. The march south took almost three weeks, giving Camelot plenty of time to prepare for a siege, and if Colwyn had stood with Geraint, our victory would have been most uncertain, for odds of slightly more than two-to-one were never that daunting to the Warband of Britain. However, when Colwyn's cohort declared their allegiance to me, halving the defender's strength and adding another five hundred men to our side, even fierce little Geraint had to admit the wisdom of surrender.

"I'd never be doing this if the King were here and himself again," he sputtered when he handed me his sword, his lime-stiffened mustache twitching like a cat's whiskers. "By God, Mordred, I thought you a good lad when Gawain first brought you from Orkney, even if you did nearly split my head that time in mock combat, and it breaks my bloody heart to see you doing this, betraying your father and your brother both. If I'd known the world would go so quickly to shit, I wouldn't have bothered getting old.''

Gwen's greeting was more fond, of course, when Colwyn escorted her to where we camped just outside the old amphitheater, for I was loath to bring Cuneda's forces inside the city walls, as that would make this seem too much like an invasion from the North. As soon as we were alone in my tent, she threw herself into my arms with nearly enough force to bowl me over, laughing and crying at the same time, and me doing both with her, until we collapsed together on my blanket, the canvas walls shaking about us. "Once again, you came for me,'' she said when she was able to talk. "Just like you said you would. When we held each other in the courtyard grove, I kept thinking, this is it, the last time, no matter what he says, we'll never have this again, or anything that matters. Oh, sweet love, I so wanted this to work, but truly, I never dared believe it would.''

"It hasn't worked yet,'' I said between kisses. "I'm barely master of the city, and I don't trust Cuneda as an ally. So many things may yet go wrong.''

Prophetic words. Nimüe had flown back to Camelot in bird-shape the morning after she'd given me the news that brought me here, and I'd not seen her since. Now Colwyn poked his head through my tent flap, as flat-faced and impassive as ever, and politely cleared this throat. "Someone to see you, my lord,'' he said, ignoring the fact that I was lying on top of Gwen. "The Queen's sister.''

I sat up and Gwen brushed herself off. Colwyn held the flap open for Nimüe, who was wearing a wide-sleeved green robe with gold brocade, this finery contrasting with her dirty bare feet and typically unkempt hair.

"Ach, Nim!'' said Guinevere. "I let you out of my sight for a day, and look at you! Where have you been? I thought you'd promised you wouldn't disappear again, the way you did after you returned from the North.''

She knelt before us, and even in the tent's gloom I could see the tear streaks on her face. "Gawain is coming,'' she said in a small toneless voice, sounding very tired. "I'm such a fool. I've ruined everything.''

Gawain is coming—three words to stop the heart. "What

do you mean? How could news have reached him so fast? Where the hell is he now?'' *He can't be close yet*, I thought. *He can't have crossed the Channel. Please let Nimüe be wrong.*

Gwen knelt beside her sister, brushing hair out of her face. ''Calmly now, tell me what's happened.''

I looked at them, Nimüe huddled close against Guinevere, and felt a touch of my old familiar jealousy, particularly ridiculous in this time and place. Nimüe stared back at me, more frightened child than powerful sorceress, and bit her lip. Ah, so that was it. ''You went to him,'' I said. ''You flew to him in Gaul, just as you flew to me in Gododdin.''

She looked down at her wide-splayed hands, pale starfish in the gloom. ''Yes.''

Guinevere's look warned me not to explode into angry reproach. ''When did you do this, Nimüe?''

Nimüe drew her knees up protectively in front of her chest and clasped her arms around them. ''Weeks ago, as soon as I was rested enough from my journey to Gododdin. Maybe it's because I can do so many things with the power that Merlin and the Mórrígán awakened inside me. To be able to do so much, yet to truly know so little, makes it easy to stumble into folly. I kept thinking how much I missed him, and how I feared what would happen when he found out that Mordred had come here and taken the city. I kept telling myself, if only I could talk to him, prepare him for it somehow, explain the why of it. And so, while Cuneda was still gathering his army to come South, I flew on bird wings over the Channel, the waves so far under me, the sky so blue above, the sun all golden in the clouds. Then there was the coast of Armorica, a land I'd never seen before, and on I went, over wood and marsh and town, to the forest of tents outside of Tours. I knew better than to appear before him as I'd appeared before you, and once back in my own shape and stolen clothes, it took me so long to find him, but I did at last. 'Please,' I said to him, 'don't come in battle, when you hear that Mordred has taken Camelot. For I couldn't bear it if harm befell you or him. He only does this because he loves my sister, not because he wants to seize the crown of Britain. Tell Arthur that he must not come here seeking war, for no good can come of that.' "

She wiped her eyes with dirty knuckles and hugged her knees some more, rocking back and forth in silence for a moment, then the rush of words resumed. "He looked at me as he never did before, cursing your name and Guinevere's, and for the first time ever he frightened me. After what he said to you in the courtyard where I was changed and Merlin died, I didn't think he'd be so angry, but he was. I begged him not to tell Arthur what I'd told him, even lied desperately, saying I'd made up the story about you coming with an army to Camelot, that I'd told him that simply because I wanted him to come back to Britain, but he was not fooled. In the end, he told me to leave him, that he could not speak to me if I was aiding you. I'm sorry, I thought he would listen to me with more kindness, that he cared for me enough that I could persuade him to do what I wanted. Gwen, you've always been so good at persuading men to do things, I thought I could do that, too."

Guinevere smiled grimly, dabbing at Nimüe's tears with her sleeve. "Oh, yes, see what my ability to persuade men has done for me. Sweets, you say this happened weeks ago, when you were gone for two days and wouldn't tell me where. Why didn't you tell us?"

Nimüe rested her head on her sister's shoulder. "I was afraid and felt so foolish. I kept hoping Mordred would get here, and Camelot would be his, and then maybe you and he could go away together, I don't know where, just away from this, and then there'd be no need for war."

I snorted. "Oh, aye, we could ride away together, but there'd still be Cuneda here, and the army of Gododdin with him, did you not think about that? I came here at the head of Cuneda's army because he wants me to rule here, knowing he cannot rule himself. I don't think I can easily persuade him to send them home." Seeking an outlet for my angry frustration, I kicked out at my own shadow on the tent wall, causing Nimüe to quail and Gwen to frown. "Now, do I take it that you know Gawain's current whereabouts, and how many men he has with him?"

Nimüe nodded. "This morning I bit my finger till it bled,

stirred the blood into a pool of water, and bade it show me Gawain. I'd been afraid to look before, but I finally had to know. I was hoping he was still in Gaul, but no, the water showed him landing on the Severn coast, with four corn barges full of men and eight of horse.''

I stood up. "That's his whole cohort, 480 men and their mounts. He'll be getting them ready for the ride to Camelot, but I cannot let him reach us. If he does, Geraint's surrender may not last, for his troops have been neither disbanded nor disarmed, and there's no time for that now. Bloody hell, I'll have to leave Colwyn's troops here, keeping an eye on Geraint, while I go to the coast with Cuneda's army. If we can meet him with a strong enough force, we can perchance force him to withdraw, to take word back to Arthur rather than meet us in pitched battle. There'll be time for negotiations then.'' Not that I really believed that.

"I've been a stupid fool," said Nimüe. "I thought I could make Gawain do what I wanted as easily as I make myself into a bird, but love's not like that, is it?"

Guinevere looked at me with her green cat's eyes. "No, child, not ever.''

I stared at them both, some part of me thinking, *Is this for what all was lost, a confused girl with more magic than sense?* But that was hardly fair, for it wasn't as if either Guinevere or I had behaved wisely.

"There's no longer any time for apologies or recriminations,'' I said, hunkering down before the two women who, between them, had, intentionally or not, dictated so much of the course of my adult life. "Nimüe, what's done is done. When I was your age, I told Arthur something unwise, thinking he'd react differently than he did. It all began with that, long before you were born.'' I reached out and stroked her cheek, even though a few moments before I'd have gladly slapped it, then leaned over to kiss Gwen.

"I wish our reunion had been less brief, but now I must talk to Cuneda and ride with him to meet Gawain. Don't ever think you weren't worth this.'' Without waiting for an answer, I strode hurriedly from the tent.

Sixteen

CUNEDA AND I stood atop the reed-fringed rise, to our right his assembled forces, shrouded by the mist that had come rolling into the valley; to our left, the slate gray Severn Sea. More fog was sweeping down the coast, hazing the morning fires of Gawain's forces where they'd camped upon the strand.

"I had a brother once," said Cuneda, punctuating the comment with a sneeze that left a strand of mucus hanging from the open tip of his nose. "I didn't go to war against him, but I could have, easily. He saved me the trouble by choking on too large a piece of mutton. Bastard always was greedy."

"It's not like that with Gawain," I said, already sweating in my helm and ringmail despite the early hour. "We never fought, not over anything."

"Well then, it's about time you started." He finally noticed what hung from his nose and wiped it on his leather sleeve. "Dammit, I spend all winter wading through snow without a single sniffle, but come South in the summer and immediately catch a fucking cold."

A rider was coming up the beach. Despite the fog and distance, I recognized the way he sat his horse. "That will be Gawain, coming to talk."

"I don't see the point, myself," said Cuneda, yawning. "It's not going to make the two of you feel any better to look each other in the face first. Unless you think you can talk him into surrender."

246

"Not bloody likely," I said. "Maybe I can convince him to withdraw, though."

Cuneda snorted. "And have him carry news back to Arthur? To hell with that. He either fights us or yields himself up."

I looked him in the eye. Unlike some of the other Northern Brits, he'd never fought against Arthur's troops, back when the throne was first being contested. "You may regret being so eager for battle."

Cuneda spit and grinned. "Maybe. I've not regretted much in my life, but there's always a first time."

Gawain was now only a hundred yards away. I started down the rise, crunching through the dry reeds. "Try not to waste too much time," growled Cuneda from somewhere above me. Below me, Gawain had reined in and was waiting, his lance held high. The reeds gave way to sand and shingle, dulling the sound of my footsteps. Beyond the man and horse, the water sighed like grazing cattle. Birds wheeled overhead, their cries echoing mournfully on the tide. The mist was a close horizon, marking a world with new boundaries and fewer choices.

He'd been letting his beard grow, making him look more bearlike than ever. There was more gray in it than on his head. His eyes reminded me of Arthur's. Not in their color, but in their weary pessimism. But they still crinkled when he managed something of a smile.

"That's better," I said, smiling back. "I feared you were angry with me."

He looked up at the rise and I knew he was trying to estimate the disbursement of troops beyond it. "I was and am, though there's no point in it now. Why did it have to come to this, brother? Loving your father's wife isn't wise, but love seldom is. Coming to Camelot with a Northern army behind you, that's different. It speaks of ambition, of treason born in the head, not the heart."

I stroked the neck of his fine black gelding, which he must have acquired in Gaul. "Is it treason to pick up what Arthur seemed so eager to cast aside? If I didn't lay claim to Camelot, someone else would. Britain won't stand united long, not with Arthur bogged down in foreign wars. In ten years, hell, in five, things would be as bad as they were when first the Saxons came. I wanted to prevent that.''

Gawain stared at me, the wind ruffling his unkempt bangs. ''Did you really? And she had nothing to do with it then?''

I gazed down at the bird-tracked tideline. ''I didn't say that. At any rate, it's too late to talk of motives, that's all in the past. We need to figure out what we are going to do now. I don't want to fight you.''

When I looked up, his eyes had a glimmer of their old humor. ''It's not fighting you I'm worried about, but that lot with you, and I think they want a fight whether you say so or not. I suppose you could always come over to my side, but then, if Cuneda wins, things would not go well for Guinevere. In you, he sees a High King that he can accept, one that will let the North do as it likes, but he'll settle for grabbing the throne himself if he has to, even though he well knows he'd have the devil of a time keeping it. Of course, you could always ride away from this and leave him and me to sort it out.''

I shook my head. ''I'd be a coward, then. Or at least someone unwilling to finish what he started. I can't do that.''

Gawain nodded. ''Any more than I can leave Arthur, as much as I'd like to. I almost did, when Nimüe came to me. She thinks I no longer want her, that I'm unnerved by what she's become, and maybe it does bother me some, since magic always makes me think of our mother, although Nim uses it less selfishly than Mum ever did. But the main thing is, I took an oath with Arthur when he was just Uther's War Duke, before I even knew he was family, and I've followed him so long I don't know any other path. Yes, what he's doing now is folly, but I didn't swear only to serve him when he was right. Beyond that rise is an army that's marched on Camelot. I have no choice but to engage it. It's what Arthur sent me back here to do when I told him what Nimüe told me.''

The wind had changed direction, but it wasn't breaking up the fog. Still, that might work more to our advantage than to Gawain's. To use his cavalry to maximum effect, my brother would need to be able to see at a distance, while we had the advantage in a disorganized melee. But I felt more of a traitor than ever, thinking of that now.

"Arthur surely didn't send your cohort back alone."

Gawain kneaded his furrowed brow. "Ach, and I should tell you our strategy? Not that it's going to make much bloody difference. Of course he didn't, but we were in the rear, and in best position to send across, for he couldn't pull back all his forces at once, and there wouldn't have been enough barges even if he could. The rest should be landing in a few days, maybe a week." He actually laughed. "Hell, maybe this war of yours will do some good, if it brings him back to Britain before the Picts and Saxons and all the local kings get too ambitious."

I looked back atop the rise, where Cuneda still waited. There was a long line of men behind him now, although I knew that most of his force was still down in the hollow. "Then there's not much left to say, is there?"

Gawain was looking that way, too. "No, I suppose not. Leastways, I can't think of anything that wouldn't take a few hours, and we've no such time."

I reached out and took his reins. "Are you going to stay on that goddamned horse, or get down and embrace me before you go? Lugh and Jesus, but it's been too long since my ribs had a good cracking."

He slid from the saddle and gripped me tight, if less painfully than usual. "Good luck to you, brother."

"And to you."

I told myself the wetness on my cheek was just spray blown in from the sighing water.

I think you know the rest, for it's where I began. The battle was all madness, the fog rolling in like a shroud, and I've no memory for the strategy of either side, the charges and formations, the bold sallies, only the muttered oaths, the impact of lance into shield and flesh, the shouts, the screams of men and horses. The only other battle I'd ever fought had been my little raid on Pictdom, and it proved such little preparation for this that I soon gave up any pretense at being in command, just rode back and forth, up the rise and then down again through the misty valley, cutting and thrusting at dim shapes, half-trying, I now think, to die.

Instead, I killed Gawain. Didn't mean to. There was blood on my face, and I seem to have been unhorsed once, although I don't remember it at all, for my whole left side was covered with mud, with mud and blood both getting in my eyes, dimming the gray figure in front of me more than the fog alone could have. Of course, I never expected him to be slashing at me from on foot, not my saddle-born brother, so that was part of it, too. I later learned, from one of their wounded, that they'd been forced to take green horses from the Gallic breeding farms, their experienced mounts all spent, and this proved their undoing, for the new steeds were unready for a Channel crossing in cramped corn barges, nor in any shape for battle immediately afterward. Gawain must have known that going in, of course, but he'd been sent to engage us whatever the cost, and there was no question of his disobeying Arthur.

Despite this, his cohort gave a good account of themselves, and I don't think Cuneda was in any way prepared for our own losses, for although he'd come South with over two thousand men, when he took count of the survivors and those who'd not been too badly wounded, he found himself with slightly less than thirteen hundred. No sooner had he numbered his forces than he began the retreat northward. I now think that was his plan all along, to pull out after the first battle, leaving the rival Southern forces to weaken themselves against each other, so that whoever won, the victor would never have the strength to wring taxes from Gododdin again. I still have Colwyn's cohort, of course, and even if Arthur wipes us out utterly while taking no casualties himself, that will leave the Warband of Britain with three-fifths its former strength.

Nimüe has not spoken to me or anyone since learning of Gawain's death. She came to the chapel where his body was laid out and threw herself upon the corpse, embracing him as I don't think she ever truly had in life. For a moment I feared she'd use her magic to try to bring him to life again, but perhaps she remembered what had happened with her cat and did not try. Remarkably, she does not seem to hate me, and I in my turn have forgiven her.

Arthur won't be long in coming now. Surely, when he does, one or both of us will die. I can see no other outcome. Perhaps Nimüe could, were I to ask her to scry the future for me, but I won't. That's where Merlin and I differ, yet are somewhat alike. He knew exactly what was going to happen to him and didn't care. I don't know such sharp particulars, but likewise find they do not matter.

Instead, I allow myself to linger on more trivial past things, holding the weighty present at arm's length. Looking out my casement at the sun-polished waves, my thoughts turn back to Orkney, small and barren and far away, but the first place I ever knew, and I find myself actually missing that realm of low horizons, restless air, and hardscrabble hills, though I valued it little enough when I lived there. My bare island had a music I've heard nowhere else; the melody hummed by the never-distant waves that murmured just beyond every hill and boomed when Mother Ocean smashed her protean self upon the black and jagged rocks; the insinuating whisper of the coarse brown grass and the rhythmic plaint of the buildings whose timbers groaned and creaked as much as those of any swell-tossed ship; the sailor songs of all the seabirds that soared on the wet salt wind or roosted in the tumbled stacks of basalt that the storm-driven sea had cut from the broken cliffs. It was a world of peat and grass and pebble, forever bounded by salt water and salt air. There is a part of me that would gladly steal back there, to live alone amid the rolling emptiness, as much of a hermit as mad Cadog in his wilderness, Merlin in his wildwood lair. But no, I've already said I will not run away.

Time to put my pen down. It will be sword time soon enough, but before then I would find Gwen in the chapel, if not to pray with her (perish the thought), at least to hold her in my arms once more. So ends my History of Mordred. When I began this testament, I said others would have to write the History of Arthur. I'm sure they will, and whether they get it right or wrong is no great matter. We'll both be remembered, at least, if he rather more fondly than me, for both his triumphs and his ultimate failure were on a much grander scale than mine, and that's the true stuff of legend, which is always better in the remembering than in the living.